Praise for *You*

'Fast paced an[...]
Harriet [...]

'A sinister standalone thriller'
Sunday Times

'I loved the characters and the dark humour.
A cracking, pacy read'
Patricia Gibney

'Trevor's inimitable voice, humanity and humour really
shone through in this locked village mystery'
Mari Hannah

'[An] edgy, electrifying modern thriller'
William Shaw

'Rip-roaring, action-packed and nail-bitingly tense'
Irish Independent

'Tense and compelling'
Daily Mail

'A propulsive page-turner'
Vaseem Khan

'Punchy, pacy and packed with powerful scenes'
Robert Scragg

'Trevor Wood has written another cracker of a book'
Nikki Smith

You Can Run

Trevor Wood has lived in Newcastle for thirty years and considers himself an adopted Geordie. He's a successful playwright who has also worked as a journalist and spin-doctor for the City Council. Prior to that he served in the Royal Navy for sixteen years. Trevor holds an MA in Creative Writing (Crime Fiction) from UEA. *The Man on the Street*, his first novel, was published to widespread critical acclaim and won the 2020 CWA New Blood Dagger. *One Way Street* was his second novel and *Dead End Street* concluded the trilogy.

Also by Trevor Wood

THE JIMMY MULLEN SERIES

The Man on the Street
One Way Street
Dead End Street

You
Can
Run

TREVOR WOOD

QUERCUS

First published in Great Britain in 2023
This paperback edition published in Great Britain in 2023 by

QUERCUS

Quercus Editions Ltd
Carmelite House
50 Victoria Embankment
London EC4Y 0DZ

An Hachette UK company

A CIP catalogue record for this book is available
from the British Library

PB ISBN 978 1 52941 486 8
EBOOK ISBN 978 1 52941 484 4

10 9 8 7 6 5 4 3 2 1

Typeset by CC Book Production
Printed and bound in Great Britain by Clays Ltd, Elcograf S.p.A.

MIX
Paper | Supporting
responsible forestry
FSC® C104740

Papers used by Quercus are from well-managed forests and other responsible sources.

For Kev. He's my brother. And not at all heavy.

THE VILLAGE OF COLDBURN

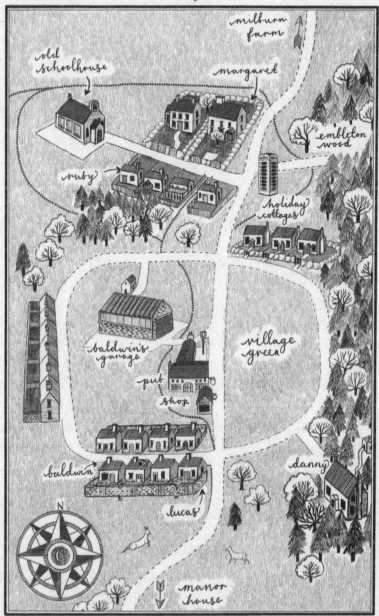

PROLOGUE

These are the things Ruby knew for sure last week:

1. She was born in Newcastle, almost sixteen years ago.
2. Her dad, Alex, is her only family in the entire world.
3. She wouldn't hurt a fly.
4. Boys are useless.
5. Nothing interesting will ever happen to her while she is stuck in a remote village in the middle of Northumberland.
6. Eating meat is the biggest crime imaginable.

This is what she knows now: None of those things are true. Especially No. 6.

1

The doorbell heralds the beginning of the end. As soon as Alex hears it ring he knows that the moment he's been dreading for almost sixteen years has finally arrived.

The man who pressed the buzzer stands back from the house, glancing nervously at the flutter of snowflakes hitting the ground around him, unaware Alex is staring right at him, hidden by the frosted glass window that he had installed for privacy.

There's a moment when Alex considers ignoring it, hoping the man will go away but, as he well knows, sometimes you just have to deal with the crap that comes your way, no matter how bad it might get, and this is another one of those moments. It doesn't mean he's not scared shitless though.

He takes a deep breath, pushes his chair back and thinks about grabbing his insurance policy from upstairs but instead heads for the front door – maybe the guy's just lost and he can get rid of him quickly. Alex unhooks the security chain, clenches his fist to stop his hand from shaking and slowly, reluctantly, pulls the door open, keeping things nice and easy, trying to look unthreatening.

The visitor is dressed like a wannabe soldier. Camouflage trousers and a black T-shirt, no logos, insignia or name badge, not quite what Alex has been expecting – younger for a start – but not a million miles away either. The ponytail is a surprise too, and there's something about the guy that would set anyone on edge; a kind of manic energy that makes it look like he's about to explode. He's shuffling on his feet, bouncing almost. Worst of all, he's got a gun.

On the plus side it's in a covered holster, clipped to his belt, rather than pointing at Alex's chest but, even so, he's struggling to take his eyes off it.

'Can I help you?' he says, looking up and smiling, trying to be friendly. Maybe the guy is just trying to find his way to Otterburn where the firing ranges are – military vehicles are a regular sight in the area. But if he's really lost why would he choose a house at the end of a cul-de-sac to ask for directions? And where's his vehicle?

'Are you Winter?' the guy says.

Fuck, that's not good. Alex nods. No use denying it. The guy points at his own chest.

'Green.'

He doesn't make it clear if that's a surname or a description but neither of them really gives a shit about the formalities. They've both got business to attend to.

'I think you've got something I want,' Green adds. 'Something that doesn't belong to you.'

Alex has thought about what he'd do at this moment almost every day for years but has never really come up with a plan that might work. There's no way he wants a fight on the doorstep though, not with Mrs Nosy Twat just across the road. He'd probably lose anyway but in the unlikely event of him winning, there'd be no way to keep it quiet. Unless he kills the neighbour too but that would definitely be a step too far. So he pulls the door wide open.

'You'd better come in.'

Green looks surprised. It's clear he's expecting more of a challenge but, unable to resist an open goal, he walks in.

'Go through to the kitchen,' Alex says, nodding to the open doorway at the end of the hall and closing the front door behind him. Green does as he's told though he keeps glancing over his shoulder, like he thinks it's a trap. He's even younger than Alex first thought and seems more nervous than a man in his line of work should be. Maybe he was expecting backup to have arrived by now.

Alex follows him in, kicking out the wedge that normally keeps the door open so Ruby won't hear the conversation. Or what happens afterwards. It closes behind him. Green already has his back to the counter, no doubt making sure that no one can creep up behind him. Not a complete novice then. The man's twitching hand hovers near the gun's holster. Alex wonders if he's on something or just gets off on confrontation.

'Where is she?' Green says.

2

Something weird is going on.

Ruby pinches herself to make sure she's not dreaming. Some randomer has just turned up at the door and her dad let him in. That is just not a thing. Ever. He absolutely hates being interrupted when he's working, which is like, always. The number of times she's had to collect a parcel from a neighbour cos he didn't answer the door – even though he can see the postman knocking from where he's sitting!

She checks the clock on her computer screen. It's 12.15. He always starts work at nine a.m. sharp and works straight through till one p.m. on the dot, so caught up in his work that you can't get a word out of him. Even though she's the only other one who's ever in the house he puts a Do Not Disturb sign on the door handle just in case she's thinking of breaking the rules. This change in routine is beyond odd.

She caught a glimpse of the mystery visitor from her bedroom window when he first rang the bell and he's definitely not a local. The camouflage trousers weren't that unusual but nobody round here has a ponytail like that, certainly not the men – they're all strictly short-back-and-sides kinda guys. Or bald. Apart from Mad Danny but there's no way her dad would let him in – he's never once let anyone from the village in.

The two of them are talking now, in the kitchen – she can hear them from her room so it must be loud. Annoyingly she can't quite make out what they're saying.

Ruby hates not knowing stuff so she creeps out of her bedroom and down the stairs, edging along the hallway towards the back of the house where the kitchen door is firmly shut. Which is also odd. Their cat, Pluto, needs to get to and from the cat flap so she can crap in the garden so it's normally wedged open. She can see the piece of wood they use pushed to one side of the hall.

She keeps to the left-hand side of the hallway as she approaches the door. There's a loose floorboard on the right and she doesn't want her dad to think she's spying on him. She is, clearly, but it's best that he doesn't know that. He's a very private person. So private that he won't even touch social media – and doesn't let her either. Though obviously she still does – her best friend Liv has taught her how to bypass parental controls and as her dad's not even on Facebook he's not likely to find out anytime soon. Hopefully.

She's almost at the door when there's a shout.

'No chance. Absolutely not.'

She stops abruptly, her heart skipping a beat. It's so sudden and surprising that she's not sure whose voice it is. It sounded like her dad but she can't remember the last time he raised his voice so maybe it was the other guy.

'You've no choice.'

Definitely not her dad this time. A strange accent. Not from round here. Southern, she thinks. A bit like the guys on TOWIE. And something threatening about it. Maybe she should go in? Would that calm things down? Or make things worse?

She hears a chair scrape across the floor.

'I'd like you to leave.'

Definitely her dad this time, calmer but insistent. She relaxes, he's got this.

'Not happening. Unless she comes with me.'

She? Was he talking about her? Must be, no other girls here, apart from Pluto, but Ruby is pretty sure the guy isn't a cat person – you can always tell.

Who is he? She puts her hand on the door handle. If this is about her she has every right to know. Something holds her back. Nervously, she puts her ear to the door, hoping to get another clue.

A loud scream from inside the kitchen makes her leap away from the door. Was that her dad? She starts to shake, her foot tapping loudly on the wooden floor. Ruby summons every bit of willpower she has to stop it, terrified that the ponytailed man can hear her from inside the kitchen. What should she do? Only one answer. Help her dad. She runs into their small front room and grabs a poker from beside the fire, sprints back down the hall and crashes into the kitchen.

She almost falls over the body lying face down on the floor in front of her. Stumbling to avoid it Ruby drops the poker and one of her bare feet lands in the growing pool of blood that's seeping over the tiles. She slips and screams. Grabbing at the kitchen counter to keep her balance, she can't help noticing the empty slot in the knife block in front of her. As she spins around she sees her dad, standing behind her, holding the missing knife, bright red blood dripping from the blade onto his hand.

3

'Ruby!'

She blinks. Her dad is holding her shoulders, the blood from his hand staining her T-shirt; the knife now on the floor by her feet. She is properly shaking now, can't control it this time.

'Listen to me.'

'But—'

'Not now,' he says, firmly. His eyes drill into hers, imploring her to pay attention, his hands gripping her arms too tightly, hurting her. He sees her wince and relaxes his hold slightly.

'Run upstairs and pack a bag, just essentials. No phones or iPad, nothing that can be traced. Make sure it's easy to carry. Like a rucksack.'

There's a groan. The other man. She glances down. He's still lying face down but inching very slowly across the floor. There's a gun lying at his feet but if he's after that he's going the wrong way.

'Ignore him.'

'He's got a gun!' she shouts.

Her dad nods, walks across the floor and picks the gun up. He ejects the magazine and slides the bullets out one by one onto the floor. Each one breaking the silence with a ping. When did he learn how to do that? When it's empty he throws the magazine into the far corner of the kitchen.

'What about the police?' she says. 'Your fingerprints are on the gun now. They'll think it's yours.'

'We won't be calling the police.' He lays the gun down on the kitchen counter.

She closes her eyes. This can't be happening. The man on the floor moans in pain and she opens them again to look back at him.

'We should at least call an ambulance,' she says.

'No!' She flinches as her dad pulls her around so she can't see the man any more. 'We have to get out of here.'

'But who—'

'No time for questions. I'll explain later. We have to move. Go. Now!'

Ruby tries to do as she's told but her feet won't budge. It's like the connection between her brain and the rest of her is broken. She can hear the wounded man dragging himself towards the back door, his boots scraping on the stone tiles. She could swear she's seen this movie. It didn't end well.

'Move!'

The urgency in her dad's voice gets her going. She runs into the hallway, finds a small rucksack in the coat cupboard and legs it up to her room. She grabs some socks but realises she has blood all over her feet. She slumps onto the floor as the tears begin. This can't be happening. It just can't. It's her birthday next week. She's supposed to be having a small party with a few friends from school in the kitchen downstairs. But it's covered in blood and there's a dying man on the floor. She laughs but not the funny kind – more hysterical. She wraps her arms around her body, as if that will keep her safe.

'Ruby! Hurry up.'

Her dad's shout shakes her out of her trance. She runs to the bathroom, leaving bloody footprints on the carpet and quickly washes her feet in the bath, pink water swirling down the drain. When they're clean and dry she puts her socks and trainers on, grabs her toothbrush and some paste and dashes back to her room. She throws some knickers, a couple of T-shirts and a pair of jeans into the rucksack. What else does she need? There's a pile of make-up on her dressing table and she reaches for the underarm deodorant but stops herself. It's not a fucking sleepover. Her phone! She knows her dad said to leave it but it's all right for him, he doesn't have any friends.

She pulls her bedclothes apart but it's not there. It's not on the desk either. Then she remembers: it's charging in the kitchen. Idiot. She dashes downstairs and back into the kitchen.

Her phone is smashed to pieces on the counter.

She glares at her dad who is holding the poker she dropped earlier.

'Why did you do that?'

'They could trace it.'

'They! Who's "they"?'

'Later, I promise. You ready?'

That's when she really loses it.

'Ready for what?' she screams, spit hitting her dad's face. 'I don't fucking know where we're going. Or for how long. Or why there's a dying man on our kitchen floor. I don't know fucking anything.'

She rarely swears in front of her dad. His face shows so many things that she can't register them all: shock, concern, fear are all there but other stuff too. He pulls her in for a hug.

'I'll explain everything later, I promise, but we have to get going. Now. OK?'

He loosens his grip and steps back, taking her hands.

'Trust me,' he says.

She nods, then realises he already has a small bag at his feet. Where the hell did that come from? He didn't even go upstairs. Was he already prepared for this?

'Thank you,' he adds, turning her around to face the door. 'Now wait in the hallway, will you? I just have to finish something.'

She starts to move but then hesitates. What does he mean? She glances at the poker in his hand. Thinks about the man on the floor. Shit.

'You're not going—'

There's a noise behind her. She glances back at the wounded man and screams. He's rolled onto his back and is pointing a small gun right at her, though his hand is shaking. He tries to say something but chokes on it and coughs up a mouthful of blood, all the time keeping the gun aimed towards the pair of them. One of his trouser legs is pulled up and there's an empty holster strapped to his ankle.

Time slows down. She can see his finger moving on the trigger and then everything happens at once. Her dad flings her to one side and she slips on the bloody floor again, cracking her head on the counter as she falls. The last thing she hears is the gunshot.

Ruby comes to, lying on the kitchen floor. No idea how long she's been out of it but she can smell rotten eggs. If that's what gunpowder smells like then she can't have been unconscious for long. She tries to sit up but her head's sore as shit and the room starts to spin so she lies back down.

She manages to turn on her side and finds herself face to face with her dad. First glance, she thinks he's dead. It feels like all the air has been sucked out of her body. Second glance, he blinks. She breathes again. Thank God. She drags herself up, ignoring the dizziness. It's obvious he's been shot. There's blood coming out of his shoulder and he seems to be in shock, barely registering her presence.

There's a sound behind her. How did she forget the gunman? She flips around but it's not him. He's flat out, on his back, his eyes closed, looking very dead, the second gun lying limply in his hand. The noise is Pluto, licking up the man's blood. It's disgusting and she instinctively screws up her face and tries to shoo the cat away. As usual Pluto ignores her so she turns back to help her dad.

Ruby drags herself up onto her knees, feeling sick but pushing through it. She's seen enough cop shows on telly to know that she shouldn't move him. She should try and stop the bleeding though. She reaches for a tea towel from the kitchen counter and wraps it around her dad's arm, grimacing when she realises that the back of his upper arm is in a much worse state than the front. She remembers that from the TV too – the exit wounds are always bigger. He's not moving, still in some kind of shock, she's not even certain he knows it's her who's helping him, if that's what she's doing. Maybe she's making things worse? She needs a professional.

Ruby doesn't want to leave him but she has to call an ambulance. She clambers to her feet and immediately sees her phone in pieces. How could she have forgotten that already? They don't have a landline but her dad has a shitty old mobile hidden away somewhere – unfortunately she has no idea where. Probably not charged anyway.

He's trying to say something. As she kneels back down next to him his eyes follow her, his lips moving. Water, she thinks. They always give people water in the movies.

She gets up and grabs a cup, filling it quickly from the sink and almost falling back down in her haste to give her dad a drink. She shoves his bag on a stool and pushes it under the counter to give her more room, puts one hand behind his head, lifting it slightly and tips the cup towards his lips. Some of it gets through but most of it runs down his chin and onto his shirt. He finally manages to make a noise but she's no idea what he's saying.

'I have to go and get help,' she says.

He grips her sleeve tightly and tries to shake his head but winces with the pain. There's no doubt what he means. And his muttering is getting stronger.

'Please,' she begs. 'You need a doctor.'

'No,' he says, clearer this time. The effort looks like it's exhausted him though he's still trying to speak. She leans right into him, her ear next to his lips. She misses the first word or two but thinks he says something about 'not safe'.

'What's not safe?' He's saying something else but it's too faint to hear. She pulls up slightly to see if she can lip read, though why she thinks she might be able to do that God only knows. She can feel the tears starting to come but bites her lip, needing to keep her shit together until she can get help.

She leans in again, more closely, to try and hear what he's saying. This time it's as clear as a bell.

'Go,' he says.

'No. Not until I've called an ambulance.'

She tries to get up but his grip is like steel and he's shaking his head more firmly. 'Safe,' he says again. Or at least that's what it sounds like. And then 'he's coming'. Maybe. And then much louder and clearer:

'Run!'

'Hello.'

Ruby jumps out of her skin, breaking her dad's grip on her sleeve, her eyes darting to the door. There's no one there.

'Come in, Green, this is base, over.' She spins around. The voice is coming from the ponytailed man on the floor. But not from him, from his waist. She looks down and realises there's some kind of walkie-talkie attached to his belt. Ruby moves towards him. She could ask them for help! Thankfully, she immediately realises that's the stupidest idea she's ever had, and that's saying a lot. Whoever is on the end of that radio isn't her friend. Maybe he's even the one who's 'coming'. Maybe he's right outside.

Ruby starts to tremble but grips her fists tightly to try and stop it. Her dad needs her. Then her eyes fall on the second gun, which is hanging from the soldier's limp hand in a pool of his blood on the floor. She has no idea whether she'll be able to use it but, holding her breath, reaches down and plucks it from him. She's momentarily distracted by the spooky-as-hell way the snake and skull tattoo on his arm appears to move when she pulls the weapon free but that's just because she's shaking so hard. He doesn't react at all. She's pretty sure he's dead but doesn't want to get close enough to check properly. She does her best to wipe the blood from the small gun with some kitchen roll and puts it in the front pocket of her rucksack, before going back to her dad.

He's mumbling 'go' repeatedly. Her lip-reading skills can just about cope with that. She bends down, gives him a quick peck on the cheek and whispers in his ear. 'I'm going for help.'

His muttering gets louder as she grabs her rucksack and legs it out of the kitchen – now he's clearly saying 'no' but she doesn't care, she can't just run to God knows where and leave him like that. She snatches a black hoodie from the hooks by the door but then hesitates. What is she doing? She's coming back, isn't she?

She pulls the front door open slowly, checking to see if anyone is around. Maybe the gunman didn't come on his own. It's quiet outside. It always is. Coldburn has so many Airbnbs now that most of the houses stand empty out of season. The snow's not settling but it is getting a little heavier and she worries that she's only got trainers on.

It's not important. There's only one thing she needs and that's the phone box at the end of the street. It's the only one in the village. It's always been a bit of a joke that the parish council insisted on keeping it when everyone has their own phone but the people here really don't like change. Right now she thinks it's the best decision they ever made.

She checks once more to make sure there's no one watching the house and sprints down the road. She can see the phone box is empty. It always is. At least she doesn't have to wait or explain what's happened to anyone hogging the phone. Not that she could.

Ruby reaches it in record time, yanks open the door and goes to grab the receiver. It's not there. Just a coiled lead coming out from the coin box and hanging down towards the floor.

Something very strange is going on.

Margaret lets the curtain drop and pats the white Bedlington Terrier on her lap as she tries to remember the sequence of events.

First there'd been the man in the phone box. A stranger. Dressed a bit like a soldier but no soldier would have a haircut like that. Nigel had never shut up about standards dropping since his day but she doubts they've dropped that far.

She'd seen the man earlier that morning, just standing on the corner looking up the street. Hadn't thought much about it at first but when he was still there ten minutes later she'd started to take an interest. He seemed to be talking to himself but then he took something from his belt and she'd realised it was a radio transmitter of some kind. She'd watched as he'd finished the conversation, put the radio away and walked down to the phone box. Why would he need a phone when he had a walkie-talkie? She was so curious that she'd made a note of it on the pad she kept by the window. He was only in there a few moments and didn't make a call. She'd found her binoculars by then and would have seen the receiver by his ear if he had.

Then he'd stepped out of the booth, thrown something over a wall, and walked back up the street, past the spot he'd been standing in and straight up to No. 8, where that quiet man, Alex, lived with his equally reclusive daughter whose name Margaret could never remember. Judy maybe? She'd been surprised when Alex opened the door, she knew from experience that he normally ignored callers – she'd taken in enough of his parcels in the past. After a brief conversation the visitor had stepped inside and the door had closed.

That had been about fifteen minutes ago. Margaret had assumed the excitement was over so she'd gone and made herself a nice cup of tea which is still sitting in front of her. It's going cold but she takes a sip anyway, not wanting to miss anything now the girl – Ruby, that was it – is out and about. Margaret doubts that phone box has seen any use in at least a couple of years – and she would know – but now twice in one morning. That's no coincidence – and the girl doesn't seem to be making a call either. And why would she need a phone box – all the young 'uns had their own phones these days, didn't they?

'There's definitely a rabbit off here, Boris,' she tells the dog.

Margaret looks up again as the girl steps out of the box, looking puzzled and more than a little distressed, glancing every which way as if she doesn't have a clue where to go next. The only place she doesn't seem to look is behind her which is ironic, Margaret thinks, because that's where the problem is.

Ruby feels the touch on her shoulder and spins around, flinging her elbow towards the man's face just like she's been taught in the karate classes that her dad insisted she took. The blow glances off the top of his head as he ducks at the last minute but it's still enough to send him tumbling to the floor.

'Christ's sake, Ruby,' he cries. 'What's that all about?'

She sighs. It's Lucas. Not a man, a boy. The class clown. Not a serious bone in his body. All she needs. He puts his hand out for her to help him back up but she ignores him.

'Thanks a bunch,' he says, clambering back to his feet and brushing himself down before turning to look at her.

'Why you crying?' he asks.

'I'm not,' she says, reaching up, the damp on her cheeks taking her by surprise.

'But you—'

'Can I use your phone?' She hasn't got time for this.

'That's a shite apology.' He rubs his head as if feeling for a bump.

'Can I?'

'What's it worth?' He grins. He's tried to chat her up a few times before, especially on the school bus that they both use when he can be arsed to go. He got no joy, obviously, but clearly he thinks he's got something to trade this time.

'Just give me the fucking phone, dipshit,' she yells.

Surprisingly, he does as she asks, fumbling it from his pocket and handing it over. She tries to use it but it's locked.

'Code,' she demands.

'1-2-3-4,' he says. She should have guessed.

She puts it in and tries to ring 999 but nothing happens. This sodding village. The whole place is like a dead zone.

'Piece of shit,' she says, handing it back to him. He glances at the phone.

'No signal? It's normally fine around here. That's weird.'

'Everything's fucking weird,' she mutters.

'What do you mean? And what happened to your head?'

She reaches up and feels a large bump from where she banged it earlier. She hasn't got time to explain things to him though, she needs a grown-up.

'Is your mam home?'

He frowns and suddenly looks lost.

'What? N-no, she's, um, away.'

'So you're no use to me at all, are you?' she shouts. He backs away and she's about to tell him to piss off and leave her alone when a movement from one of the houses nearby catches her eye. It's the old biddy's house, the one who used to be in the Neighbourhood Watch, Maureen, no, Margaret. Thinks she's Queen Bee, just because she's got one of the biggest houses in the village. She's always watching out of her window – this'll be the most exciting thing she's seen in months. Ruby bets she's got a phone though. She starts to cross the road when she hears a siren in the distance. Whatever it is, it's clearly heading towards them as it gets louder and louder. It can't be, can it? Ruby can't believe her luck. How is this happening? Who called them? Not her dad, surely? He never carried his phone – and he'd have let her do it if that's what he wanted. She remembers the dead guy's radio. Maybe he isn't dead after all?

A few moments later an ambulance flies around the corner and speeds past them, squealing to a halt right outside her house. She's about to run towards it when she realises there's something wrong. It's definitely an ambulance – there's a big red cross on the side. But the rest of it is green. It's military. She grabs Lucas by the arm and pulls him behind the phone box so they won't be seen.

'What's gannin' on?' Lucas asks. 'Has something happened to your dad? Is that why you wanted the phone?'

She nods slightly but doesn't answer him, too busy watching as two men leap out of the ambulance, one from the passenger side and one from the rear, the latter carrying a stretcher, and run into her house. Who cares where they're from, they're going to help her dad. She should be with him. She starts to move forward but then a third man gets out of the driver's door, which stops her in her tracks. What the fuck? He's dressed exactly like the prick who shot her dad; black T-shirt and camo bottoms. Much bigger though, like the Hulk on steroids. The other difference is the hair – which even from this distance she can see is a standard military buzz cut. And then her brain catches up. The other two who went into the house were in the same outfits too. And that ambulance is just plain wrong.

'He doesn't look like a paramedic,' Lucas says, stepping out from behind the phone box. Ruby says nothing, though he's right. More like a soldier. She tries to pull Lucas back out of sight but is too late. The guy with the buzz cut looks around and sees them. He grabs something from his belt and puts it to his mouth. It's another walkie-talkie, exactly like the first man had. A few seconds later he puts it back and starts running towards them.

This is his own fault. Alex lies there, bleeding, thinking all the way back to how it started: Emma's disappearance. Could he have dealt with it better? If he'd gone after her straight away things might have been different.

He hears the front door open and is immediately back in the moment, praying that Ruby hasn't come back. The rush of heavy footsteps is strangely reassuring. Whoever it is, there's more than one of them. It's not good but at least it's not her.

Two soldiers, dressed in exactly the same gear as Green, rush into the kitchen, stretcher in hand. Alex had heard the wounded man mutter 'man down' into the walkie-talkie earlier. That's why he insisted Ruby should run – but he didn't expect them to come so quickly.

'Fuck me,' the smaller of the two says as they run past Alex to their injured colleague.

'No pulse,' the other one says – a Scottish accent this time.

Alex can hear them trying to revive Green, lots of huffing and puffing and exhortations to 'go again'. It should be the perfect opportunity to escape but he's already tried to move twice and the pain in his shoulder is unbearable. He's pretty sure he briefly passed out the first time he attempted to get up. The bullet must have hit the bone on the way through.

'It's too late, Red,' the first man says. 'He's gone.'

So he's a murderer now. No regrets. Ruby's safety comes first. Always.

'Stupid twat,' Red says. 'What was he thinking? He was only supposed to be on recon.'

Alex readies himself for the attack that's surely coming – he's killed one of their own. He tries to move again but the pain's still too great so he feels around for the knife that he dropped earlier. His fingers brush against the handle.

'What a car crash.' The one called Red appears from around the corner and boots Alex in the ribs with his steel toecap. There's an audible crack but not much more pain than he already has. The knife has slipped away again though.

'This what you're after?' Red asks, picking up the knife and placing it against Alex's neck.

Alex tries to pull away but his damaged shoulder makes it impossible to move. He's sure he's about to get sliced and diced when the other guy intervenes, placing a hand on Red's shoulder.

'Pack it in, Red. Green messed up, jumped the gun. The kid should have waited for the rest of us.'

Alex flinches a little at the word 'kid', wonders how old he was.

'Didn't deserve to die for it though, did he?' Red says, shrugging the guy's hand away.

'Up to you, sunshine. But the boss will want him in one piece. He's bait.'

'You're a right brown-nosing bastard, aren't you, Silver? Bet you'd love to tell tales.'

Silver shrugs. 'Your call.'

Alex can see that Red wants to ignore the advice, desperate to get revenge for his dead colleague, but he's obviously been trained to follow orders. After a moment's hesitation he puts the knife back down on the floor and gets right up in his face, making sure that his spit flecks Alex's cheeks as he speaks.

'Temporary reprieve, dickhead. If we didn't need you you'd be dead already. But soon as we've got the girl, you and I will be spending some quality time together. And we'll see how many pieces you end up in then. Just one thing you need to tell me first,' he adds, pressing firmly down on Alex's injured shoulder. 'Where the fuck is she?'

Stranger and stranger, Margaret thinks as she walks over to her house phone. She must tell Sally what's going on. The woman will never forgive her if she keeps this to herself. She puts the phone to her ear but there's no dialling tone. She clicks the little button on the top – what do they call those things? It makes no difference; the line is dead.

'Bugger,' she mutters to herself, glad that Nigel's not there to tell her off. 'Potty mouth,' he'd say. She misses him sometimes but he couldn't half be a sanctimonious old sod at times. And that wasn't his worst fault.

She goes back to the window. The two kids and the ambulance driver have disappeared around the corner now, which is a shame, but there's more action back at the girl's house. The medics who ran into the house have come back out with a stretcher covered in a sheet. That's not good. They only cover them up if they're dead. They put the stretcher into the back of the ambulance and go back into the house again with a second one. Why is it an army-style ambulance? And what on earth has happened in that house? She remembers those House of Horror stories she's seen on the news – like the Fred West thing where they found all those bodies. That couldn't happen here, surely? Though now she thinks about it, that was what the neighbours in those stories always said, wasn't it? 'It's such a nice place to live, and he was such a quiet man, always kept himself to himself.'

Jesus H. Christ. That was Alex to a T. 'Blasphemer,' Nigel would have said.

A few minutes later the two men come out with the other stretcher though this time it looks like the patient is alive. Margaret can see that the top of the man's body is uncovered and his head is moving. She picks up her binoculars to take a closer look but it's too late; by the time she has them refocused the stretcher is in the back of the ambulance. One of the men clambers in after it while the other walks around to the passenger side door. When he gets there he stands scratching his head, looking around, clearly wondering where the driver has gone.

She wonders whether to pop out and tell him, but thinks not. Best to stay out of it until she knows what 'it' is. Eventually the man shrugs, goes around to the driver's side and gets in. A moment later the ambulance moves off.

Margaret puts the binoculars down, makes a note on her pad and smiles. Sally's going to be furious that she missed all the action.

This is not what Silver signed up for. It was meant to be a straight in-and-out mission. Cut the phone lines, jam the signals, find the target and get the hell away. One last earner before he packed it in and started afresh while he was still young enough. Somewhere quiet, down south, where they didn't talk funny and live on Greggs. Maybe he could be a postman or, even better, a window cleaner? Plenty of fresh air, cash in hand and no dead civilians or screaming kids to haunt him.

No one was supposed to get hurt this time, especially one of their own. But now he finds he's signed up for another shitshow. Not as bad as the last one, in Syria – or Kurdistan, depending on who you asked – where the civilian casualties were off the scale, but that was a pretty high bar to set.

He looks behind him. Green stares at him accusingly. He reaches across and closes the dead man's eyes. What was the kid thinking, going in alone? Why didn't the stupid twat wait for backup like he was supposed to? Now this could take days. And Gold is going to have to bring in more men to seal up the village and carry out a house-to-house search. Good job there's a Plan B and they've already set up a base just in case it all went tits up.

On the other side of the ambulance the father has passed out again. Silver checks his vitals but he's stable. For now. He's not losing any more blood at least. They'd been told he was an unarmed civilian, an easy target. They'd been told wrong. He hopes this is just a temporary setback – he's promised to take his wife out for dinner on her birthday – the day after tomorrow – and she's not the forgiving type.

A bit like Red. Absolute psycho. He's pretty sure the jock headcase would have killed this poor bastard back in the kitchen if he hadn't intervened. Silver makes a mental note to try and switch places with one of the others tomorrow – last thing he needs is another partner who can't control himself. He'd had that in Rojava and far too many innocents had died as a result. He shakes the images from that day out of his head before they can take root, still ashamed that he stood by and said nothing. Either at the time or since.

He'd thought those days were over. But now look at him – sat in the back of a knock-off ambulance with a dead oppo and a wounded civilian that he has to keep alive. For the moment.

11

Ruby's heart is trying to beat its way out of her chest. She has never run so quickly in her life. She's barely ever run at all but the sight of that humongous soldier sprinting towards them was all the encouragement she needed.

Even so she is already several metres behind Lucas. She sees him turn down the small side street and run under the arch that leads to Mr Baldwin's garage. Ruby pumps her arms harder, gasping in pain as she slips on the wet, icy pavement, her hand clipping the wall when she tears around the corner.

Lucas is nowhere to be seen. Despite the fear of being caught she slows down, wondering where the hell he's gone. As she does so an arm snakes out from a doorway to her right and pulls her inside the pitch-dark room, the door slamming closed behind her back. A hand closes over her mouth.

'Divvn't scream.' Even though he's whispering she knows it's Lucas. He's got that distinctive Northumbrian burr where some of the letters seem to last forever. He's facing her and they're so close she can feel his breath on her forehead.

'OK?' he says.

She nods and he moves his hand away. They stay silent and still until they hear footsteps pounding down the road which fade away into the distance. It's only then that she notices the smell. It's rank.

'What is this place?' she whispers.

'Used to be a bin store but now it's Baldwin's emergency loo. He pisses in a bucket so he doesn't have to go back to his house to do it.'

Ruby gags at the thought of it, the smell somehow becoming worse now she knows what it is. She takes a deep breath and holds it for as long as she can, all the time terrified that their pursuer is going to fling open the door any moment. She's also conscious of how small this place is. She and Lucas are squeezed tightly up against each other. It's the closest she's been to a boy since she snogged Mark Johnson at Sophie Watson's birthday party for a dare last month. She counted *that* as brave back then.

She can feel something nudging up against her waist. Seriously?

'Have you got a hard-on?' she whispers.

Lucas shakes his head but pulls away from her slightly. Boys are unbelievable. It stinks of piss, they're being hunted by a massive psycho and he's still thinking about sex.

Ruby's eyes are adjusting to the light and she can see there's a curtain behind Lucas's back.

'What's in there?'

He turns to look.

'Just tins of old paint.'

'How do you know about all this?'

'Baldwin pays me to tidy up the place now and again.'

Suddenly Ruby freezes as the footsteps return, right outside the door this time, then she hears someone cough, as if they've been running. The door begins to open, bashing into her back. Light streams into the small space.

'Who's in there?'

She sighs with relief – it's not the soldier, it's Mr Baldwin. She imagines his giant belly entering the room a few seconds before the rest of him but Lucas has other ideas.

'It's just me, Mr B,' Lucas says, squeezing past her and out through the gap, pulling the door behind him. 'I got caught short.'

'Cheeky little bastard. I should charge you for using the executive facilities,' Baldwin says, but she can hear the laughter in his voice.

'When a man's gotta go . . .' Lucas says playfully.

'You're not a man yet, sunshine, don't wish your life away or before you know it you'll be like me. Having to piss every five minutes. Talking of which . . .'

The door starts to open again.

'Maybe I should empty the bucket first,' Lucas says, clearly doing his best to keep Baldwin from discovering her.

Ruby quietly pulls the curtain in front of her to one side. The space is tiny – literally the depth of the tins piled up in there – but so is she and though it's tight she squeezes into a gap and closes the curtain again.

'I only emptied it this morning, lad, unless you piss like a horse it'll still be fine.'

Ruby hears the door open fully and can see more light edging around the curtain. She wonders about saying something – maybe he can help? But what's she going to say – I think my dad's just killed a man? And everyone knows Baldwin's a drunk who you wouldn't trust for a second – her dad has warned her several times to keep away from him. She can smell the stale beer and sweat on him from here. Lucas seems to like him though so maybe he's not all that bad?

Her mind is made up by Baldwin's piss starting to trickle into the bucket. She'd be way too embarrassed to say anything now. The curtain is so near she daren't move an inch so can't even put her hands over her ears. It stops and starts several times before the man sighs and calls a halt. She's so close she can hear him do his zip up before he goes back outside, leaving the door open. The smell is even worse than it was when she got there which she would have sworn was impossible. She waits for as long as she can bear it and then creeps out from behind the curtain, checks that the coast is clear, and steps outside.

12

Lucas is waiting for her around the corner. She doesn't see him at first as he's crouched down behind a parked car on the other side of the road but then he stands up and whistles to get her attention. There's no sign of the soldier.

She joins him and they both stay down together, keeping out of sight just in case the soldier suddenly appears again. It's the first time she's had the chance to properly think for a moment but the delay hasn't helped. She has no clue what is happening. Her world has been blown apart in the space of – she checks her watch: 12.45 – barely half an hour since the ring on the doorbell which started this all off.

'What's gannin' on, Rubes?'

She hates that version of her name but lets it go. Despite his faults, she's grateful that he's there, he's been useful – without him the driver would have caught her easily. She'll send him packing later once she knows more about what's happening.

'Who was that guy chasing us?' he adds.

'I don't know.'

'OK,' he says. 'Why don't you tell us what you do know?'

She looks up at him, he's staring at her intently, serious as cancer. Maybe she's misjudged him. Lucas has always been one to avoid really, the kid who was always messing about at junior school, cheeking the teachers and that. Once they'd moved up to the big school, he disappeared into the lower groups, rarely seen again, usually sitting at the back of the bus, occasionally flashing his arse and generally acting like a right dickhead – which is why it's never been exactly difficult to resist his cheesy chat-up lines before. She prefers this version of him.

Everyone reckoned he was the one who'd set fire to the school gym last year, which is the only time she's really thought about him again, but no one was ever officially blamed for that. Before today he would have been the last person she'd have wanted by her side in a crisis.

Lucas sighs. 'You don't have to tell me if you don't want to.'

'It's not that—'

He turns away, cutting her off.

'We can go to my house,' he says, glancing back over his shoulder. 'The signal's fine there. If you're worried about your dad you can ring a friend or another relative, maybe? Someone you trust.' He's obviously pissed off with her.

'I don't have any other family.'

He looks puzzled, as if everyone must have a family.

'Right. Well, you could try the hospital then.'

She nods, not having a single alternative idea in her head. She needs somewhere to clear her mind and it's as good a place as any. A small part of her remembers the hard-on but she pushes the thought away. Lucas is a twat but he's not that kind of twat – that was just a lad thing, they can't help themselves. There are a few at school that you wouldn't want to be left alone with but all the girls know who they are and Lucas isn't on anybody's shit list – at least not in that way.

They make their way carefully through the village, using the back lanes. She and Liv – who's the only friend her dad's ever allowed to sleep over – used to play a game to see if they could go from one end to the other without being seen and it's paying off until they come out onto a small side road and the soldier who chased them is standing on the corner, ten metres away, talking on his radio.

Luckily, he has his back to them and they manage to scramble back unseen. A few seconds later they hear a vehicle pull up and Ruby takes the chance to peer around the edge of the wall. It's the ambulance. Their chaser climbs into the passenger seat and it speeds off towards the south end of the village. She's certain her dad is in the back of it – she can feel it in her bones. But they're not using their siren any more and she doesn't want to think about why there's no hurry this time.

Ruby and Lucas cross the road into another back lane which threads its way behind what used to laughably be called the village centre – one pub and a small shop, both long closed and up for sale – and manage to avoid anyone else until they reach his house.

Lucas lives at the arse-end of Coldburn, only a few hundred metres from Ruby's place but it might as well be on another planet. It's a small cottage – not the rose-coloured kind from a Disney movie but a tumbledown wreck of a place that badly needs some work doing. Ruby realises she knows next to nothing about Lucas, his mum was as much a recluse as her dad and Lucas only started junior school in her last year there. 'Incomers' the locals called them – a label they applied to anyone who hadn't lived in the village for several generations, including her and her dad even though they'd been there for almost her entire life.

They approach the cottage from the back, through a decaying door in a wall that's also beginning to crumble. There's no back garden, just a concrete yard with a couple of pot plants. It's tidy though, like someone cares about its appearance – there's a stiff brush propped against the wall in the corner.

Lucas must notice her glance at it as he smiles at her.

'It's one of my chores. I have to sweep it every other morning.'

'It's cute,' she says, to change the subject. Truth is she's embarrassed that, apart from some cooking, she does so little around her own house, leaving most of it to her dad – who sometimes calls her a spoilt princess. She's always thought he was joking but maybe he was right.

Once inside, Lucas grabs a couple of cans of Diet Coke from the small fridge and guides her into the tiny front room, which is also tidy. He sits on the only armchair in the room and nods towards a ragged two-seater sofa that takes up most of the space. Both things point towards an ancient telly in the corner.

Ruby takes five, glugging from her drink, still not quite sure how she's ended up there. It's no time at all since she was sitting in her own room without a care in the world, other than the school project she had to finish. It takes her a moment to realise that Lucas is staring at her.

'What?'

'Your arm,' he says.

'What about it?'

Ruby lifts her arm up and realises that the underside of her sleeve is covered in blood. She's not sure where it came from, or even whose it is.

'I cut my hand on a wall when we were running,' she says, holding it up to show him, but her voice catches and it's such obvious bollocks, there's barely a mark on it. Suddenly the room seems freezing and she starts to shake. She tries to control it but can't and in moments she's crying big time and there's snot streaming from her nose like someone turned a tap on. She tries to wipe it away and cover her face with her arms at the same time but Lucas comes over and takes her hands.

'You're safe here,' he says. 'You can stay as long as you like. But that's a whole lotta blood for a scratch and what about the whopping bump on your head? When we've got you cleaned up, how's about you tell us what's really gannin' on?'

13

Ruby slips on one of Lucas's plain white T-shirts that he left outside the bathroom door for her while she cleaned herself up. She sniffs the armpits. It smells of boy.

She's puzzled by his calmness and wonders what he's seen in the past if the sight of so much blood doesn't shake him. He's a bit different than she believed, more mature. She stares at the mirror on the front of the small bathroom cabinet above the sink and almost smiles. She's changed too. She's not even the girl she was this morning. She looks down at the bag by her feet. That girl would never have had a gun in her rucksack like she does – she's brought it up with her just in case Lucas was thinking about having a little nose around in her absence. What he doesn't know can't hurt him.

She decides she needs him for the moment and should trust him a little more. Though maybe not completely.

'A man came to our house earlier,' she says, as soon as she's sat back down in the living room. She pauses, editing her story as she goes along, not wanting to make her dad look like the villain. 'He shot my dad.'

Lucas starts to pale. He'd obviously known that something odd was happening but someone getting shot probably wasn't on his shortlist.

'You serious?'

She nods.

'Like with a gun?'

'No, with a fucking peashooter.'

Neither of them laugh.

'But why?'

'I've no idea.'

'Is he . . .'

She can tell he's looking for an alternative to 'dead'. Almost feels sorry for him.

'. . . OK?' Of all the choices he could have made it's probably the best one.

'I think so. There was a lot of blood but I think I stopped it. He was conscious, talking a bit.'

Lucas looks like he has other questions but fortunately he moves on.

'So *you* called for that ambulance?'

'No, that's the weird thing. One of the weird things. I wanted to but my dad wouldn't let me use my phone. That's why I ran to the phone box but it had been vandalised.'

She gives him a bit of a look. Whenever anything like that happens in the village, Lucas's name gets a mention. He visibly bristles.

'It wasn't me.'

'I didn't say it was.'

'I know that look. I see it all the time round here. You're probably one of those tossers who reckoned I burned the gym down just because I like to play the odd prank on people and have a laugh.'

Ruby can feel her face going red. She definitely was.

'I'm sorry. I didn't mean anything by it.'

'Sure,' he says, clearly annoyed but trying to control it. 'So if you didn't call the ambulance, who did?'

'I've no idea.'

'It's good though, right? He'll be OK now, won't he? Getting treatment and that.'

'Maybe. But that wasn't a normal ambulance, was it? And why did that man start chasing us? He was dressed exactly like the one who shot my dad, like some kind of army guy.'

'That was mental,' Lucas agreed. 'He was huge. Looked like one of those 'roid rage guys I've seen shooting up in the gym bogs in town. I reckon he could have picked me up in one hand if he'd caught us.'

Neither of them speak for a moment but then he glances up with a bright idea look on his face.

'Just to be sure, why don't you try and ring the hospital now? He could be there. If he is you can find out how he's getting on – they'll talk to you cos you're family.'

'I haven't got my phone.'

'Use mine. Like I said, signal's fine here.' He pulls his phone out of his pocket and passes it over. 'The code's—'

'1-2-3-4,' she says, grinning. 'You told me before, remember.'

'My mam's always reckoned I lack imagination,' he says,

laughing and then stopping, like he thinks it's not appropriate.

Ruby tries to Google the number of the local hospital – there's only one anywhere near them so it has to be the right one – but the internet's not working.

'D'you have Wi-Fi?'

He nods. 'It's a bit patchy though. Just ring 999, they should be able to put you through.'

It's a good idea. She hits 999 and waits but nothing happens. She glances at the screen. The call has ended. She tries again. Same result. Still no signal.

'I think your phone is busted,' she says, handing it back to him.

'It was working this morning,' he says, moving to the window and trying himself, then frowning when the same thing happens. 'Try the landline instead.' He points at a small table beside the sofa where an old phone sits.

'Why didn't you mention that before?' she complains.

'I forgot. I never use it. It's my mam's thing. She doesn't like technology much.'

Ruby picks it up but it's dead. She shakes her head.

'Maybe she should have paid the bill.' She regrets it as soon as she says it. Everyone knows that Lucas and his mum are poor. He used to get free school meals. Probably still does.

He pretends to ignore it but she can see he's hurt.

'Lines must be down again,' he mutters.

Suddenly, there's the sound of someone shouting from outside. They both leap up and dash to the window.

'Keep out of sight,' Ruby says.

They stand on either side, looking out. At first there's nothing to see but the shouting is getting nearer and clearer and eventually she can make out the words.

'. . . it is safe to leave.'

An open-top army jeep is moving along the street very slowly. Another of the black-shirted soldiers is standing in the back with a megaphone. He begins again.

'Please stay inside and lock your doors. An escaped prisoner has been sighted in the village. We are carrying out a controlled search of the area. To ensure your safety please stay inside until you are told it is safe to leave.'

He pauses for a moment as the jeep passes Lucas's house then begins again:

'Please stay inside . . .'

As the jeep disappears from sight, the man's words fade away.

Ruby glances across at Lucas who looks excited.

'D'you think that's who it was at your house? The escaped prisoner! Maybe you should go and tell them about it? He might still be hiding there.'

Ruby closes her eyes and flicks through her memory of what happened earlier. The man ringing the bell, her dad letting him in, the shouting in the kitchen, the fight. There's just no way.

'He was no prisoner,' she says. 'He came to our house specifically, it wasn't just chance. My dad wouldn't have let him in otherwise.'

'But maybe that's why he escaped, to find your dad. Maybe they knew each other from before.'

Ruby shook her head though she could feel a splinter of doubt in there somewhere. Could that have been what happened? What did she really know about her dad's past? She remembers him ejecting the bullets so efficiently. She had no idea he could do that.

'My dad is a good man,' she says, firmly.

Lucas frowns. 'I never said he wasn't. But didn't you say you have no family?'

Where is he going with this? She nods, hesitantly.

'What if you're in witness protection?'

'What do you mean?'

'Maybe your dad was a witness to whatever put this guy in prison. Maybe he was given a new identity and the man found out where he was and escaped to come after him.'

'You watch too much telly,' she says.

It does actually make some kind of sense though. Not just about this morning but about her dad's lack of friends. Then there's his obsession with privacy and his weird reluctance to talk about the past. There's only one problem.

'Why would that man have been dressed exactly like the ones who've just driven past?' she says, nodding at the window. 'And like the guys in the ambulance and the one who chased us. He was one of them.'

That shuts him up. They stand in silence for a minute or two.

'I didn't mean your dad was a criminal,' he says.

'I know. And I'm sorry for what I said about the phone bill. That was mean.'

'OK, quits,' he says. She nods but knows it's not quits, not really, she hasn't been honest with him.

'I think the man was dead.'

'The prisoner . . . I mean, the guy who came to your house?'

'Yes.'

'But I thought he shot your dad?'

'He did. But then my dad managed to stab him.' It was a small lie; she wasn't ready to tell him her dad had started it. 'I think he was dead when I left.'

'So the ambulance crew, the soldiers, would have found his body?'

She nods.

'Then who are they looking for now?' He glances towards the window as if the soldiers are still out there.

Ruby sighs. She knows this is going to sound paranoid. But she remembers the first soldier talking about 'she' and how urgently her dad told her to run. Slowly she raises her hand and points at her own chest.

'I think it might be me. But I have no idea why.'

'Shiiiit,' Lucas says, leaning back against the windowsill. They stay like that for what seems an age before he stands up straight again, excited.

'We should go back and check out your house,' he says.

'No chance,' she says immediately. Then, 'Why?'

'If it is you they want there must be a reason. Something to do with your dad's past, maybe. You said you don't have any family. Where else can we look to find out what that might be?'

She shakes her head, terrified at what they might find. What if her dad's body is just lying there on the kitchen floor?

'No. They might still be there.'

'But we saw the ambulance. It was heading out of the village. They'll have done their searching by now. If you think about it, it's the last place they'd expect to find you.'

She's about to contradict him when she realises that he's probably right. If they're looking for her they'll do it methodically, house-by-house, won't they? So it makes sense to hide in the place they started searching.

'I could go on my own, if you like,' he continues, misreading her hesitation. 'Just to check it out. You need a rest anyway, you look wiped out.'

She almost accepts his offer, she's exhausted and it's nice of him, but knows it's the wrong thing to do. She has to woman-up.

'I can't ask you to do that. It's my problem.'

'A problem shared . . .'

'Is what?'

'I dunno, do I? My mam used to say it.'

She rolls her eyes but he doesn't seem easy to discourage. He reminds her of Tigger from *Winnie-the-Pooh*, bouncing around with boundless energy. Maybe he's on drugs? That would explain a lot. She shakes her head, realises she's just being a cow again.

'How about we go together then,' he says.

She nods, though Ruby can't help thinking that whatever they find it's not going to be good. If Lucas is right, and her dad really isn't who he says, then who the hell is she?

14

Dearest Ruby

If you're reading this you're either 16 (Happy Birthday!) and old enough to know the truth about how we ended up here, or something has happened to me. I really hope it's the former but if it's the latter I pray that you have found a place of safety. Don't trust anyone.

Please believe me that everything I've done has been to protect you. I'm sure I've made many mistakes along the way but please understand that whatever I've done has come from a good place. I've loved you with all of my heart from the first time I set eyes on you and keeping you safe has always been my number one priority.

I'm sorry that I haven't prepared you for any of this . . .

15

Danny Barnes is furious. The last time someone threatened him with a gun he shot first and asked questions later. If he was armed now he'd be tempted to do it again. But it's a long time since he was serving in Belfast. And anyway, this time, the guy in front of him, who is just putting the last barricade in the roadblock in place, is the soldier. Sort of.

'I have to get to the supermarket,' he tells the armed man.

'No one in or out, I'm afraid, sir.'

'My dog needs feeding.'

'Not my problem, sir. Just turn your vehicle around, head back to your house and stay indoors until someone tells you it's safe to come back out.'

'What is he supposed to eat? I've got nowt in.'

The man laughs. He looks too young to be a soldier. But everyone looks young to Danny these days.

'Dogs will eat anything, sir. You must have some food in the cupboard. Give them some baked beans.'

He's not wrong but Danny's never really liked doing what he was told – which had seen him up on the occasional charge back in the day. Since he left the army he hasn't really had to answer to anyone, which is exactly how he likes it. He taps the barricade.

'Just between us, I used to do this, a few years back. In Belfast.'

'Thank you for your service,' the soldier deadpans.

'Come on, man, what's really going on?'

'Like I told you, there's been a sighting of an escaped prisoner in the area and we believe we've got him pinned down in the village.'

'And he's an ageing pensioner with long grey hair and a gammy leg, is he?'

The soldier smiles. 'No, sir, he isn't.'

'It's not me then, is it? So why can't I leave?'

'Those are my orders, sir.'

A memory flashes through Danny's head. It's like déjà vu, only it's him standing on the other side of the barricades making a similar argument to one of the locals. It seems like yesterday rather than almost forty years ago. He shakes his head and starts to move away before turning back one last time.

'How long's this going on for?'

'Until we catch the man, sir. Or until we establish that he's not here. Whichever comes first.'

'So I just have to try later, is that what you're saying?'

The soldier nods. 'Exactly, sir.'

Danny sighs. He's starting to feel a little guilty, getting on the man's case. He's only doing his duty, and doing it well. The barricade stretches right across the road and there's a stinger lying on the tarmac twenty yards further back, just in case anyone tries to drive through the first obstacle. And another barrier stopping people entering the village even further along. Textbook stuff. Almost. Both barricades should be manned, at the very least. He's heard about defence cutbacks – maybe they're short of numbers?

'I suppose one of your mates is at the other end of the village?'

The soldier nods again. 'I'm afraid so, sir. So don't go trying there as well.' He indicates the radio on his belt. 'I'll be reporting your registration number as soon as you've turned around.'

There's one last thing that's been bothering Danny.

'Where are you based?' he asks.

'Need-to-know basis, I'm afraid. And you don't need to know.'

'It's just that you don't have any insignia on your uniform. Why's that?'

The soldier looks a little confused by the question, like he either doesn't know or maybe doesn't want to answer.

'Just get yourself home, sir,' he says, raising his rifle slightly. 'We wouldn't want anything bad to happen to you, would we?'

16

There's total silence as they make their way back to Ruby's house. No cars on the move, no people stopping to chat to each other. It's creepy as hell. Clearly the few villagers still living there are doing as they're told.

To limit the risk of being seen they waited until the light began to fade but they may as well have set off earlier, there's no one to see them anyway. The place is like a ghost town. Ruby shivers, imagining whose ghost it might be.

They are halfway there when a noise stops Ruby in her tracks. There's someone behind her and it's not Lucas. He's ahead of her, peering around the corner of the alley into the street.

She turns slowly, the rucksack on her back catching the edge of the fence. She's trying to look casual, not show any fear, pretending her world hasn't imploded.

A monstrous three-legged black cat is staring at her, claws out, hackles raised. It hisses, feral as anything. She likes cats but this one is nothing like her lovely Pluto. It first appeared in the village a few months ago and no one has dared to try and take it in. She jerks her foot towards it, hoping to scare it away, but it doesn't flinch, instead letting out a yowl that would wake the dead.

Lucas is suddenly beside her.

'Jesus!' he says. 'That's ginormous.'

They back away slowly but the cat follows them, keeping the same distance, growling as they move, like they've invaded its territory. They're near the end of the alley when a pair of headlights sweep into the road in front of them. Startled, the cat bolts but there's no time for them to do the same so they press themselves against the edge of the wall, hiding in the shadows. Ruby's glad she made Lucas wear a black hoodie that almost matches her own – it makes them harder to see. The army jeep drives straight past them and turns the corner, away from view.

'That was close,' Lucas says. 'The cat slowing us down probably saved us.'

They continue on, shooting straight across the road and down a small path which brings them out fifty metres from her house, which looks deserted but she's taking no chances. They're not going in the front door, especially as the lights in No. 1 across the road are blazing and she's not letting Mrs Nosy Parker see her again.

'This way,' she says, grabbing Lucas's hand and heading back the way they came to pick up a narrow trail which snakes behind the houses, almost completely hidden from view by the tall hedge that blocks off the gardens.

The trail would eventually take them down to a stile into a field, where the public footpath sign points to Rothbury, the nearest town, about ten miles away. Ruby almost suggests they take it, see if someone there can help them, but it's dark and Lucas is already turning right, heading towards the back of her house, so she follows him.

'Which one's yours again?' he asks, as they get nearer to the rear of the four houses that back on to the field.

She nods to the one on the far left. She can see her dad's curtains moving in the breeze – he always likes the windows open when he sleeps and never shuts them in the day – claims that fresh air is all you need to stay fit and well. Which she always thought was bollocks. Now she knows it was. An image of him bleeding on the kitchen floor flashes into her head but she shakes it to clear it out again. If she's going to help him she needs to stay focused.

There's a hedge at the back of the house but it's got a big enough gap to squeeze through. Her dad jogs to keep fit and he's always used it as a shortcut down to the footpath. He tried to get her to go with him a couple of years back but when she told him she'd need some sports bras he got embarrassed and never brought it up again. It was nonsense, obviously, her boobs are tiny, but there's no way he would have wanted to talk about that. Although it was excruciating at the time she'd give anything to have that kind of conversation with him again.

The house looks quiet, though there's a light on in the kitchen, but they take no chances, edging slowly along the side of the garden, using the trees for cover and crouching down until they're both underneath the window. Ruby, terrified of what they are about to confront, feels herself starting to panic, her heart racing. Lucas touches her arm gently.

'I'll have a quick look first,' he says. She nods, relieved for a change that someone else is making the decisions for her.

He takes a deep breath and pops his head up, glancing around but not saying anything. After a few moments of that he stands up fully, still alert though.

'Oh. My. God.'

'What?' she says trying to scramble up.

'Nothing,' he grins. 'Just winding you up. It looks deserted. No one in the kitchen, anyway.'

For a moment he's the boy she remembers, always taking the joke too far. He can tell by her face that she's not impressed.

'Sorry,' he says. 'It's just nerves. I didn't mean anything.'

She gets up and stands next to him. He's right, there's nothing there. She can't even see blood on the floor but most of that would have been behind the island. They're going to have to go in.

'Ready?' Lucas says. She nods.

He sidles over to the door and opens it slowly – there's never been any need to lock it, until now. There's no sound from the inside. She closes the gap between them and they both step into the kitchen. The floor is gleaming, no blood where she last saw the dead gunman but there is a tell-tale smell of disinfectant. Someone has cleaned the place up. She moves past Lucas to the end of the counter, where she last saw her dad. Again, there's nothing, no body, no blood, just clean tiles. No bullets either. She glances across to the corner of the room. The magazine her dad threw over there has disappeared too.

'It's pretty tidy, considering there was a shoot-out,' he says. 'You're sure this is where it all happened?'

'Of course I'm sure. Unless you think I'm making it all up.'

He is actually considering it. She can tell. He does his best to hide it though.

'No, course not. It's just it all looks so normal.'

Ruby sees the knife block is full again now and bets that they will all be sparklingly clean too.

'Nothing about this is normal,' she says.

17

There's a sharp rat-a-tat-tat at the door.

Margaret turns the CD player off and heads into the darkened front room to see who it is. She watches from the window as a man in a black T-shirt and camouflage trousers steps back from the glow of her security light and looks straight at her. Behind him, sitting in the middle of the road, is an open-top jeep with a driver waiting patiently. As usual, her net curtains do a great job of hiding her so the man at the door has no idea she's staring straight back at him, examining him. Though he's dressed the same, he's not the man who went into No. 8 or the one who chased those kids. How many of them are there? And what exactly are they doing in her village?

He looks up at the other windows but seeing no movement there either, he steps forward and knocks again. This might be fun, she thinks, and shuffles out to the door. She waits until he starts a third knock then wrenches the door open quickly so he stumbles a little. She likes to catch people off guard; when you're getting on a bit you need to find ways to even things out.

The man steps back, clearly trying to regain some composure and give her a bit of breathing space. There's a pool around his boots where the recent snow has melted.

'Good evening, ma'am,' he says.

'No need for the ma'am, young man, I'm not the Queen.'

He looks confused for a moment so she presses home her advantage.

'What's a handsome chap like you doing calling on an old lady like me?'

She smiles as he opens his mouth and then closes it again.

'What do you think my husband would say if he saw us?'

'Is your husband in?' he asks eventually.

'I hope not,' she says. 'He's been dead for two years.'

She's got him so far on the back foot now that he's starting to look down the street, planning his escape, no doubt convinced he's found the local madwoman.

'Don't stand there gawping, you'll catch flies. What can I do for you?'

He holds his hands up, as if to show he's unarmed, which is weird because she can see that he's carrying a sidearm.

'Nothing for you to worry about, ma'am—' He stops, belatedly remembering not to call her that. He waits, like he's expecting her to give him her name, but hell will freeze over before that happens, he should do his homework.

'Did you hear the announcement?' he says, instead.

Margaret has no idea what he's talking about but when she glances behind him she can see a megaphone on the bonnet of the jeep. Whatever it was must have been drowned out by her Abba CD – can't beat a bit of 'Dancing

Queen'. Nigel always used to turn the volume down when he was around, terrified of upsetting the neighbours. When there were neighbours. Now they've all sold their soul for some rental income and Nigel's gone she can do what the hell she likes.

'I had some music on,' she says.

'We're just asking everyone if they could stay indoors for a little while.'

'Why?'

He looks a little nervous.

'Like I say, there's no need to be alarmed. It's just a precaution. But there's been a report of an escaped prisoner from HMP Northumberland being seen in the area and we need everyone in the village to stay inside until we make sure it's safe.'

'How did he get here?'

'What do you mean?'

'HMP Northumberland is thirty-odd miles away. And he couldn't just hop on a bus outside the prison, could he? Not that we get many buses through here on a weekend.'

'We think he stole a car.'

'Came here for the nightlife and the girls, did he?'

The soldier says nothing. She can tell he's just making it up as he goes along. She had plenty of experience of that with Nigel.

'Who's "we" anyway?' she asks.

'I'm sorry?'

'You said "we're" asking. Who's we?'

'Um, we're operating on behalf of the prison service.'

'You army?' she asks, knowing full well that he's not. The man hesitates but then he clearly notices the photo of Nigel on the wall behind her in his full dress uniform and smiles.

'That's right. Did your husband serve?'

She smiles right back at him. 'Coldstream Guards, 5 company.'

He nods. Clearly impressed. Margaret's not. There is no 5 company. As she suspected this man has never been anywhere near the proper army. She wonders about asking him for his ID but doesn't want to show her hand just yet. Better to keep him off-balance.

'What's he look like?'

The man hesitates for a moment too long.

'The escaped prisoner. You know, the one you want me to keep an eye out for.'

'Right. Yes. He's, um, tall, about six three, well built, long black hair.'

'Clothes? I assume he's wearing some.'

He smiles. 'Hope so. Grey trackie bottoms, a white T-shirt and a donkey jacket.'

He's clearly getting better at making stuff up; Margaret would bet a month's pension that there's no such prisoner.

'I'll keep an eye out,' she lies. 'What about my dog?' she adds.

'Your dog?'

'He needs to do his business. Outside.'

'Oh, right, yes, of course. Do you have a back garden?'

'Yes, but his piss kills off the grass.'

She can see he's shocked by her language. She's playing

with him now, enjoying it. Hasn't had this much fun in ages. Nigel definitely wouldn't have approved. As well as bad language, he didn't like jokes.

'I'm afraid you'll have to live with that.' He points at her window. 'I knocked because I saw your sticker.'

There's an old symbol of the local Neighbourhood Watch group on the lower pane, peeling off at the corners. Been there for years. She used to run quite a big group but once most of the houses had been sold off for second homes, and the shop had closed, there wasn't much call for them any more. Maybe she should tell him they disbanded years ago? No, she thinks, information is power.

'The Neighbourhood Watch. What of it?' she says.

'You're just what we need around here. Eyes and ears on the ground, so to speak. Someone who will notice if anything unusual happens and report it.'

'That is what we do.'

She can sense his impatience growing. He's not enjoying having to work so hard to win this grumpy old woman around.

'And have you?'

'Have I what?'

'Seen anything unusual?'

She senses a chance to get more information from him.

'There was something going on at No. 8 this morning,' she says, pointing up the street. 'An ambulance, I think. Looked serious. It was too far away to see properly.'

He doesn't even look at the house. It's clearly not what he was hoping for.

'That's all under control. No need to worry about that. Anything else?'

She thinks about the girl, Ruby, and that daft lad Lucas, running away from something. It certainly counted as unusual. He sees her hesitation and smiles, hoping for something he can take back to his superiors. He's clearly someone who likes to collect brownie points. But he's going to be disappointed.

'No,' she says. 'Nothing at all.'

18

Ruby watches from her bedroom as the soldier looks up at the house. Thank God she didn't put the light on. She's certain the poisonous old cow is talking shit, blaming everything on the incomers. She's pointing straight at Ruby's house. No doubt exaggerating what she saw this morning, her and Lucas – the sad loner and the bad lad who lives at the wrong end of town – fleeing the scene of the crime. Slagging off Ruby and her dad because they haven't lived there for like a hundred years.

At least she didn't see them come back. Ruby's certain of that, it's why she made sure they came in through the garden. Otherwise they'd have to get the hell out of there sharpish before he came over to investigate. They'll still have to find somewhere else to hide out though – once they've finished looking for anything that might help her understand what's happening.

'He still there?' Lucas asks. 'D'you think she's telling him to come and look up here?'

Without taking her eyes off the soldier she shakes her head.

'Maybe we should leg it anyway?'

'And go where?' she asks. Ruby knows he's right but they've only just got there and she needs to try and find out what's going on. Maybe, like Lucas said earlier, it's the last place they'll think of looking? She glances back at him but Lucas shrugs. He's clearly all out of good ideas. But not good questions.

'Why would anyone want to attack your dad?' he asks. She turns her gaze back on the conversation that's continuing at Margaret's house but carries on talking.

'I have absolutely no clue.'

'What does he do? He's not a spy or something, is he? Or some kind of master criminal? A bank robber?'

'Don't be stupid. He's self-employed, a graphic designer, creates logos, websites, that sort of thing. That's why he could work from home all the time. Everything he does is on his computer.'

'D'you know the password?' Lucas asks. 'There might be something on there that explains what's been gannin' on?'

She smiles. Can't help herself.

'Course I do,' she says.

She leaves Lucas keeping watch on the soldier, to make sure they don't have to leg it out of the back quite yet, and heads down to her dad's office. The door is closed and she has a sudden horrible thought that his body is lying on the leather sofa in there. She pushes it open and gasps in shock. The room's a tip. All the desk drawers are lying on the floor, upside down, the contents scattered everywhere. There are bits of stationery all over the place, a stapler under the desk, hundreds of paper clips tipped out, pens and pencils strewn around like there's been some kind of explosion. She rarely sets foot in there but she's never seen it like this. Her dad is insanely neat. Someone else did this.

Ruby has a compelling urge to tidy the place up and actually makes a start, picking up some of the paper from the floor. But then she realises that's not the biggest problem. There's a big space on her dad's desk. His computer is missing.

She slumps down amongst the mess, can feel the adrenalin that's kept her going draining away. It's just too much to bear. Tears start to flow again and this time she makes no attempt to stop them.

She has no idea how long she sits there for, feeling sorry for herself, but eventually she gathers the strength to move. She has to. They need to get out of there in case the soldier comes up to check the place out again.

Lucas hasn't made a peep in all that time and when she goes back up to her room she finds him lying on her bed, flicking through her diary, using his phone as a torch. She should have guessed she couldn't trust him. There's a cold cup of tea sitting on her bedside table from earlier that morning – she hasn't inherited her dad's tidy genes – and she's tempted to throw it over him but resists, ripping the diary from his hands and heading to the window instead. The soldier's gone.

Ruby turns and throws the diary at Lucas but he blocks it with his arms.

'You were supposed to be keeping watch,' she yells.

'Sorry,' he mumbles. 'The soldier left. I thought you'd only be gone a minute or two so I just sat down on the bed.'

'And started reading my private diary.'

'I thought there might be something in there about me.'

'As if.'

He laughs.

'You and Mark Johnson, eh?'

'That was a dare!' She hates it that she feels she has to explain herself to him and is glad the light's dim so he can't see her blushing. It gets worse when he pats her duvet.

'Comfy bed.'

Is he inviting her to join him? She's about to tell him that she'd rather sleep in Baldwin's piss-house when he rolls over and off the bed.

'Did you find anything?'

She shakes her head, too angry to tell him about the mess and the missing computer.

'What now then?' he says, as if he's been busy as hell and exhausted all his options.

'How about you fuck right off—'

There's a noise downstairs. That soldier trying the front door, maybe? She glances out of the window again but there's still no one there. Another noise, a door creaking open. Is he inside the house already? Maybe he came in the back way?

'Who—'

'Shhhhh!' Ruby shuts Lucas up before whoever it is hears them. She looks around for a weapon, seeing nothing at first, but then her eyes fix on the rucksack, which she left on the floor by the bed.

She grabs it and opens the front pocket, pulling out the small gun she took from the dead soldier's hand just a few hours ago. Lucas's eyes are on stalks, his mouth opening and closing like a fairground goldfish.

'Where did—'

She puts her finger to her lips and he gets the message, putting his hand over his mouth, keeping his eyes on the gun as if he's worried she might shoot him if he speaks. Which had crossed her mind.

Ruby signals to him to move behind the door so if someone comes into the bedroom they won't see him straight away. She kneels behind the bed so that she's half-hidden herself and points the gun at the door. The only sound she can hear now is her own breathing which seems loud enough to be heard at the other end of the street. Lucas is pressed up against the wall behind the door, like he's trying to blend in with the wallpaper, clearly scared shitless. He's not the only one. The hand holding the gun won't stop trembling and she has to use her other hand to keep it steady. She's gripping it so tightly that after a few moments she begins to cramp up and has to loosen her grip a little, lowering it down towards the bed.

Almost immediately there's another noise and the bedroom door slowly opens. She raises the gun again and takes aim at the door. She can see Lucas edging as far away from her line of sight as he can. She can't blame him as she's never shot a gun in her life and has no idea what she's doing. She doesn't even know if there's some kind of safety catch she should have released and it's too late to start looking for it now. Her heart is pounding as the door keeps moving. It's almost fully open and she can see through the gap onto the landing. There's no one there.

Suddenly Lucas starts to laugh. She's heard that people can get hysterical when they're terrified but that's ridiculous. This is exactly why people think he's a dick. Then he bends down and picks something up from the floor. It's Pluto.

She drops the gun onto the bed and collapses back onto the floor, exhaling loudly. These bloody cats creeping around are getting on her tits.

'Fuck!' she yells at no one in particular and closes her eyes, hoping that when she opens them everything will be back to normal. But when she does all she sees is Lucas standing over her, still holding the cat, with a worried look on his face.

'You OK?' he asks.

'Peachy.'

He looks like he wants to ask her a question but is too scared to actually say it.

'What?' she says, getting slowly back on her feet.

'Would you really have shot the soldier if he'd come through the door?'

She thinks about if for a moment then nods.

'One hundred per cent,' she says.

If anything, Lucas looks even more scared than he did before.

'Did you really not find anything on your dad's computer?' he asks.

She shakes her head. If he's scared now, wait until he sees the state of her dad's office. At least he might believe her then.

'It's gone,' she says. 'Just like my dad.'

'And you're sure you don't know anything about his past? About what he did before you came here? Where he lived? About your mam?'

Ruby shakes her head.

'He never liked to talk about the past. The one big thing I know for sure is that my mum died giving birth to me. I tried to speak to him a few times – I wanted to know more about her but, other than her name, Sylvie, and the fact that she was a bit younger than him, I know next to nothing. He told me she was funny and brave, didn't take any shit from anyone but talking about her always made him sad. It upset him so much that eventually I just stopped asking.'

Lucas gives her a look.

'What?'

'Nothing.'

'No, go on. I can see you want to say something. Spit it out.'

'It's exactly the kind of cover story someone in witness protection would have. Saves them telling too many lies. I've seen it on the telly.'

'He is not in fucking witness protection!' she shouts back at him.

Without realising it she has stepped closer to him, one arm raised aggressively. He's backing away, a scared look on his face. She looks down, she has picked up the gun in the other hand.

'I think you should leave,' she says.

He looks puzzled, confused.

'But—'

'Just go. Now. Before I fucking shoot you.'

She turns her back on him and stares out of the window, checking again that the coast is clear. When she turns around Lucas has gone.

19

When Alex wakes up he can't move his arms.

It's nothing to do with the bullet wound in his shoulder; it's because there are four broad leather straps securing him tightly to a metal single bed, two for his arms and two across his legs. He strains against them but there's very little room for movement. Despite his limited mobility he can move his head from side to side so he can see most of the room he's woken up in.

There's a drip standing next to the bed with a line running into his hand. He's tired and his head is foggy as hell but he's strangely pain-free – almost certainly morphine, he thinks. He's naked from the waist up apart from a dressing on his shoulder which seems to have been applied by someone who knows what he's doing. It looks like they want to keep him alive. For now. Which gives him a chance to escape. He surveys the room looking for weaknesses, opportunities, anything that he can exploit.

He's definitely not in a hospital ward. No big surprise there – whoever these guys are, they're not official, that's

for sure. The room's about the size of a large double bedroom. The walls are bare – not just undecorated but hardly
painted at all, long neglected. And it's not just the only
bed in the room; it's the only thing in the room, with the
exception of the drip, a small bedside cabinet and a solitary
camping chair on the other side of the bed. The floor-to-
ceiling curtains are drawn on the windows and the light is
coming from a bare bulb in the middle of the ceiling. Even
if he could get free there's nowhere to hide and nothing to
use as a weapon except the flimsy chair.

Alex tries to move his feet, there's some wriggle room
there. He can work on that. The same with his hands and
fingers. He checks for possible escape routes. There's only
one door that he can see – it's possible there's another
behind the curtains – and it's closed. He wonders if there's
a guard outside it; is pretty sure there will be, though he
can't see him through the small frosted window in the
top half of the door. These don't seem like the kind of
people to leave anything to chance. And knowing who
they're probably working for they won't be short of manpower, his bottomless pockets will have made sure of
that.

That idea is almost immediately confirmed by the sound
of voices in the corridor outside. He can't hear what they're
saying but there's a distinct military nature to the conversation, short, sharp and precise.

The door opens and a new face appears. He's dressed in
exactly the same uniform as the other men Alex saw this
morning but is older, late forties maybe, silver hair and a

thin moustache giving him a more polished look than the others.

'You're awake then,' he says.

Alex says nothing, making him work for whatever it is he wants. The longer he keeps them occupied the more time Ruby will have to get away.

The soldier stops a foot or so away from the bed and stares at him.

'I'm Gold,' he says. 'And I'm here to help you.' He smiles awkwardly, as if it's something he's only just learnt to do and hasn't been practising.

Again, Alex keeps his counsel. He's encouraged by the fact that he's still alive. If they had Ruby they wouldn't need him; though there's surely a price to pay for what he did to that kid Green in the kitchen.

The soldier nods like he's seen this kind of resistance before.

'You don't look too well, Mr Winter,' he says. 'Would you like something to eat?'

Alex wonders when the bad cop is going to show up. When he doesn't reply again the man sighs and perches on the lone chair, tapping him gently on the leg. His long thin fingers and immaculate nails underline the thought that he's not the guy who does the dirty work out in the field.

'I know what you're thinking. But there's really no need to make things unpleasant for yourself, is there? You may as well do what you can to make your stay here as comfortable as possible, surely? It won't be long – after all, it's only a matter of time before we find Ruby.'

Alex grimaces at the mention of his daughter's name, which Gold smiles at. The man is clearly trying to press his buttons but he shouldn't be letting him know how well he's succeeding.

'My man, Red, is very keen on that moment coming sooner rather than later, of course. You've rather upset him by killing his young friend and I'm sure he's already plotting some payback. I think it would be best for the girl if I find her before he can get his hands on her. So to speak.'

So Green is definitely dead. Alex checks again to see if he can find any remorse but there's nothing. He'd do exactly the same thing again if he had to. He'd do the same to this Gold guy right now if he had the chance. The names were a concern: Gold, Green, Red – obviously not their real ones, which wasn't a good sign at all. It reminded him of that Tarantino film. Didn't everyone die in the end?

'How's the shoulder?' Gold says, edging his chair towards the dressed wound. Alex tries to pull away but the straps stop him from moving more than an inch or so.

'Don't worry, I'm not going to torture you, not yet anyway, I'm not a complete monster. I was just hoping you might see the sense in cooperating with me. You've met some of my men – killed one of them, it would seem – and you've probably noticed that they're not exactly a disciplined elite. They can all get a bit "handsy" with people, especially women. I do my best to control them but you know, if they followed orders they'd probably be in the regular army and not the, um, irregular one that I have to manage, for my sins.

'So it really would be best if you just told me where she'll be hiding out so I can go and pick her up personally and we can avoid all that unpleasantness.'

Alex's stomach lurches as he imagines that Scots twat, Red, manhandling Ruby. She's a tough cookie, in her own way, and he's never doubted that she can look after herself, but dealing with teenage boys is a bit different to managing violent psychos like him.

'She'll be long gone by now,' he says.

'I don't think that's the case. We're certain she's still in the village.'

He must be lying. Alex told her to run. Why would she stick around? Immediately a host of reasons flood into his head. Maybe she couldn't get out of the village? There's only one road in and out so it's easy to blockade the place. And even if she took one of the footpaths, where would she go? There's nothing for miles around once you've gone through Embleton Woods except fields and wild moorland, quite literally nowhere to hide. And if the snow has got any worse she'd be easy to spot from the air, what with the footprints, and he'd bet they've got a chopper on standby. He'd chosen Coldburn because it was so isolated but he's now realising that was a curse as well as a blessing.

'Well?' Gold says. 'What do you say?'

'Fuck you,' Alex says. 'Fuck you and the rest of your stupid Poundshop Reservoir Dogs shit-heads, Mr Fucking Gold.'

Gold sighs.

'Suit yourself. But when she finds out who you really are and what you've done I'm pretty sure she won't want to see you again anyway.'

20

First things first. Your mum's real name was Emma, not Sylvie, as I've always told you. By the end of this story I hope you will understand why I misled you. What is it they say? 'The names have been changed to protect the innocent.' In this case you were the innocent and I wanted to keep it that way for as long as I could. Which meant protecting you from the truth.

Emma was a wild child, lippy, rebellious and cool as all hell. I loved her to bits right from the start and we would talk for hours about how we were going to take the world on and win when we were older. Despite some difficult circumstances life was sweet. And then, in the spring of 2006, she disappeared.

Turned out her foster dad was starting to give her those looks – like the ones she often got from old pervs in the park – and finding reasons to brush up against her when his wife was out. She ran away before he took it to the next level. She didn't tell me then as she knew I'd try to stop her leaving or would want to go with her. I was 19, a couple of years older than her, and saving for a flat so we could move in together. It wasn't easy, as I was studying by day – on my graphic design course – and working in the evenings and weekends but I was getting there. To this day I wish she'd said something and I still wonder why she didn't trust me enough to confide in me.

I had no clue where she'd gone and it was months before I heard anything. Then, out of the blue, she contacted me. It was just an email telling me she was safe and well but it was a start. It was weeks before I heard from her again. This time she at least told me why she'd left – no gory details, just broad-brush stuff – and that she'd got a job and somewhere to live. Told me not to worry, that she was safe – as if that would work. Worrying about her was all I did at the time.

I later discovered that the job was occasional waitressing work for a big catering company. Terrible pay and hours on what we'd call a zero-hours contract these days. They'd just call her up when they had a big job on and needed extra pairs of hands. I didn't know any of this at the time – her flatmate Rosie contacted me when she got in trouble. I'll get to that.

Her real problems started on one of the catering jobs. She got into an argument with someone she was serving at a posh banquet. Apparently the man was a real arrogant twat who called her a 'thick bitch' because she brought him the wrong meal. It wasn't her fault so, typically, she snapped back and it escalated from there. She threw a glass of red wine over him and he tried to slap her but hit another guest, which started a free-for-all. The host, the CEO of a big security company, had to step in. Surprisingly, perhaps, he threw the arrogant guy out and apologised to Emma for the way she'd been treated, insisting she be sent home on full pay.

I wonder now if the host had staged the whole thing and

was already grooming her. He's the kind of man who plays a long game. A few days afterwards he rang her to make sure she was all right and offered to buy her lunch at The Ivy – a very swanky restaurant in London – as an apology for the way she'd been treated.

I'm sure that she'd normally have said no, she wasn't naive, but her flatmate later told me that Emma had been surviving on porridge, Big Macs and whatever she could scrounge from her catering gigs for months and the offer of a proper meal out was too good to turn down. She should have known there's no such thing as a free lunch.

21

Ruby stares at the mess in her dad's office.

When Lucas left she realised how alone she was now and hoped coming back in here would help but it hasn't. It's done the opposite. It's even worse than she first thought. The place has been taken apart, piece by piece, quite literally in some cases; her dad's noticeboard is broken in two, one half leant against the wall, the other lying on the floor next to it; a hole in the wall where it's been ripped away.

The desk is completely bare but the place where the computer used to be is plain to see, a thin layer of dust covering everything but that one square in the middle. Even the carpet's been ripped up in places, the searchers looking for God knows what.

Ruby feels herself welling up for the umpteenth time. She knows how upset her dad would be to see this mess. How many times has she heard him say 'cleanliness is next to godliness'? It always made her laugh because he didn't believe in God. Doesn't believe in God. She kicks herself for thinking about her dad in the past tense. He's still alive. She has to believe that.

She flops down on the floor as if her strings have been cut and lies flat on her back. If they come back for her now then so be it. She's got nothing left.

Ruby doesn't know how long she's been asleep but when she wakes up she's lying on the floor amongst the debris. It's now pitch black outside. As her eyes get used to the dark she can see Pluto stretched out on the sofa. She looks around to see if Lucas is there and then remembers. They had a fight. She sent him packing. Fucking idiot. Her, that is, not him. She needs all the help she can get.

She's about to get up when something catches her eye. A tiny glimmer of light coming from a couple of holes in the wood panelling on the back wall of the office, only notice-able because all the lights are off. As she moves closer she realises it's just where some knots have dropped out of the wood. The thought triggers a memory from earlier that day, something her dad tried to say to her.

Ruby places her fingers carefully in the holes, grateful that she hasn't got sausage fingers like her dad, and pulls. Nothing happens. She tries again and can feel something give. She thrusts her fingers further into the holes to get a better grip and tries once more. This time the bit she's pulling on and the two panels either side come out in one piece. She gasps. There's a small safe with a digital keypad and an LED display hidden behind the panelling. Her dad hadn't whispered 'Not safe.' He'd whispered 'Knots. Safe.'

What the hell is in there that was so important to him? Maybe it's something that will explain why these people are after them. All she needs now is the passcode. Luckily she already thinks she knows it. The same as his computer. Her birthday. She taps in 160207. Nothing happens. Shit. She was so sure. She tries again. There's an immediate beep and the display features the word OPEN. Ruby breathes a sigh of relief, she must have hit the wrong key first time. She turns the small handle to the right of the keypad and the safe door springs out.

The first thing she sees is another gun. She's not even surprised – which shows how quickly her life has changed. It's very similar to the one her dad dismantled earlier. She takes it out and puts it to one side. If Lucas was still around they could have had one each but it's too late for that now.

The only other contents are an envelope and a small gift-wrapped packet. Her birthday present. She opens the gift first, nobody ever accused her of being patient. She rips off the paper and is surprised to find a chunky heart-shaped key ring inside – with just one key attached. Not what she was expecting or hoping for. Just another fucking mystery. What is the key for? She has no idea. Why has he made this so hard? Maybe what she's looking for will be in the card. But it isn't.

It's a straightforward sixteenth birthday card with 'Happy Birthday, Ruby, you'll always be in my heart' inscribed inside in her dad's incredibly neat handwriting. There's a beautiful hand-drawn heart under the writing. You can tell he did Art A level.

Ruby sighs. In a different world, the one she lived in when she woke up that morning, she might have found this intriguing, but in this new messed-up version she really needs something more useful. She pulls the safe door wide open and feels around inside just to make sure she hasn't missed anything but it's empty.

She has no idea what to do now but there's a more immediate problem to deal with. She can smell burning.

22

Ruby stuffs the key ring in her pocket and edges out of her dad's study, the new gun in hand. She doesn't even know if it's loaded but it makes her feel less vulnerable. Not much use against a fire though.

She creeps down the hallway. The smell of burning is much stronger here but there's no smoke. Which doesn't mean anything. Her dad had fire doors installed in the house, so, if there is a fire in the kitchen and they're doing their job, the minute she opens one of them the flames could still burst through the gap and envelop her. She hesitates but knows she has to do something. Ruby takes a deep breath and flings open the kitchen door. The room is empty and the smell stronger but there are still no flames, just a few wisps of smoke near the ceiling and the back door is wide open. She steps into the kitchen. Her hand tightens on the gun as she slowly moves around the counter towards the doorway.

Lucas is standing at the back of the garden, scraping something from a grill pan into a dustbin. He finishes what he's doing and turns to head back towards the house. He jumps as he catches sight of Ruby, clearly startled by her sudden appearance. Or more likely by the gun in her hand. He slowly raises his hands as if he's being held up. Despite herself Ruby laughs; he's still holding the grill in one hand and she can see crumbs from it falling into his hair. There's a plate of blackened sausages on the ground beside him.

'Don't shoot,' he says. 'I didn't mean to burn the bangers. I can make some more.'

'I'm a fucking vegetarian, you idiot.'

'I guessed that, they're Linda McCartney's – whoever that is – I found them in the freezer.'

He leans down and picks two sausages up, handing her one. They both take a bite. They're crisp but not inedible.

'I thought I told you to leave,' she says, taking another bite.

He nods. 'You definitely did. Do you still want me to go?'

She doesn't. He's not perfect but he's all she's got for now. She has never felt as lonely as she did back in her dad's office.

'I suppose not. But you need to stop with all the witness protection bollocks.'

'Sorry. I was halfway home, calling you all sorts, when I realised I was being a dick. I came back up to say sorry but you were fast asleep. So I thought I'd make you some sausages. Stop you from still being hangry when you woke up.'

'You think I shouted at you because I was hangry?' She can feel her temper coming back.

'D'you need another sausage?'

'Fuck you.'

'Joke,' he says, holding his hands up. 'I deserved the bollocking. Like I said, I was being a dick. But seriously, how long is it since you've eaten?'

'A while. Breakfast, I guess.'

'Have another one then. Two even.'

Ruby realises he's right. She's actually starving. She grabs another sausage and wolfs it down. So does he.

'It's important to stay strong,' he says as he chews. 'An army marches on its stomach.'

'What the hell is that supposed to mean?'

'I've no idea, it's something Danny says to make me eat properly.'

'Mad Danny?'

He glares at her. 'Don't call him that. Danny's all right.'

Now she's curious. Mad Danny is the village oddball, a scruffy, long-haired, eccentric loner who's rumoured to be a bit dodgy, and another man, like Mr Baldwin, that her dad has urged her to avoid. She had no idea he and Lucas were so pally.

Lucas has moved closer now and can clearly see the puzzled look on Ruby's face.

'He keeps an eye on me,' he explains. Ruby wonders why Lucas needs keeping an eye on – where is his mum in all this? She's not at the house and has someone else looking out for her son, which seems a bit off.

'Is he your uncle or something?'

Lucas shakes his head. It's pretty clear that he doesn't want to talk about it so she lets it go. He takes her silence for more doubts about Danny, which it probably is.

'Look, he's not as bad as everyone says, just a bit different. He was in the army when he was younger.' He looks around as if someone might be listening in. 'Mam reckons he had a daughter once but she died in some kind of accident, drowned, I think. He doesn't like to talk about it though.'

Ruby didn't know any of that. In fact, she's beginning to realise that she knows almost nothing about anyone in the village. And most of what she does know seems to be wrong. Maybe she's actually the odd one, the loner?

'D'you think he would help us?' She doesn't know where the 'us' came from, they're both obviously still holding stuff back, though Lucas doesn't seem bothered by her choice of words, which is kind of nice.

'Deffo. He's not a big fan of the authorities – if that's who sent these people. And he knows this place like the back of his hand. Plus, he can hunt.'

He clearly sees her scrunch up her face and looks puzzled.

'I just told you I was a veggie.'

'Probably why you're so pale.'

'Fuck you very much. Anyway, it's illegal, isn't it, hunting? Has he got a special licence or permission from the land-owner or whatever you need?'

'I doubt it. Have you got a licence for that?' He nods at the gun in her hand.

She laughs. 'Fair point. He must have a few weapons though?'

'Aye. For sure. Couple of shotguns, a rifle and a canny crossbow. He let me have a go with that once. Just firing at a tree, like. It was mint.'

Lucas's eyes are shining like he's going through some kind of religious experience. It's weird. It sounds like Danny is his proxy dad. She has no idea what's happened to his real dad and realises that it's not just the oldies she knows nothing about, it's everyone in the village, including Lucas. He really should despise her. She makes a mental note to find out more about her new friend. Though maybe not right now. They need to move on.

'Maybe we should talk to him. Any idea where he'll be now?'

Lucas glances at his watch.

'Aye. A pretty good one, actually. But he wouldn't be very pleased to see us there.'

23

Danny holds down the top strand of barbed wire with one hand and climbs over the fence at the edge of the wood. His legs are only just long enough to manage it so he presses the wire down even further just to be on the safe side.

'Gotta look after the crown jewels,' he mutters to himself. Once over he lifts up the bottom wire so his Labrador, Scout, can scramble underneath.

The half-moon sheds a little light but not enough to see where he is going. He reaches towards his backpack for a torch but with the bogus soldiers around he decides to only use it as a last resort. No point getting shot. Instead, he stands for a few minutes until his night vision begins to improve and he can make out the tree line. He picks out a gap between two large yew trees and a vague track which leads to the river and moves off again.

He's been there before, several times, but nevertheless he walks slowly, eyes down, making sure to avoid tripping over one of the many exposed tree roots until the ground grows softer and he can hear the river ahead. He used to be able to do this blindfold but since last year's storms took down so many trees it's like an assault course.

Danny heads to his usual spot, a bank that overhangs the river. He places a waterproof picnic blanket on the wet ground to avoid getting soaked then lies down on his stomach. At least it's stopped snowing. Scout settles beside him. Danny takes a breath to steady his movement and reaches slowly under the overhang, keeping his hands as close to the bottom of the river as he can.

He leans forward, as far over the edge as he dares, and moves both hands about a yard apart, until he can feel the riverbed on the back of them. The water's freezing. He slowly moves his hands towards each other, fingers stretching upwards to feel for the trout. There's nothing there but he's a patient man. He moves down the river to another promising-looking overhang and tries again. Still no joy.

Danny sits back on the blanket and takes out a hip flask from his jacket pocket. Just for the warmth, obviously. When he'd lost his job and told Lucas what he was going to do to put food on the table the lad had thought he was joking.

'You're a postman not a poacher, Danny,' he'd said.

'Used to be a postman,' Danny had replied.

The government had put paid to that when they'd sold off the post office to their rich pals, who'd immediately put the cost up and halved the deliveries. Bastards. They should try getting another job in rural Northumberland. No chance he was going to pick fruit for a living – not with his back – even though the money had gone up now they'd made it much harder for the Romanian lads to get into the country.

A splash in the water brings him back to the job in hand. He puts the hip flask away, moves another few yards downstream and tries again. The whisky seems to have done its work as it doesn't feel so cold this time. Perhaps he's just getting used to it. At first he thinks he's drawn another blank and is just about to give up when he feels something with his right hand, a small movement, nudging against his fingertips. He adjusts his hand slightly. Slowly, slowly, he thinks.

He strokes the trout's belly gently, steering it towards his left hand until he has it in the perfect position, one hand beneath the gill plate, the other under the tail. He takes a deep breath and pounces, taking a firm grip with both hands, heaving the fish out of the water and onto the bank. The trout is about a foot long. Not bad. It slips out of his hands and flaps around on the ground as if it's trying to throw itself back into the river so he grabs a small spanner from his other pocket, holds the fish down with his free hand and taps it sharply on the head.

'Danny one, trouts nil,' he whispers.

He takes another sip from his flask to celebrate. He's not sure what the fuck is going on with these soldiers but they seem to have the village locked down and people need to eat. Be nice to give the boy something other than baked beans – might even let the dog have some if he can catch a few more. Suddenly there's a noise behind him, a sharp crack of a branch then leaves rustling. Scout gets to his feet and growls quietly. Danny turns and stares at the edge of the wood, his heart pounding, as he imagines the end of a rifle appearing through the foliage. He pulls his own shotgun from the holster on his back. Just as he is beginning to think he'd imagined it there is another rustling sound, much closer this time, and a fox emerges from between the trees. It stops, aware of his presence, and stares back at him, probably wondering if he can steal the fish. Danny puts one hand on Scout to hold him back, picks the dead trout up and drops it in the small cool box he's brought with him. After a few moments the fox turns and heads back into the wood.

Danny can sense rain in the air so he takes out his waterproofs and slips them over his clothes before moving further along the bank for one last try. He reaches deep into the overhang and this time it is his left hand that feels something. He moves further forward and brings his right hand along the bank, grabbing his catch with both hands and heaving it onto the bank.

'What the fuck?' he says to himself, louder than intended, staring in disbelief at the catch. He pulls his torch out and flicks it on to get a better look, the bitter taste of whisky coming back up into his throat. There's a man's arm lying on his picnic blanket, its colourful snake and skull tattoo glinting in the torchlight.

24

Margaret, as usual, decides not to do what she's told. Nigel used to call her 'difficult' but that was more his problem than hers. He didn't really like women to have their own opinions. Hence the thing he started with that brain-dead organist slapper who wouldn't say boo to a goose. Stupid man.

Anyway, the bottom line is that Boris eats for England and if he doesn't get his exercise and do his business he'll probably burst and that really wouldn't do. It's not because she likes the stubborn thing – truth be told, she can't stand the yappy little shit. She just wouldn't want to clean the mess up.

She's not stupid though, she's not going out the front like she usually does, she's seen the jeep patrolling around the streets and with her knees she isn't quick enough to hide if it suddenly appears on the scene. So she heads out the back door and through a gate in the fence that takes her onto the quiet footpath there. She only intends to walk around the block and back, just enough time for Boris to evacuate his bowels, but as she rounds the old schoolhouse – still disused since the last big family moved out of the village five years ago – she sees lights on in the kitchen of No. 8 and her curiosity gets the better of her. She's always been a bit nebby, she knows that. It's exactly why she formed the Neighbourhood Watch in the first place – it was nice to have an excuse to keep a close eye on things.

As she gets nearer the house she can hear voices in the garden. She stops just behind the trees and peers through. Lucas and the girl, Ruby, are standing near the bin talking quietly. She had never seen them together before that morning but there's something about their body language that looks almost intimate. Dirty little beggars. She's about to move away – even she doesn't want to see teenagers necking on – when Ruby steps to one side and Margaret sees the girl's hand. Is that a gun? She instinctively pulls away but the movement annoys Boris and he whines in that horrible small dog way.

'Who's there?' The boy, Lucas. She sees him move towards a gap in the trees but it's too late to do anything about it. She'll brazen it out instead, pretend she doesn't know what's going on. Years of living with Nigel taught her that ignorance is bliss where men are concerned.

'Hello?' she says. 'Who's that?'

The boy steps out onto the path. 'Mrs Carr?'

'Good evening, Lucas,' she replies. 'Nice night for it.'

He looks confused and glances back towards the garden, clearly hoping the girl will help him out but there's no sign of her yet. Margaret senses she's just behind the trees, probably wondering what to do with the gun.

'For what?' he says.

'Just being out. Warm and that.' He looks even more puzzled now because it's actually freezing.

'Ah, right, yes. You just walking the dog then?'

'No. Thought I'd go out for a jog.' Sometimes she can't help herself.

He's shuffling from foot to foot now, the very definition of nervous. Luckily for him the girl decides to make an appearance. She must have hidden the firearm.

'I hope I haven't disturbed anything,' Margaret says, mischievously. Even in this light she can see them both starting to blush. 'I didn't realise you two were courting.'

'We're not—' Both kids start and stop speaking at the same time. Awkward as all hell. Margaret's actually beginning to enjoy herself. Until there's a whirring noise somewhere above them.

They all look up at the sky and Boris starts to yelp. He hates bats, somehow knows they're cleverer than him. In reality there are trees cleverer than Boris.

'I'm sorry,' she says. 'He's scared of bats.'

'That's not a bat,' Lucas says. 'It's a drone.'

25

Ruby tears through the house, stopping only to grab the gun and her rucksack and legs it out of the front door, closely followed by Lucas.

They'd left the old woman by the trees, figuring that it wasn't her the drone was spying on. Obviously it couldn't follow them into the house so Ruby hopes that whoever is operating it takes a minute to realise they've gone straight through and out the other side.

She tries to look up as she runs but can't see anything.

'D'you think we've lost it?' she shouts.

'Doubt it,' Lucas says, drawing up alongside her. 'It could be way up in the sky and still pick us out.'

'In the dark?'

'If it's got a good camera. Some of them have night vision.'

Ruby already feels like her lungs are going to burst. She can't run much further without a break. She wishes she had gone jogging with her dad when he wanted her to. There are a lot of things she wishes she'd done with him now. Hopefully it's not too late. She has to believe that.

Up ahead she sees a chance to hide from view. Sort of.

'Over there,' she says, darting across the street and under the ancient bus shelter, still standing even though hardly any buses come through the village these days. The glass has long since been smashed out but there's still a metal roof to hide them. She leans back against the rear wall and sucks in some air, grimacing at the stitch in her side.

Lucas joins her, looking like he's barely drawn breath.

'How come you're so fit?' she says.

He grins, flicking his hair back. 'You think I'm fit?'

He really could do with a slap sometimes.

'Don't be stupid, not like that, you dick.'

Lucas doesn't drop the smile, arrogant sod, but leans out of the shelter, glancing up at the sky.

'I cycle a lot. Do the odd triathlon.'

She can't quite see his face any more so isn't sure if he's joking, can't even envisage him in sports gear, he's such a gothy kind of a guy.

'What are you doing?'

'Shhhh!' he says.

After a moment he pops his head back in.

'I reckon it's gone. Can't see anything and they've normally got a little light on them. Though fuck knows if I'd be able to pick it out among all those stars. But I can't hear it now.'

'How come you know so much about drones?'

'Danny's got one. He let me have a play with it once.'

'Why's he got a drone?'

Lucas frowns, and starts scratching his arm.

'Well?' she presses.

'He uses it to look out for gamekeepers. I told you, he's a poacher. Fish mainly but deer sometimes.'

'That's horrible. Meat is murder.'

Ruby's been a veggie since she's been allowed to make her own food decisions. Her dad wasn't exactly thrilled at first but he soon came round when she offered to do half the cooking. Not that she entirely kept to her promise, of course.

'Man has to eat,' Lucas says, glancing up at the sky again.

'He could grow his own veg instead,' she grumbles, but suddenly realises that she doesn't care as much as she thought she did. Bigger fish to fry now. Despite everything she giggles at the irony of that weird saying – she's picked it up from her dad without ever thinking about it.

'We could head to his house, see if he's back yet,' Lucas says. 'It's as good a place to hide as any.'

'I don't want to hide,' Ruby says, 'I want to find my dad.'

He turns back to face her, his serious face back on again.

'That's why we need a hunter.'

26

Danny's cottage is the last house at the south-east corner of Coldburn, sat on the very edge of Embleton Woods, which Ruby supposes is ideal for a poacher.

It's not exactly derelict, it appears solid enough and it's in better nick than Lucas's place, but it's a long time since it's seen a lick of paint. The outside is more like a scrapyard than a garden, bits of what looks like a car engine, or several car engines, scattered to the four corners. A couple of dismantled bike frames and a single car wheel to one side of the door add some finishing touches to the chaos.

Lucas knocks on the front door but there's no answer. He tries the handle but it's locked.

'Must still be out,' he mutters. He turns and sees her screwing up her face as she stares at the mess around them.

'He likes to fiddle about with engines,' Lucas says defensively. 'He keeps all this stuff for spare parts. It doesn't half piss Mr Baldwin off cos Danny sometimes sorts people's cars out for a cheaper price. He can fix almost anything.'

'That's good,' she says, not wanting to be a twat about it.

'He's doing his bit to save the planet if he's helping recycle stuff. My dad's hopeless with things like that, he always has to get someone in.'

Thinking of her dad in normal times is like a punch in the stomach and – even though he's clearly kept some secrets from her – she has to blink back the inevitable tears. Again she wonders if she'll ever see him again. So much for a positive mental attitude. She shakes her head to throw the thought out. Or at least to try.

Somehow Lucas's hand has ended up on her shoulder and he squeezes it in sympathy. Normally she'd be embarrassed but his touch is reassuring, welcome almost. It's another confusing moment in a completely messed-up day. She's glad he came back after their fight.

'If anyone can find him, Danny can,' he says.

Alex is woken by shouting in the corridor. Something about an old woman throwing stones. Or maybe that was a morphine-induced dream.

He's surprised that he managed to sleep at all but the drugs probably had something to do with that. He tries to move again but there's no sign of any slackening in his leather bindings. And his shoulder is starting to hurt like hell. Escape seems a million miles away.

There's still a drip attached to his hand. In fact, nothing at all has changed. Apart from the shouting, which is getting closer. Gold eventually pushes through the door, followed by a sheepish-looking Red, the Scots twat from the house. From the look on his face it's obvious he was the one on the receiving end of whatever the bollocking was about. It's clear who the leader is here. Alex wonders if he can use the in-fighting to his advantage somehow.

'How are you feeling?' Gold asks him.

'Tip-top,' Alex says, his voice cracking a little from lack of use. He turns his head to cough and goes again. 'Ready for breakfast, in fact. Two eggs, bacon and sausages with some strong black coffee to wash it down, please.' Another cough follows, longer than the first.

'It's ten o'clock at night.'

Alex is surprised. He thought he'd been out for much longer.

'D'you not do all-day breakfast here then?'

Gold smiles. 'Give the man some water, Red,' he says. For some reason the Scot sniggers but he does as he's told and grabs the glass from the bedside cabinet, holding it close enough that Alex can sip from it.

'Humour's good, Alex,' Gold continues. 'Important for keeping your spirits up when the shit hits the fan. Red here likes a joke, don't you, Red?'

The Scot nods but looks like he'd probably scalp the next person to tell him one. Alex takes the risk. If Red reacts badly Gold might reprimand him again and it could all kick off. It's not much to hope for but maybe he can spread more dissension in the ranks.

'What's the difference between a lawn mower and a bag-pipe?' he says. Gold plays along.

'I don't know. What is the difference between a lawn mower and a bagpipe?'

'You can tune a lawn mower.'

Gold laughs. Red's face betrays nothing, but he does put the glass back down a little too firmly. Alex hopes he's never left alone with the twat.

'Anyway, I'm glad you're in a good mood because I've got some bad news for you,' Gold adds.

Alex automatically tries to sit up but the straps are way too strong. He strains against them anyway. If they've hurt Ruby in any way he'll kill them all. He lies back down and closes his eyes. Immediately realising what a ridiculous thought that was. He can't lay a finger on them in this state and there's no way they're going to even free his arms.

'As I thought, I'm afraid the lovely Ruby definitely hasn't taken your advice to get out of town. She's still here.'

It looks like he was right about the difficulties of getting away. Maybe the snow has got worse. Why else would she stay? He immediately realises that *he* is the answer. She would want to make sure he was safe before she went anywhere. *He's* the problem here. It would have been better if they'd killed him. Unless Gold is lying.

'I don't believe you.'

'Sadly, it's true. I've seen the footage of her and her young man running out of your house about thirty minutes ago. Unfortunately, Red here somehow got distracted by a pensioner and managed to lose track of them after that.'

What fucking young man? Ruby has never shown much interest in boys and he can't imagine why she'd start now. Although she has seemed a little secretive lately. Did she have a boyfriend?

'So I need two things from you, Alex. And I'd rather not have to hurt you to get them. One: who is this young man? And two: where or who would she be running to?'

Alex has no idea what the answers to either of those questions are. Which is a good thing – he can't possibly help them even if they try to torture it out of him.

The rain begins to fall heavily as Ruby and Lucas head around the side of Danny's house to try the back door. It's locked as well.

Neither of them are really dressed for the sudden downpour. Their almost-matching black hoodies are good for hiding in the dark but they're no protection against this deluge.

'Danny!' Lucas bangs on the door but it's obvious he's not there. The place is in total darkness.

'Maybe we should break a window,' Ruby suggests.

Lucas shakes his head. 'We can shelter in the storeroom,' he says.

Ruby glances around and spies a building set back amongst the trees. It's about the same size as a standard garage with a corrugated iron roof and only one door she can see. It's definitely not a garage though as there's no way a car could access it from the road and the only door is way too small to get a vehicle through it.

Lucas grabs her hand and guides her along a narrow track which goes through a gap in the bramble hedge up to the door. Thankfully this door's unlocked. He leads her into the building; it's pitch black in there.

'There's a light here somewhere,' he says, feeling around on the wall.

Ruby moves out of his way but as she does she bumps against something solid hanging from the ceiling. She shrieks, jumps back and hits another object which seems to swing away from her before bashing her on the shoulder. A rancid smell makes her gag. She rubs her arm and her hand comes away covered in a sticky substance which she tries to wipe off on her jeans. She steps forward and stumbles over something which clangs on the floor. Lucas finds the switch and a low light comes on. Ruby screams.

She's in the centre of half a dozen skinned rabbits hanging from the rafters of the room. There's a bucket lying on its side on the floor and a small pool of blood, which she's now standing in, surrounding it. Her hand, sleeve and jeans are both stained red too.

'Jesus,' she whispers, ducking down and moving away from both the dead animals and the mess. 'It's a slaughterhouse.'

'Hardly,' Lucas says.

Ruby can't bring herself to look at the swinging bodies so turns to face the wall.

'I told you he hunted stuff,' Lucas says. 'We do live in the countryside, you know.'

'Doesn't mean I want my nose rubbed in it.'

'So you'd rather get soaked.'

'No, but you might have warned me.'

'I didn't know what'd be in here, did I? I mean, I knew what he used it for but I didn't know it'd be like this. He must be stocking up or something. I was only trying to help.'

Ruby realises once again that she's being a cow but it was a bit of a shock and the smell is disgusting.

'Why are you helping me anyway?'

'Because you needed me to,' he says simply.

Despite the rabbits she turns around again.

'But I was always horrid to you.'

'No, you weren't. You just ignored me. Everyone else was happy to slag me and my mam off to my face just because we were poor. I remember one time on the school bus you telling them to leave me alone.'

Ruby has no memory of that and feels awful that it's the best thing he can recall anyone doing.

'I'm sorry. Kids can be horrible.'

'Tell me about it.'

'And thank you. I'm not sure what I'd have done without you today.'

Lucas opens the door and looks out again. It's absolutely lashing down now.

'You'd have got wet, that's for sure,' he says.

'I do remember one boy she used to talk about.'

'Excellent,' Gold says, smiling. 'Name?'

'Justin something. Give me a moment, it'll come to me ...'

Alex pretends to be thinking. If he could move his arms he knows he'd be scratching his head like a bad actor. He has no idea if Gold is telling the truth about her still being in the village – he hopes not – but he is sure that the more time he can buy her the better chance she has of keeping away from these bastards.

'I know,' he says. 'Bieber, that was it. Justin Bieber.'

The smile drops from Gold's face and he nods to Red who turns around and walks out of the room.

'There's really no need for any of this, you know. We've got no intention of hurting Ruby; in fact, we'd be in serious trouble if we did harm her.'

'From whom?' Alex says, although he knows the answer. It would just be good to hear it said out loud.

Instead Gold shakes his head, mimes zipping his mouth shut and changes the subject.

'I'm genuinely sorry we've ended up in this situation. This wasn't part of the plan. I put it down to the exuberance of youth. Young Green was only supposed to have a watching brief. He jumped the gun, if you'll pardon the expression.'

'So you were just going to take Ruby? You're a snatch squad? Is that it?'

'That's one way of describing it, I suppose. Wouldn't be my choice but, you know, it's all semantics.'

Gold seems a bit pissed off and doesn't speak again until Red comes back with a small jug, a cloth and a grin plastered on his face.

Shit, Alex thinks. He's read about Guantanamo Bay and seen enough movies to know what comes next. Red puts the jug and cloth down and moves to the foot of the bed where he activates some kind of mechanism that tips the bed backwards. Alex's head goes down while his feet go up.

'Wait,' he shouts but they ignore him. He tries to squirm out of his bonds but it's no use. Gold takes the cloth and holds it firmly over Alex's face. He tries to turn his head to shake him off but the man's grip is like steel. Alex can't see a thing through the cloth and is trying to hold his breath when the first water is poured onto his face. He gasps in shock and almost immediately starts to choke. It's fucking terrifying. Then it stops. Before he can get his breath back it starts again. He's sure he's going to drown and pushes his head to one side with all his might to try and find some air but it's hopeless. Then the water stops and the cloth is pulled away.

Alex takes in large gulps of air while Gold stands quietly at the side of his bed, cloth in hand, shaking his head sadly. Behind him, Alex can see Red exiting with the empty jug, no doubt to refill it.

'This is all so unnecessary,' Gold says. 'Just tell us who the boy is and where we can find her and you can go back to sleep.'

Alex can hear the rain pouring down outside as if the gods are mocking him. He sucks in a final mouthful of breath.

'I have no idea,' he says.

Gold looks disappointed though Alex suspects he's not. The man's a sadist in sheep's clothing.

'You're only hurting yourself, I'm afraid.'

Red returns with the jug, slopping a little water on the floor as he barges through the door.

'Still not talking?' he mutters.

'I'm afraid not.'

'Good.' The Scot grins at Alex, clearly keen to start all over again.

'But he will,' Gold says, suddenly ramming the cloth back over Alex's face.

Before he can close his mouth the water pours through it. He's going to die this time for sure. With his last breath he strains every sinew to get away but the straps hold him tight and the cloth barely moves. Then it stops. Alex sucks in air as quickly as he can but there's no time – the water again floods his mouth and nostrils almost immediately and there's nothing he can do. He gives up. He's a dead man.

The cloth comes up again.

'Last chance,' Gold says, stepping away from the bed.

Alex sucks in air as if it's his last breath, which it might well be. It's pathetic but he simply can't face that again. He has to give them something. Alex has no real clue who the boy might be. There are two or three teenage boys living in the village but he's never paid them any attention and, as far as he knows, neither has Ruby. He couldn't put a name to any of them. But he can give them another name and a place. The one man he knows Ruby would never go anywhere near. It'll buy them both a little time. He's reluctant to send these monsters his way but he's also the one man in Coldburn who might actually be able to do something about them if they approach him in the wrong way.

Gold steps forward with the cloth again.

'Try Danny's house,' Alex says. 'Danny Barnes. He's a friend. She might have gone there.'

The rain stops almost as quickly as it came. One minute the tin roof is vibrating to the sound of a thousand raindrops, the next it's silent. Lucas opens the door and steps out, hands held out like a preacher but he's clearly not feeling anything.

'Let's go,' he says.

Ruby happily joins him outside and sucks in the fresh air. Anything is better than staying in there with those carcasses. The house is still in darkness though. It doesn't look as if Danny has returned while they were sheltering.

'Where is he?' Lucas says. 'He should be back by now.'

They're only a few metres outside the door when he stops suddenly.

'Shit,' he says, looking up to the sky again.

Ruby doesn't really need to look up. It's not the rain that's worrying him this time. She can hear the same whirring sound they heard earlier, coming from somewhere in the heavens. When she does eventually follow his gaze she sees a small light flickering in the sky about twenty metres above them. The drone is back.

There's a sudden boom and she's pelted by something falling on her. She crouches down and puts her hands over her head for protection. The sliver of light coming out of the storeroom means she can see several bits of hard plastic hitting the ground around them and once the echo fades she realises there's no whirring sound.

'It exploded,' she says.

'Not an explosion,' Lucas says. 'A gunshot. Danny's back.'

27

Ruby watches Danny emerge from behind the storeroom, a shotgun in one hand and a cool box in the other. A brown Labrador plods quietly at his heels, seemingly unbothered by the shooting. He's obviously used to it. The poacher nods at them.

'All right, lad?' he says to Lucas. 'Quick cuppa?'

Lucas glances down at the remains of the drone. Ruby can tell he's thinking the same as her – shouldn't they be running?

'Don't piss about, lad, we haven't got long. I need to get these waterproofs off and I'm parched. Might be our last chance for a brew for a while. Keys are under the wheel.'

Lucas nods and heads towards the house leaving her alone with Danny.

'I'm Ruby,' she says nervously.

'I know who you are,' Danny says and heads towards the house himself.

'Shouldn't we get—'

Ruby's wasting her breath. He's not paying her any

attention. She hesitates, still thinking they should run, but the man seems so relaxed about what he's just done that in the end she simply follows him.

The kitchen is just off the front door. Lucas already has the kettle on and is taking a carton of milk out of the small fridge.

'Leave that open,' Danny says. He takes the lid off the cool box and pulls out a large fish which he puts into the fridge before shutting the door.

'First things first,' he says, reaching back into the box. 'Anyone know who this belongs to?'

Ruby screams as he places a severed arm on the kitchen table. Lucas turns around to see what the fuss is about and drops the milk carton on the floor in shock.

'Christ, Danny, you might have warned us.'

'We haven't got time to waste, lad. I hope you haven't spilt all that milk, I'm gasping.'

Lucas picks the carton up and finishes pouring the tea, handing a cup to Danny.

'You'd better stick a few sugars in young Ruby's cup,' the old man says. 'She's had a bit of a shock.'

'You think?' Ruby says.

'You OK?' Lucas hands her a cup.

'It hasn't got any fingertips,' she says, pointing at the arm.

'They probably chopped them off to avoid identification,' Danny says, as if it's the most normal thing in the world. She shudders but can't take her eyes off the arm. Then she realises she's seen it before.

'That tattoo. That soldier who came to our house this

morning had one exactly like it. The one my dad stabbed before they took him.'

Danny's mouth opens in surprise.

'Your dad stabbed someone? There's some weird shit going on around here but that might be the most unlikely thing I've heard so far. I don't believe it.'

Ruby drags her eyes away from the severed arm to confront Danny.

'How would you know? You don't know anything about him.'

'I know him well enough.'

'How?'

'I taught him to shoot.'

Now *she's* momentarily lost for words. Instead of the severed arm all she can see is her dad efficiently emptying the bullets from a magazine in their kitchen. Why the hell would a graphic designer take shooting lessons from Mad Danny? Especially when he's always warned her to keep away from him.

'When was this?' she asks but Danny ignores her, glances at his watch, drains his cup and stands up, heading towards the door.

'If they've got your dad and you want my help to find him we'd better get going. They'll be here soon. You can bring me up to speed on the way.'

'On the way where?' she asks but he ignores her, which really winds her up.

'Who'll be here soon?' she yells at his back.

He turns around to look at her.

'Now that is one thing I don't know. Yet. Come on, let's walk and talk.'

'Not until you tell me where we're going.'

'To see a friend. If anyone knows what's going on around here it'll be her.'

Danny hangs his waterproofs in the small porch and puts on an old Barbour jacket. He swaps his shotgun for a rifle that he carelessly seems to keep propped up just inside the door and they head out the way he came in, skirting the edge of the woods as much as they can. The dog, whose name appears to be Scout, leads the way, some ten metres or so in front of them, obviously familiar with the track. It's slow progress as the man stops regularly to listen for danger.

Ruby spends most of the journey telling Danny exactly what happened in her house that morning. The time for protecting her dad's reputation is long gone. It's clear that he hasn't been exactly honest with her for years – maybe nothing he's told her about her past is true? When she gets to the bit where she barges into the kitchen and finds the soldier dying on the floor Lucas interrupts. He's barely spoken since they left the house.

'You kept that quiet.'

'I told you what had happened,' she says, knowing full well she hadn't. Not exactly, anyway. Lucas may not be school-smart but he isn't stupid. He knows she hasn't been completely straight with him.

'No you didn't. You told me the soldier attacked first.'

'Does it really matter, lad?' Danny says. 'More important stuff to deal with than who said what, eh?'

Lucas glares at him, clearly pissed off that he's been corrected in front of her – boys are such soft shites under all that macho bullshit, she thinks.

'And you have no idea what it was all about?' Danny continues. 'Or where they've taken him?'

She starts to say no but the image of her and Lucas almost being caught earlier comes back to her.

'The ambulance was heading south, out of the village, I guess.'

'You might have mentioned that before we set off in the other direction,' Danny says grumpily. 'Anything else you've forgotten to tell me?'

She shakes her head. But then remembers the key ring.

'Wait,' she says, stopping in her tracks. She digs around in her pocket and pulls it out. 'My dad had a safe, I found this key in it when we went back to the house earlier. But I have no idea what it's for.'

She holds it in her palm to show the other two.

'You didn't mention that either,' Lucas mutters.

'I forgot,' she says, though that's not strictly true either. She'd been baffled by the present. She has no idea what the key might fit. She knows every inch of that house – she's lived there her whole life, after all – and there is nothing there with a lock on it. Though she didn't know the safe existed until today so maybe she was wrong about that too. Or maybe her dad has a secret lock-up that he's never mentioned?

The heart attached to the key ring was really out of

character too – her dad wasn't the sentimental type. She'd wanted to think it through properly before she showed it to Lucas. Now she realises that there's no time to waste on thinking, action is the only thing that matters.

'You can trust me, you know,' Lucas says.

'I know,' she says. 'I'm sorry.'

'When you two lovebirds have finished making up can we move on?' Danny says. 'Have you opened it? Seen what's in it?'

She looks at the key and back at him.

'What do you mean? Open what? I don't know what the key is for. Do you?'

He sighs, takes it from her hand and fiddles around with the heart. Nothing happens so he hurls it against the nearest tree, startling a sleeping pheasant which takes flight from one of the higher branches.

'Jesus,' Ruby says, running over to find it amongst the wild garlic. When she gets there the heart has broken in two. If that's not fucking symbolic I don't know what is, she thinks. The piece that has fallen off is lying a few inches away from the rest of it, but when she picks it up she realises it's not actually broken, more like a lid that's come off. The rest of it is still in one piece but she can see it's not what she thought at all – it's a memory stick.

She grabs it from the ground and turns back to Danny.

'How did you know?'

'I've read a lot of crime books in my time,' he says. 'Whenever a chunky key fob turns up there's always a memory stick inside it. The key's probably a wotsit – a red herring.'

She can't decide whether he's taking the piss or not but he doesn't seem the type to joke around and, as she's already realised, there isn't time to care about that kind of stuff any more. She has to find out what's on this thing.

'All we need now is a computer,' she says.

'Your dad said you were bright,' Danny says.

28

After Emma's first emails I tried everything I could to find out where she was. I rang around all her friends but none of them knew a thing. I tried to hunt her down on Facebook but got no joy – hardly a surprise as it was pretty new and no one our age was really using it back then. All I'd had from your mum in the months since her first email were a couple more messages saying she was fine and that she'd met someone. Obviously I wasn't happy. I'd have been even less happy if I'd known who it was.

Her flatmate Rosie later told me that Emma had returned from her first lunch with 'Simon' as high as a kite and more than a bit pissed. She swore blind that nothing had happened and that he hadn't tried it on with her but Rosie could tell she was interested in the man. In retrospect I think the trouble was that your mum believed she could handle anything and anyone. But she hadn't met anyone like this guy before – he was playing in a different league.

That lunch was the first of many, apparently – about once a fortnight, Rosie reckoned. She was getting worried that Emma was being sucked into something sordid. Simon was married and though Rosie didn't know anything specific about him other than his Christian name she knew that he was very well connected and came from a wealthy family – your mum had made sure to drop that into the conversation a few times. I was blind to most of her faults but even I would admit that she liked to show off.

The first time she'd gone to lunch with Simon, Emma had borrowed one of her flatmate's best dresses but after a couple of months of seeing the man Rosie realised that she'd acquired a brand new wardrobe of her own. She was pretty sure she knew who'd paid for it. They had their first ever fight about it, apparently. Rosie called her a tart, your mum accused her of being jealous and they only made up when Rosie went out and bought a cheap bottle of plonk from the local offie to share. Even then it nearly kicked off again when Emma complained that it wasn't as good as the stuff Simon bought her at their lunches together. She was clearly being sucked in deeper and deeper.

It must have been around this time that I got my final email from Emma. It said that her new man – she still hadn't told me his name – had a proposal for her, something that would blow my socks off. She said that she would tell me all about it once she'd decided whether to accept it or not.

I never heard from her again.

29

Margaret sits in the back garden with a shotgun on her knees waiting to see if the drone comes back. Throwing stones at it earlier had been a hoot – she'd christened it 'Nigel' which improved her aim no end – but although her efforts seemed to send it scurrying away she knew that if she wanted to really damage it she needed to, quite literally, bring out the big guns. She's not having these invaders watching her every move. If anyone's doing any spying around these parts, it's her.

Boris is confused. He doesn't normally have free rein outside at night and at first he patrolled the edges of the garden, making sure there was no danger – he's scared of cats, especially that monstrous stray that hangs about in the alleyways. But he's not making the most of his unexpected freedom now. Just sitting quietly under the camping chair she's set up in the middle of the lawn. He's getting on a bit and it shows. She's already decided to try and get a smarter dog as soon as he's popped his clogs.

There are no lights on in the house as Margaret was

worried they'd be able to see her sitting there with their eye-in-the-sky. She tried to do some research on the internet about the capabilities of drones but there seems to be some real connection problems at the moment. Maybe these people have got some kind of blocking thing in place. Was that even possible?

She wonders again what happened in that house up the road. Was it really only this morning that all hell had broken loose? She's sure they took at least one dead man out of there. She was so tempted to sneak in and have a look after the kids had done a runner, and probably would have done if it wasn't for that drone watching her. Whatever it was, those young 'uns were clearly terrified, both this morning when that 'soldier' chased them and tonight when the drone suddenly appeared. They'd been off like a shot without even a by your leave.

'What do you expect?' Nigel would have said. 'No manners these days, the younger generation.' Pots and kettles, she thought. Over the years she had realised that Nigel was not just the angriest man she knew but the rudest too and he got worse with age. Always banging on about bringing back national service, and immigrants. Once he'd shuffled off it hadn't taken her long to appreciate the peace and quiet.

She hasn't really missed him at all until now. He'd have been quite useful in this situation, with his knowledge of the way soldiers operated and thought. And he knew his way around guns – the shotgun on her lap was one of many that he had stowed away around the place. Typical that he'd bugger off before he finally came in handy.

She takes a sip from her flask of tea and starts to make a plan. The only other man in the village who might be able to work out what's going on is Danny. He'd been in the army too, more recently and for longer than Nigel, in fact. She'd actually picked up the phone earlier to ring him but that still wasn't working either, which has given her a bit more time to think about it. He's always been difficult to read, even when they were younger, and though they had history – she smiles at the memory – she wasn't absolutely sure where he'd stand on this. Maybe with his background he'd be on the side of the soldiers?

They haven't spoken for years, ever since a furious row about the Neighbourhood Watch. He'd hated them with a vengeance. 'Sticky-beaks' he'd called them. Still, it's all water under the bridge now and there's no doubt she needs another pair of eyes on the situation. And she doesn't mean those things in the sky. She glances up again and her mind is made up. She isn't a woman who sits on her hands waiting for something to turn up like some northern Mrs Micawber. She's a doer. She'll go and find Danny in the morning – like her, he's a stubborn old sod but he dislikes outsiders even more than she does so she's pretty sure he won't be happy with this siege – which is what she's started to think it is. For now though what she needs is a good night's sleep.

She puts the lid back on her flask of tea, stands and folds up the chair. Boris, typically, doesn't get the message so she nudges him firmly with her foot and he stirs, slowly climbs to his feet and heads back to the house, no doubt hoping he'll get a midnight snack.

That's when the shooting begins.

30

The soldier appears out of nowhere. Ruby steps out of the trees to head back into the village and he is just standing there under a streetlight, about four metres away but with his back turned. She freezes but it's too late. He hears her, spins around and points his rifle straight at her.

'Don't move,' he shouts. 'Put your hands on your head and kneel down.'

She thinks about running. Would he really shoot her? From the look on his face the answer's yes. She curses her carelessness. Why didn't she just do what Danny told her and stay on the forest path?

'Now,' he screams.

Ruby starts to raise her arms when he fires. She collapses to the floor. Bizarrely, she can't feel any pain apart from the impact of her knees on the ground. And as she starts to check for a wound or blood she sees that the soldier has dived for cover behind a car. It takes her a moment to realise that it wasn't him who fired. It was Danny. Another shot pings off the side of the car, the soldier ducking down to keep out of the line of fire.

'Run,' Danny shouts, firing again from behind the trees. She doesn't need telling twice, leaping to her feet, turning and running back into the trees towards him. 'Get out of here,' he adds, nodding in the other direction.

She instinctively does as she's told but is only just past him when she stops dead. This isn't going to plan. She turns back again, thankful that the shooting has stopped for a moment.

'No. I'm not going anywhere. You said you'd help me find my dad.'

The poacher stares at her for a moment. She thinks he's going to shout at her again but then he nods.

'I will,' he says, turning away from her to keep his eyes on the soldier. 'But you have to leave that with me. Tracking down things is my skill-set, not yours. If you want to help you should find out what's on that memory stick.'

He's right. He's a hunter. And she really wouldn't know where to start. She turns and sprints past Lucas who doesn't react immediately despite her grabbing at his arm as she goes by. But then Danny yells at him too. 'Look after her,' firing again at the car as if for emphasis.

The shot acts like a starting gun for Lucas and he's quickly on her heels as the pair of them escape as fast as they can, putting as much distance between them and the gunfire as possible.

*

Danny is privately cursing himself. Why is he getting involved in this shit? He has a certain loyalty to the boy, he promised his mam he'd look after him, but this is different level stuff. Whatever it is the girl's father has done is down to him. She's not Danny's responsibility: just because he couldn't save his own daughter doesn't mean he has to help every other bugger's. It won't bring her back. And maybe he's on the wrong side of this one? These soldiers could be the good guys.

Even if he has ended up on the side of the angels he's not sure that he's doing them any good. He should have stayed at the back, keeping watch, as he did at the start, instead of dropping his guard and letting the girl lag behind him and wander out of the trees at such a public spot. He's losing his touch. Maybe he lost it years ago. Maybe that's why the army – and even the Post Office – were happy to wave him off.

He can see the soldier peeking out from around the side of the car and fires another shot just to keep him on his toes. If he can keep him pinned down or lead him in the other direction at least the kids can get away. Though where they'll find shelter or safety God only knows. And as for finding the girl's dad, he has a couple of ideas but that's a job for another time. For now he's got this situation to deal with.

He waits a few minutes as the stalemate continues, the soldier letting off a couple of aimless shots that clip the trees to his left, until he hears the man speak into his radio. He's not sure what he says but is certain he's calling for backup. Which leaves him no choice. He has to resolve this quickly. He fires once more to give himself a head start before turning and tearing back into the trees. Well, not exactly 'tearing', his gammy leg isn't up to much more than a quick hobble. He glances back once to make sure the man is chasing after him and not the kids and then veers off towards the old mine workings, Scout at his heels. Danny's too old to outrun his pursuer for any distance but he has one big advantage: he knows these woods like the back of his hand.

A chunk of tree trunk flies away close to his head as the soldier finds his range. Danny starts to slalom through the trees, keeping obstacles in between him and the firing line. Another shot ricochets around. From the height of the shots he knows that the soldier is aiming to kill. But he also knows how difficult that is on the run, especially when it's dark as hell, like it is now. He also knows for sure now that these are not the good guys.

The threat makes his mind up though. He knows where this will end. He tries to speed up but it's like the red light's flashing on his fuel supply. Despite the cold he's soaked in sweat and he can feel his legs beginning to go. Thankfully, he's almost there. He stumbles over a tree root but somehow keeps his balance. Then he sees it. The small marker he painted on the tree the first time he found this spot, only just visible above a small white flash of snowdrops that have sprung up since then. Thank fuck he used luminous green paint or he would have missed it. *Fail to prepare, prepare to fail* as his old CO used to say. Danny veers to the left, making sure his movement is spotted by crashing through more branches than he needs to, runs straight towards the mark, then slams on the brakes and hides behind the biggest trunk he can find, holding his breath as best he can so the soldier can't hear him. Scout is just behind him, lying prone on the ground, as he's been trained to, awaiting further instructions.

There's no chance of the soldier hearing anything, though, as he is pounding along the path Danny's carved through the trees, making enough noise to scare off every animal for miles. And he clearly has no idea where Danny is or where he's going as he flies past his hiding place and straight into the sinkhole that Danny has led him to. If the poor bastard's charging around hasn't woken the dead his scream will as the swamp swallows him up to his neck in a second. His best bet would be to stay still but he's clearly young and inexperienced. Panic sets in as his head starts to go under. He's flailing around desperately but there's no way he's getting out of there without help and his movement is making it worse. Danny remembers the first time he discovered the sinkhole when he was tracking a full-size deer which disappeared in an instant after running into the swamp.

The soldier's head reappears again as he desperately tries to stay afloat but he's clearly tiring as his arms barely hit the surface. Danny steps out from behind the tree and walks slowly over to the edge of the sinkhole. The soldier catches sight of him and gasps for help before his head goes under again. Danny glances at a large branch lying on the floor beside his feet. It's probably the man's only chance. If only there was someone there who gave a fuck.

Air bubbles continue to pop out of the swamp for a moment or two before everything goes still again. He remembers the arm he found in the river, almost certainly from the guy that Ruby's dad took out. Two down now, Danny thinks. But how many more to go?

31

Ruby is nearing the edge of the village when she hears shouting. She stops dead, not taking any chances this time. Through the trees she can see a barricade set up on the road to stop people leaving. Or coming in. An armed soldier is standing on the village side of the barrier and a man, a civilian by the look of him, is on the other side. He's the one doing the shouting. He seems quite old, maybe because he's stooping, and strangely familiar. Annoyingly she can't hear what he's saying and can't edge any closer for fear of being seen. There's a car just behind the man with its headlights on. The driver's door is wide open and she's guessing that he wants to drive into the village and the soldier won't let him.

Lucas taps her on the arm and she jumps.

'Who's that?' he whispers. They haven't spoken at all as they jogged through the woods, neither seeming to have a plan apart from putting as much distance between them and the shooting as possible. Now it looks like they are going to have to turn back.

'No idea,' she says. It's dark but the car's headlights make the scene feel almost staged. It's started snowing again and the flakes are floating through the beams. Under other circumstances it would be beautiful. The older man's got a hat on – not a beanie or a bobble hat but an actual proper hat like they wear in those black and white movies her dad sometimes watches. He must be ancient because nobody under forty would be seen dead in one of those.

Eventually the man storms off, still shouting, and gets back into his car. He sits there for a moment and Ruby wonders if he's deciding to just go for it. The soldier doesn't seem too bothered. He makes a call on his radio then lights a cigarette and takes out his phone. Maybe the problem with the signal has been sorted. She'll get Lucas to check his phone once they're out of sight. Eventually the driver seems to give up, reversing the car around and driving off.

The soldier is completely oblivious to Ruby and Lucas's presence and he hasn't looked around once, just perched his arse on the barrier as soon as he was on his own, and rested his rifle against it. He's tapping on his phone now and Ruby's pretty sure he's playing some kind of game. She's starting to think that whoever these men are, they're not exactly disciplined. Ruby's never had any contact with the real army but she's pretty sure that this isn't it.

'We should move back,' Lucas whispers. She nods and they retreat into the denser bits of the woods.

'What do we do now?' he says, quietly. They're out of sight of the soldier but she still guides him further away before answering. Who knows how far sound travels when there's nothing else around? Apart from that drone the village has been eerily quiet all night. It's very late and the place is never exactly buzzing but there's normally the sound of a car or at the very least a dog barking to disturb the peace. It looks like the earlier warning has convinced everyone else to stay indoors. And if that hadn't worked then the more recent sound of gunfire has probably done the trick – though with all the hunting that goes on around here the locals are pretty used to that.

'I don't know.'

'We could get away, you know,' he says. 'There are plenty of footpaths through here that would take us out of his sight. We could head to one of the other villages and raise the alarm.'

Ruby shakes her head.

'In this weather? It's miles to the nearest village and by the time we get out of the woods the snow could have covered all the paths. We'd probably get lost and die of hypothermia. Remember those two shepherds who died trying to get home in the snow over Alnham way back in the sixties? They didn't get halfway and they knew the area really well. There's a big cairn there to mark where they found the bodies. My dad and I went walking there last year. Mrs Morrison told us about it in junior school. Remember?'

Lucas shakes his head. Stupid question really, he'd probably been too busy messing about at the back of the class to pay attention.

'You can't have forgotten that! She got into trouble cos little Davey Cox got scared and wet himself.'

He laughs. 'I remember that!'

She sighs. Maybe he isn't as different now as she'd hoped.

'Seriously, Lucas, even if we did manage to get somewhere, who would believe us? If they can block the roads they must have some kind of official backing. And what happens when they find out that my dad started it by stabbing that soldier? He could end up in prison, if he's not already dead. I won't leave until I know what's going on and, more importantly, what's happened to him.'

Lucas looks unconvinced but doesn't offer up a plan B. Luckily, she has one up her sleeve.

'Look, you might be right,' she says. 'Maybe we should just run. But before I do anything else I need to know what's on this memory stick.' She pulls it out of her pocket and examines it, as though the answer will be written on the side or something. 'I just need a computer.'

'I know where we can find one,' Lucas says, taking her hand and leading her back the way they came. His grasp is firm and even though she'd never say so, it makes her feel a little safer. Which in turn makes her angry as she should be stronger than that. And she can't blame her 'girliness' on anyone else. It's all down to her. Her dad is so PC it's laughable. She's seen all her baby photos and he always dressed her in neutral colours, never pink or blue. And it was him who sent her to self-defence classes so she could protect herself. Though after what's happened today she can see now that he might have had other reasons for that.

She pulls her hand away just to spite herself. Lucas looks a little pained but keeps his mouth shut.

'Just follow me then,' he mutters eventually, walking quickly away from her.

A few minutes later they come out behind a row of three houses on the east side of Coldburn. Lucas heads through the back gate of the end one and goes into the shed. As she follows him a security light comes on and she freezes.

'What if someone sees us?' Ruby asks.

'These are all holiday homes,' he says from inside the shed. 'There's no one staying here at the moment.'

'How do you know that?'

'I look after the gardens for them,' he says, as he emerges with a key in his hand. 'They tell me when there are people here so I don't disturb them.'

She remembers him saying earlier that he sometimes did some work for old man Baldwin in his garage.

'How many part-time jobs do you have?' she says.

'A lot. Some of us don't have a trust fund.'

'I don't have a—'

He winks at her to show he was teasing. She can feel herself blushing. She needs to get a grip. Now really isn't the time to be going soft on a boy. Especially this one. A day ago she would have crossed the road to avoid talking to him.

Lucas heads to the back door and unlocks it, stepping into the kitchen. He looks back at her.

'You coming or not?'

She nods and follows him in, shutting the door behind her. The place smells of fresh paint and looks immaculate.

There's a small basket of goodies on the counter, all ready to welcome the next set of holidaymakers.

'Computer's in the bedroom,' he says.

'How do you know that? I thought you just did the gardens.'

'My mam used to clean for them. I helped her sometimes.'

The boy's clearly a workaholic, she thinks, feeling guilty as she's never had to get a part-time job. Her dad came up with a scheme to reward her for doing some of the cooking and getting good reports from school. Easy money. Compared to Lucas she supposes she kind of did have a trust fund. From the bank of Dad.

Lucas heads towards the stairs and she follows him, closing the curtains in the lounge as she passes just in case one of the soldiers wanders by and glances in. She doubts they'd have noticed they were open before – they don't seem that observant.

There's an old-fashioned desktop computer in the corner of the main bedroom, one of those with a separate hard disk storage below. Maybe that's why the owners left it behind. Lucas moves out of the way while she sits down and works out where everything is. She can see that it's all connected properly and there's a green light shining on the hard disk. She clicks the on switch and hears the system start to warm up. A few seconds later the screen comes to life and after a series of images there's a prompt: Username and Password. Fuck.

Ruby slumps down in the chair, her forehead against the desk. She feels like smashing it up and down until something gives and she doesn't much care whether it's her skull or the desktop. Lucas puts his hand on her shoulder and she's so weary that she doesn't shrug him off this time.

'I'll see if I can find the handbook they leave out for visitors,' he says. 'Might be something in there.'

She doesn't hear him leave the room but when she sits up he's gone. The screen is still showing the prompt and she thinks about trying to guess but knows that's ridiculous. Behind the computer she can see that, aside from a couple of street lights, the entire village is in darkness. She draws the curtains just in case. There's a clock on the wall in the bedroom which shows it's well past midnight. It's no wonder she's exhausted. She puts her head down on the desk, only lifting it again when she hears Lucas return.

She sits up and spins the chair around. He shakes his head slowly, without needing to hear the question.

'Just the Wi-Fi code. And that's not working. There's still no signal either.' He yawns. 'Maybe we should get some sleep and try somewhere else in the morning.'

'My dad's still out there,' she says.

'But we don't know where yet. You heard what Danny said. Leave it to him, he knows what he's doing. And at least we're safe for now. They're not gonna search every house and they'll never think of looking for us here.'

She knows he's right but how can she possibly rest without knowing where her dad is? Or what's on this bloody memory stick.

'I won't be able to sleep,' she says. 'I have no idea where

my dad is or if he's even still alive. You have no idea what that feels like.'

Lucas glares at her. She can tell that he's pissed off but isn't sure why.

'Don't I?' he says, eventually. 'I know all this is really fucked up but you're not the only one with problems!'

32

'My mam's in rehab,' Lucas says, as they lie on the double bed, separated by the welcome basket he liberated from the kitchen. They're eating by the light from the computer screen as they were too scared of being noticed to put the bedside lights on.

They've already demolished the shortbread biscuits and the crisps and are halfway through the little chocolates they found next to the small packets of coffee by the kettle. They've even opened the bottle of red wine the owners left behind as part of the package.

Ruby knows that Lucas has more to say but gives him some room. It's pretty obvious he hasn't spoken to many people about this before.

'She's an alcoholic. Has been since Dad left her, before we moved here. She has a lot of accidents. Hurts herself. Sometimes I'm not even sure they're accidents.'

Maybe that explains why the blood on her sleeve earlier didn't freak him out.

'Jesus, I'm sorry.'

'You weren't to know.'

Ruby has read about actors and pop stars going into rehab but never ordinary people like Lucas's mum. She has no idea how that works.

'Isn't rehab really expensive?' she asks quietly.

Lucas nods.

'Is that why you do all those jobs?'

'Sort of,' he says. 'Though that doesn't come anywhere near to covering the cost.'

She nods but is still confused.

'So how . . .'

'Danny helps us out,' he says. 'He found a place run by an old friend of his and got a massive discount. He chips in as well.'

That throws her.

'Are he and your mum . . .?' She almost says 'shagging' but stops herself at the last minute. But he clearly gets it.

'God no, that's gross,' he says, going red. 'At least I don't think so.'

'But where does he get the money from?'

'I don't know and I don't care.'

She gets that. When Danny offered to help find her dad she didn't ask for a CV and a bank statement. Sometimes how you get something doesn't matter as long as you get it.

'How's she doing?' she asks instead.

'I'm not sure. Danny says she's OK but she won't let me see her until she's better. It's been a couple of months now.'

'And you've been on your own all that time?'

'I'm not twelve,' he says. 'I've been doing everything

myself for a lot longer than that anyway so if anything it's easier when she's not around.'

Ruby can see how hard that was for him to admit and how difficult he finds it to talk about the whole thing so she squeezes his hand.

'I'm sure she'll be home soon. And at least she's not getting caught up in this shit.'

He nods. Even in the gloom she can see his eyelids are starting to droop and she realises that, unlike her, he hasn't slept at all. The wine's probably not helping.

'You're not exactly a party animal, are you?' she teases.

He smiles, opens his eyes slightly, shakes his head.

'Proper lightweight, me.' His head slips down on to the pillow, his eyes closing. 'It's your birthday next week, isn't it?' he adds quietly.

'How do you know that?'

'I saw the invitations in your bedroom. Mine must be in the post.'

They both know he wasn't going to get one. She's too embarrassed to look at him even though he still has his eyes shut.

'Maybe we should try and get some rest,' she says. The next time she glances over he's fast asleep. She stares at the ceiling, unable to turn her brain off, wondering what is happening to her dad.

33

Alex is woken by someone fiddling with his restraints.

'Don't move,' Red says, 'or I'll shoot your dick off.'

'What's going on?'

'The boss says you can have a toilet break.'

Alex looks past Red and sees Gold nodding in the doorway.

'You scratch my back,' he says.

What does that mean? The last time they spoke Alex had sent him on a fool's errand.

'Your girl was exactly where you said she'd be,' Gold continues. 'I thought you were playing me but I was wrong.'

Alex tries to hide his bemusement but fails miserably as panic starts to set in.

'What do you mean? Where is she? What have you done with her?'

Gold frowns and looks like he's about to break the bad news but then his features crack into a sick smile and he laughs.

'Relax, *Dad*! They got away. For the time being.'

'Who's they?'

'Ruby, this man Danny and the boyfriend, whose name we don't have yet. Unless you want to give us that too now?'

'I already told you I have no idea. You better not have hurt her.'

'Or what?' Red mutters. 'You gonna try and bite me to death?'

Alex is so busy trying to process what he's been told that he barely notices the second restraint come off his upper body. What the hell is Ruby doing with Danny?

'You can sit up now,' Gold says, 'give your arms a stretch. But no sudden movements. I doubt you'll survive a second bullet.' He waves the pistol he's holding in his left hand just in case Alex hasn't got the message.

Red moves on to his leg restraints. When the second one is released Alex stretches his legs out but is immediately hit by a wave of pain. He yells out as Red laughs.

'Cramp can be a bitch,' Gold says.

'Not as bad as a bullet though,' Red adds, stepping back and making sure Alex can see his rifle.

'Try standing up,' Gold says. 'I'm a patient man but I haven't got all day.'

Alex is massaging his calves, playing for time again. While he's keeping them here there are fewer people looking for Ruby. He wonders how many of them there are altogether. At least two more, to his knowledge – the other man from the kitchen, Silver, he thinks Red called him, and the big guy they picked up. Any others must be out there searching because he hasn't seen another soul here.

'Let's go,' Gold says, clearly becoming impatient.

'D'you want me to come with you, boss?' Red asks.

'I think I can handle it,' Gold says smugly. 'Walk slowly past me and keep going straight on,' he tells Alex. 'I'll be right behind you so don't piss about.'

Alex does as he's told. They'd let him piss in a bottle earlier but now he's dying for a crap. And he wants to try and get a handle on where they're keeping him. He shuffles across the room and through the doorway, Gold following close behind. They're in a corridor now, a couple of doors on one side, and another one at the end. Alex glances around but there's nothing to see really. Red flock wallpaper covers the walls but there are no pictures or photos, no clues to where he is.

He slows down as he passes the first door. It's open. The curtains are closed so he can't see outside but inside is a desk and a chair and not much else apart from a weird plastic box with about a dozen aerials sticking out of the top.

'Keep going,' Gold says. 'Second door on the right.'

'What was that?' he asks.

'Never you mind.'

'It's not like I can tell anyone, is it?'

'True,' his captor says, nudging him in the back to keep him moving. 'And I have been told that taking away someone's hope is worse than killing them. Seems like horseshit to me but maybe you can confirm it one way or another.'

Alex doesn't turn around but he'd bet that weird half-smile is on Gold's face again.

'It's a jammer,' he continues. 'We've got them all over,

sending out electromagnetic waves that mess up everyone's signals. Couldn't have your neighbours chatting about all this on the phone or social media, could we? I mean obviously we cut the phone lines too, which is a bit more old-school. Belt and braces and that. So don't think the cavalry will be coming over the hill any time soon.'

As Gold predicted, Alex feels a little more hope drain away. That had been one of his few optimistic thoughts – that someone might get the word out that there was something weird going on here and alert the authorities. Though whether they'd do anything about it was anyone's guess – they might even be a part of it given who was involved. He reaches the second door and nudges it open. It's a gents' toilet, a small urinal and two traps. He moves towards the first trap.

'Keep the door open,' Gold orders.

There's a window above the toilet – it's frosted glass but it's the first glimpse of the outside he's seen in a while, though obviously it's dark out there. He thinks it's the middle of the night but in truth he's lost all track of time in this place so he could be way out.

On closer inspection the window looks like it hasn't been opened in years, several layers of thick paint covering the edges. As far as he can tell there are no bars behind it so he makes a mental note: possible escape route. Though how that might happen God only knows. As he stares at the window he thinks he sees a shadow pass across it. He blinks but it's gone. Probably just another guard on patrol.

'Get a move on,' Gold says.

It's demeaning but Alex does as he's told, turning around to face the soldier, dropping his pants and sitting down. As he evacuates his bowels Gold at least offers him a little dignity by glancing to the side.

'Now that you've seen I'm a reasonable man,' he says, 'I hope you'll be a bit more cooperative. Maybe tell us who this boy is.'

Alex ignores him but he hasn't finished.

'Did you know that the last Winter who upset the authorities around here was hanged just down the road?'

Alex shakes his head.

'I don't get out much.'

'Place called Winter's Gibbet, aptly enough – there's still a plaque there to celebrate it – the people up here do love a good lynching. Maybe we should give them another one? Just pick someone at random to encourage you to be a bit more cooperative. I'm sure my men could knock up a quick scaffold on the village green. What do you think?'

'Just call me the fucking Deer Hunter,' Silver mumbles to himself.

He's standing high up in a small wooden tower that was built for the hunting, shooting and fishing brigade that inhabits this part of the country. He imagines that hunting must be a piece of piss around here, what with the miles of open space between Coldburn and the next town. There are very few places to hide – which is why he's tucked away in this thing. Apparently it's called a blind and with the snow now falling heavily around him that seems entirely appropriate. He can't see for shit, which is doubly annoying as he likes to stargaze when he pulls a night shift and one of the other lads reckoned Northumberland was the best place to do that in the country. Something to do with a lack of light pollution apparently.

Be careful what you wish for is his new watchword. Complaining about having to partner up with Red has won him the graveyard shift, making sure that no one tries to leave the village on foot. And then tomorrow he's being teamed up with Black instead. Another day, a different psychopath. First of all they give him a jock headcase who wants to kill everyone, and then, when he volunteers to patrol the village instead of doing house-to-house, he gets the night shift and a new partner who never speaks and looks as if he spent his childhood torturing people's pets for kicks. Yesterday, at the morning briefing, he could have sworn he heard the man humming the theme tune from *The Exorcist*.

Whoever put this group of lunatics together must have spent too much time watching *The Dirty Dozen* on repeat. Silver wonders what that says about him. Maybe he was the only medic on their books who was available – that's what he's going to choose to think, anyway, otherwise he has to consider that he's got a screw loose as well and that he actually belongs with these muppets.

At least he got a half-decent nickname when they were handed out. Silver makes him feel like he's the number two on the team even though he isn't. Typical of Gold to give himself the most prestigious colour, mind.

He shivers. He knows that the weather's a blessing really, most people will be happy to stay cooped up in their nice warm houses, leaving them to search for the girl without hindrance. But as soon as this jaunt is over he's going to book that foreign holiday he's been promising the girls, south of France or maybe one of the Greek islands – it's always hot there, isn't it?

Silver yawns, struggling to remember when he last slept; if this goes on much longer they're all going to be zombies. He's tempted to head off somewhere for a kip – surely no one's going to be trying to leave in this – but just as he's wondering where he could hide away he sees a small light flashing in the trees. It appears to be heading towards him. Obviously he was wrong, someone is stupid enough to try getting out. He slips on his night vision goggles and waits.

A few moments later he sees what looks like a young lad climbing over a stile into the open field. He's got a torch in his hand. As he lands he slips and falls onto the sodden ground. The light goes out. The kid gets to his feet and seems to be searching for something – the torch probably – but he has no luck. After a moment or two he trudges on in the dark, turning right and heading across the field towards the path that eventually leads to Rothbury. Though he's got a hell of a way to go in these conditions.

Silver sighs. He was hoping for a quiet night and a kip but now he's got to leave his shelter and stop this idiot. He wonders if it's the mysterious boyfriend they've been told to look out for but if that's the case why wouldn't the girl be with him?

The kid trudges on, getting nearer, becoming an easier target by the minute. Fortunately for the lad, Silver's brief is to stop people leaving, not to shoot them – he's not in the Middle East now. He's not even supposed to take prisoners – they don't need the grief and haven't got the capacity to guard them anyway – so this should be pretty simple.

He climbs down from the tower to a quad bike, which is parked on the narrow track below. He switches on his head-lights, turns on the ignition and swings the bike around, heading along the outside of the field towards the same gate the stumbling idiot seems to aiming for. The impact of the lights and noise is instant and clearly scares the shit out of the kid who starts to run but immediately falls again and this time he stays down.

Silver stops the bike and watches carefully – the kid could be playing possum, hoping he'll move on and leave him lying there. He thinks about discarding the bike and going in after him. If it is the boyfriend he will know where the girl is. But that's a big if. And the truth is, he can't be arsed. He's tired, it's a quagmire out there and he's no longer sure that he gives a shit whether they find this girl or not.

Eventually the kid slowly rises to his feet. He looks towards the quad bike's lights, seeming to realise that he's going to get cut off at the end of the field if he keeps going. So he turns and runs back the way he came. As Silver watches he sees the poor sod slip at least twice more before climbing back over the stile again, heading back into the village.

Maybe now he can get some kip.

35

A red kite soars above Danny's head looking for prey. He's been watching Milburn Farm for an hour or more, recceing the buildings from behind a drystone wall as the sun begins to rise. Assuming they're keeping him nearby, there are only two places they're likely to find Alex, here or the manor house. He knows the girl said the ambulance had headed south but this was the nearest one to the sinkhole so it was worth checking out first. The snow has finally stopped again but he's still freezing his arse off, truly thankful that he put his thermals on to go out poaching last night.

The house looks deserted but it could be clever camouflage. These guys might not be the actual army but they're by no means amateurs. And an empty farm is an ideal place to hold someone hostage without anyone noticing. Someone like Ruby's dad.

There are no vehicles in the yard – any tracks there might have been long covered by the snow – but there is a large cow barn off to one side of the big farmhouse that could easily house a whole pool of them. The house itself is in darkness but it's early and it's possible the power is off anyway. Danny hasn't been home since he fled with the two kids so has no idea what steps the 'soldiers' have taken. He'd be very surprised if they're not running some kind of jamming device on comms in the area and the next obvious step would be to take down the power lines. That's what he'd do. Even though most of the houses have generators it still added a buggerance factor that would keep people off balance.

After waiting another thirty minutes and not seeing a damn thing he makes his move, creeping around the edge of the yard just in case someone is keeping watch, staying in the shadows of the outbuildings. He has to keep his eyes peeled as there are various bits of disused farm machinery lying around on the ground, a couple of rusting feeding troughs which have been left to rot too. Once he's negotiated his way past these he jogs the last twenty yards across the open space to the side of the house.

He's never been inside the place before – just used to buy eggs from the wifey there occasionally – so doesn't know the lie of the land. The Milburns gave up the farm a few years back when the EU subsidies stopped; the irony of being avid Brexit supporters seemingly lost on them. It's been empty since then but bizarrely it still smells like shit, as all farms do. He wonders how long it takes for that to fade.

The first window he passes is frosted glass so he can't see inside. A bathroom or downstairs loo, he guesses. As he moves around the house there's no sign of life at all. The next window offers him a glimpse of the kitchen, there's a microwave on the worktop but it doesn't look like it's been used in years. Everything is covered in dust and some of the cupboard doors are hanging off. He works his way to the back door, which has a padlock on it, and, as he continues around, the rest of the house is equally unpromising. The front door is also firmly closed and bolted. It looks like whoever owns it now has fitted a couple of newish sturdy locks to deter break-ins – which makes him more than a little curious. Why bother with new locks? It's out of the way and Coldburn isn't exactly a haven for vandals. Maybe he is in the right place after all.

He heads towards the large barn. If they are staying here then there'll be signs of it in there; if not vehicles then at least a tyre track or two with no snow to hide them. He guesses they could even use it to hold a prisoner if they didn't want to use the house for some reason. He crosses the yard and presses his ear against the large wooden door. It's as quiet as a graveyard. Danny removes the bar that's securing the door, grabs the handle and hauls it open. It's completely empty. The place is a bust.

36

Ruby hears the siren getting nearer and nearer. She's sprinting down the middle of the road looking for some way of getting out of the ambulance's path but it's impossible. There are high walls on both sides and no pavements. Any second now she's going to be crushed under its wheels. She glances back and can see the driver grinning as he closes the gap. She starts praying but knows there's no escape. The siren is so loud now she can't even hear the sound of her own voice.

Ruby wakes up. There's an alarm going off downstairs and no sign of Lucas. She leaps off the bed, still fully clothed, and runs for the stairs. The noise is much louder on the landing and there's smoke drifting over the banister. She flies down the stairs two at a time and turns the corner at the bottom to see Lucas standing in the kitchen in just his boxer shorts waving his hands frantically at the toaster. His fuckwittery knows no limits.

'Open the window,' she yells, noticing that the world outside is covered in snow.

He mouths 'sorry' and does as he's told, moving quickly across to the sink and pushing the window behind it open. Still the alarm goes on. Ruby scans the room and sees a smoke detector on the ceiling. She pulls a chair out from under the small kitchen table and jumps up on it, just managing to reach the device on her tiptoes. She quickly twists the cover off and pulls the battery out. The alarm stops. She glares at an obviously repentant Lucas, who's trying to avoid her gaze.

'Again! You've got to be kidding me! I thought you said you could look after yourself.'

'It's not my fault,' he protests. 'The toaster's full of crumbs.'

'No more cooking, right? I don't even like toast.'

'We have to eat,' he mutters.

'You ate your own bodyweight in biscuits last night.'

She notices that the clothes he was wearing last night are on the radiator.

'What happened to your clothes?'

'Nothing.' His growing blush makes it obvious that's nonsense. She waits him out, knowing he'll crack quickly.

'I went out.'

'Went out where?'

He sighs. 'I couldn't sleep so I went out to see if I could get some help. They can't cover all the ways out so I reckoned I could get over to one of the other villages towards Rothbury while it was still dark, raise the alarm.'

'Weren't you listening when I told you about those shepherds who died? You could have got lost.'

'But I didn't, did I?'

'What did happen, then? Why did you come back?'

'One of them saw me, chased me on a quad bike. I got a bit wet but I managed to get away.'

'And you led them back here?' Ruby looks out of the window. There are footsteps leading from the back gate to the door. Lucas sees what she's looking at and hangs his head.

'Sorry. I panicked. I lost the torch. I was soaked and freezing. I didn't know what else to do. I was just glad the owners had shown me how to work the heating just in case the guests needed some help.'

Ruby knows she's being a total bitch. At least he tried to do something positive. What has she done so far apart from hide away?

'Thanks for trying. It's not your fault you completely messed up.'

He grins. 'Harsh.'

'But it was brave of you to try. You could've been shot. But now that you've literally raised the alarm the whole village will know where we are. We have to get out of here before they find us.'

Almost immediately there's a loud knock on the front door.

They both freeze. Lucas stares at her as if she's some kind of weird psychic.

'Christ, that was quick,' he says.

'Shhhhh!' she whispers, putting her finger to her lips.

There's a second knock. Louder and longer. Neither of them moves.

'I know you're in there. Open the door.'

A woman's voice. Not a soldier.

Ruby edges over to the front window and tries to see through a small gap in the curtains. Margaret is peering through the same gap from the outside. The old woman points to the front door. 'Let me in,' she mouths.

Ruby goes to the door and, though Lucas tries to protest, maybe because he's still only got his boxers on, she opens it anyway. Margaret is holding a bicycle and kicking the snow around outside the door. She sees Ruby's puzzled look.

'Don't want anyone to know that I'm here, do I?' she says before wheeling her bike into the house, her manky dog dragging its heels behind her.

'Shut it quickly,' the older woman says. 'Before someone sees us.'

Ruby obeys instantly. Margaret does a double take when she sees Lucas standing there in his pants.

'Have I interrupted something?' she asks.

'No,' they both say immediately. 'Lucas got his clothes dirty so he had to wash them,' Ruby explains.

'You're not exactly clean yourself,' Margaret says.

Ruby glances down at the bloodstains on her sleeve and jeans from her unfortunate meeting with the skinned rabbits. She had thought about washing them last night but couldn't find anything else to put on in the house and there was no way she was wandering around in her underwear, not like Lucas, who grabs a jumper from the radiator and throws it on.

'You two really need to get a grip,' Margaret says. 'I could hear you from the other side of the village. It's like you're begging to be picked up by these mercenary bastards! Pair of fucking idiots that you are.'

Lucas looks at Ruby and then back at Margaret, clearly wondering if he heard her right.

'What!' Margaret says. 'You think you teenagers have got a monopoly on cursing? I've forgotten more swear words than you've had hot dinners. My uncle was a sailor. He couldn't finish a sentence without slipping in at least a "bastard".'

Despite the circumstances Ruby can't stop a laugh slipping out and Lucas quickly joins her.

Margaret shakes her head.

'Kids,' she says in apparent disgust before sitting down at the kitchen table. 'Now stick the kettle on, lad, make me a brew, and tell me what the hell is going on in my village.' Her dog sniffs around Ruby's feet as Lucas fills the kettle up.

'Don't mind Boris,' Margaret says. 'The lazy little shite hates following me on the bike. He'll be asleep in a heartbeat.' As if on cue the dog moves under the table, settles down and is snoring gently in moments.

Ruby's not sure what to make of this woman. She's not at all what she expected. It was difficult enough to accept that Mad Danny was on her side but now it looks like she might have another unlikely ally. She's always avoided any contact with Margaret, mostly because her dad told her to keep well away from pretty much everyone in the village – but also because she seemed way too scary to approach. The woman's built like an ageing discus thrower, stocky and compact, and has an almost permanent scowl on her face. Even her dog looks irritated most of the time. Can she really trust her?

'Have you got a computer?' Ruby says.

'No, I rely entirely on Ceefax and a good encyclopaedia.'

'What?'

'Of course I've got a fucking computer. I'm not stuck in some weird time warp. There's no connection at the moment, though, if you want the internet.'

'Danny thinks they're jamming the signals,' Lucas says, as the kettle begins to boil.

Margaret seems to perk up a little.

'You've spoken to Danny?'

Lucas looks guilty as if he's given away something he shouldn't have. Ruby can't see a problem so jumps back in.

'Yes. He shot down that drone we saw yesterday when we were with you.'

'Great minds think alike,' Margaret mutters.

'What do you mean?' Ruby says.

'I was going to try and do that last night but the bloody thing flew off and never came back. I'm not surprised Danny's on your side though. People here may not be over fond of each other but we hate outsiders even more, especially those who think they can push us around. D'you know where Danny is now? I was just on my way to talk to him.'

'No idea,' Ruby says, curious that the woman and Danny have a connection of some kind. She'd always thought he was a real loner but it seems he's actually everyone's friend. 'We nearly got caught by one of the soldiers and Danny kept him occupied while we got away.'

'Was that what the shots were late last night?'

Ruby nods.

'Don't think I haven't noticed that you still haven't told me what's going on,' Margaret says. 'Now either shit or get off the pot. What is it that these men are looking for? And don't tell me it's an escaped prisoner. I wasn't born yesterday.'

'It's not a "what",' Lucas says. Ruby shakes her head, she's still not sure she trusts this strange, sweary woman, but he ignores her and presses on. 'It's a "who".'

Margaret looks from Lucas to Ruby and back again. It's like having one of those teachers who won't stop asking you a question until she gets the answer she wants. Ruby gives in.

'I think it's me. I think they're after me,' she says.

'Why?' The old woman's brow scrunches up, adding to her many wrinkles. She looks a bit like a bulldog, Ruby thinks. Acts like one as well.

'Hurry up,' Margaret says. 'I haven't got all day.'

Ruby wonders exactly what pressing engagement the impatient old bat might have but lets it go.

'I don't know,' she says, truthfully. She pulls out the memory stick from her pocket. 'But I think the answer might be on here. My dad left it for me to find.'

'Where is your dad?'

Ruby takes a deep breath. She decides to take a chance on Margaret. It's not like she's spoiled for choice.

'I don't know. I don't even know if he's still alive. One of them shot him yesterday.'

'I saw them carrying two people out of your house on stretchers. One of them was alive, I think. I hope it was your dad.'

Ruby nods. She can feel the tears starting to form.

'So do I,' she whispers.

'I won't ask who the other one was. Or what happened to him. Yet.' Margaret stands up.

'Where are you going?' Ruby asks.

'I thought you wanted to use my computer,' Margaret says. 'Let's find out what's on that stick thing.'

Ruby's starting to realise how wrong she's been about these people. First Lucas helps her, then Danny and now Margaret.

'Why are you doing this? I thought you all hated me cos I haven't lived here for like a century,' she says.

Margaret looks puzzled, as if she's been asked the most obvious question ever.

'We're Northumbrians, pet. No one can just turn up here and take what they want. We've been fighting off invaders since the dawn of time. It's in our blood. Why do you think there are so many castles in these parts?'

She taps the sleeping dog with her toe.

'Come on, Boris, we're going home.'

Margaret glares at Lucas.

'Might actually get a cup of fucking tea there.'

37

Margaret cycles home on her own – unless you count Boris, which she rarely does. The temptation to race ahead and leave him behind is strong, he'd never find his way home, but she resists. For a change he's serving a purpose.

It's like the opposite of safety in numbers. If these men – and she's pretty sure they're all men – are patrolling the village they're more likely to spot a group of people than an individual that's doing their best to keep out of sight. Though the snow's not helping; it's easy to follow her trail in the white blanket. Hopefully it'll keep falling and cover up her cycle tracks quickly.

It's not such a problem for her anyway. Firstly, she doesn't give a shit if they stop her, and secondly she's got the dog for cover and her age as an excuse. It's amazing the things you can get away with when you're old. There's almost a free pass for being awkward, argumentative and not listening to anyone else. Like it's expected. And she's always been happy to take advantage of that – it makes up for the years of taking Nigel's crap and not speaking her mind, like the lady her parents, and her husband, had expected her to be. Bollocks to that for a game of soldiers.

Thankfully, things have changed these days. Young Ruby seems to have a bit of spunk about her. Margaret sniggers, knowing full well that that's not a word that's kept its previous meaning. Regardless, the girl shows promise. Though Christ knows why she's tagging along with a dunderhead like that Lucas lad. The boy's a liability. Canny legs though.

She hears the jeep before she sees it, the engine purring ever closer from behind her. She ignores it, continuing to pedal towards her house as if she hasn't a care in the world. Eventually it pulls past her and then stops a few yards in front, blocking her way. The same soldier who came to her house gets out, rifle in hand, and stands on the road waiting for her to get closer. He's now wearing a camouflage jacket over his black T-shirt, which is hardly surprising given the weather, though she notices the driver is still under-dressed. Obviously reckons he's a hard man.

She considers cycling straight past them to see what would happen but even she thinks that's probably a little too provocative so she stops. She glances at the driver who has remained in his seat and hasn't once turned around to look at her. He's enormous, so wide that his arm is outside the frame of the vehicle. Could well be the man she saw chasing the two kids the day before.

'Good morning,' she says.

The soldier makes a kind of clucking sound, smacking his lips in disapproval. It's oddly like something her judgemental mother would have done.

'You're not supposed to be out on the streets, Mrs Carr.'

Margaret's pretty sure she didn't tell him her name last time they spoke.

'Says whom?' she asks.

'I thought I'd explained. It's not safe.'

'I'm not scared. Boris needed some exercise and he can be ferocious if he thinks I'm under threat.'

She glances down. Boris is currently eating some other dog's shit in the snowy grass at the side of the pavement.

'Maybe so,' the soldier says. 'But he can't stop a bullet.'

'Are you threatening to shoot my poor dog? Or are you saying this escaped prisoner is armed?'

The soldier hesitates.

'That's only two options but by all means take your time. It's not like I'm freezing my bits off or anything.'

'It's possible he's armed,' he says.

'Anything's possible. How do you know my name?'

The change of direction throws the soldier. He glances at the jeep as if seeking help but there's no reaction from his colleague.

'We've been briefed on the more important people in Coldburn.'

She smiles, can't help herself. It's true, obviously, but it's nice to have it acknowledged by officials. Not that she thinks this man and whoever he works for are necessarily official.

'I think you should return the favour then. It's only polite. What's your name?'

'Silver,' he says.

'Is that a Christian name or a surname?'

'Just Silver.'

'Like Madonna, eh?'

The soldier yawns.

'Am I keeping you up?' she says. 'Don't mind me if you want to go and lie down.'

'Have you seen anyone while you've been exercising the dog?'

'Anyone who looks like an escaped prisoner, you mean? Short, slim, long brown hair?'

He nods. Idiot. That wasn't the description he gave her yesterday. If you're going to lie at least be consistent.

'Have you still not found him? Her? Or maybe it's a them? I understand that's a possibility these days.'

The soldier smirks. She imagines he's not particularly in favour of non-binary options.

'Anyone at all.'

She pretends to think.

'Strangely, no – it's as if people have been told to stay indoors.'

'Maybe you should join them.'

'That's where I'd already be if you hadn't stopped for a chat.'

He steps to one side.

'I won't keep you any longer.' He pauses. 'Stay safe, Mrs Carr.'

'Thank you, Silver. And you. And try and get some sleep. You look worn out.'

She gets back on her bike and moves off, Boris reluctantly

trotting slowly behind her. She's a yard away when she decides to throw down another gauntlet, putting her brakes on and turning back.

'I don't suppose you've got any ID on you, Silver?'

The soldier ignores her and gets back into the jeep. As they pull away the driver gives her a look which is colder than the snow around her ankles.

38

Lucas is the next to leave the house. His clothes are filthy but at least they've dried out on the radiator. Ruby watches him from the kitchen window as he heads off into the woods, deliberately taking a different route to Margaret to make sure no one who might be watching connects the pair of them. And to avoid leaving a trail that can easily be seen on the streets. The snow is not on their side. She checks her watch. They agreed to leave at ten-minute intervals but she's going to break that agreement. She never really had any intention of sticking to it.

Before she goes to Margaret's house she wants to have one more look inside her own. She knew Lucas would insist on going with her if she said anything – he clearly has some kind of hero complex, why else would he have dragged himself out into the freezing cold in the middle of the night to try and get help? Maybe she should leave him out of all this? Before he got himself killed.

More than anything else, though, she needs some time alone to clear her thoughts. If she leaves quickly it won't be obvious that she took a detour on the way, it's close enough to Margaret's that she doubts the woman will notice the delay. She can't just sit on her hands and hope that Danny finds out where her dad is being held. She needs to actually do something.

Ruby also heads out of the back door but she locks it behind her, keeping the key, just in case they need to use the place again. The back alley is deserted as the whole village still seems to be and, aside from Lucas's footprints in the yard, the snow is pristine – no one else is out and about in this – so she makes quick progress towards her house. The only moment of danger being the quick dash across the road between alleys where they were nearly captured by that soldier last night. She wonders what happened after they'd run off and hopes that Danny is OK.

She's only a couple of minutes away from her house when she turns a corner into an alleyway and walks straight into the man. It's so unexpected that she bounces off him and lands on her arse. She scrambles up, preparing to run for her life, when she catches a whiff of alcohol and sour body odour, a combination that she's experienced quite recently. In Baldwin's piss-house.

'You should watch where you're going,' Baldwin says. 'Nearly knocked me off my feet.'

Given the size of him that seems highly unlikely. She has to shield her eyes to look at him as the winter sun reflecting off his shiny head combines with the glare from the snow. She's always thought it funny that Baldwin was actually bald – Mrs Scott, her English teacher had told her that having a name that was particularly suited to you was called an aptronym. When she told her dad that he said that she'd been called Ruby because she was so obviously a gem. Thinking of her dad makes her want to cry again so she tries to move on swiftly before the tears come and embarrass her in front of the mechanic.

'I'm sorry,' she says. 'I wasn't expecting anyone else to be around.' She goes to step around him but he's too wide.

'Why not?' he says. 'Lovely crisp day like today. Perfect for a stroll. Especially the morning after the night before, eh?' He laughs, tapping his nose as if she should know what he's talking about.

'Did you not hear the warning?' she asks.

'What warning?'

'About the escaped prisoner. There's a curfew. The army asked everyone to stay indoors.'

'The army? News to me,' he says. 'I've been having a marathon poker session with old Bob Lumley. A bottle of single malt and a nice bit of AC/DC on the record player, can't beat a bit of vinyl. I doubt I'd have noticed if they'd detonated an unexploded bomb in his back garden. Didn't even know it had been snowing till I came out the front door just now.'

He stops to think a moment.

'Wait just a second. If there's a curfew what are you doing out and about?'

He's got her there. She thinks about conjuring up some medical emergency or something but he laughs.

'Oh, I get it, the walk of shame. Don't worry, love, I was young once, sneaking out at night to see my girlfriend. Your secret's safe with me, pet.' He taps his nose again. 'I saw you and young Lucas together yesterday. Or was it the day before? It's all a bit hazy, truth be told. He's a keeper. No offence, love, but you're punching above your weight there.'

Ruby tries to imagine a context in which that wouldn't be offensive but can't. Lucas was lucky to have her. Or would be, if they were a thing. Which they aren't.

'We're not together,' she says.

Baldwin gives her an exaggerated wink. 'Whatever you say, love.'

'He's just a friend.'

'Friends with benefits, eh! Like me and Peggy from the mobile library.' He taps his nose again. 'Mum's the word.'

Ruby thinks she might gag imagining Baldwin and Peggy snogging in the back of the library van, knowing immediately that if this shit ever ends she's never going to set foot in there again. She'd rather get the bus to Rothbury.

'Be careful who else you tell, though, if you want to keep it a bit quiet, there's some right gossips around here. That Margaret Carr for one. Wouldn't trust her as far as I could throw her.' He laughs. 'Which wouldn't be very far with the size of her.'

Given that his large belly is wobbling over the top of his belt the man's got a nerve but Ruby's way past caring about his obvious sexism.

'Why not?' she asks. Whether you could trust Margaret was something she was very interested in. Her dad had drummed it into her that you couldn't trust anyone, including the man in front of her, and she was finding it a hard rule to ignore. Even Lucas still had a bit of work to do to fully gain her confidence.

'She's a snitch,' Baldwin said. 'When her and her Neighbourhood Watch cronies were operating she regularly informed the authorities about stuff that wasn't her business. She reported me to Environmental Health once for burning the wrong things. Just a few old tyres. I reckon it's cos her old man was in the army, a stickler for following orders and that. I bet she'll be the first one to dob people in for breaking this curfew thing. I'd keep well away from the scheming cow if I were you.'

Ruby goes around the back way into her house again. After the conversation with Baldwin she doesn't want Margaret to see her – or Lucas for that matter.

The kitchen remains untouched from their last visit. She can even see the empty packet of veggie sausages on the worktop by the oven. But she's not there to tidy up.

She moves past the cooker and there it is. The getaway bag her dad had packed, still tucked on the stool under the counter where she'd moved it. In their haste to search his room the soldiers must have missed it, as she'd hoped. She'd forgotten about it when she and Lucas had come back the first time but now realises how important it could be. If her dad had prepared it in advance, and she was certain he had, then there just might be something in there that he couldn't bear to leave behind. Something from a past she knows nothing about. She unzips the bag and fumbles around, nothing obvious comes to hand so she removes the clothes from the top, a jumper, a couple of shirts and two pairs of trousers. She digs deeper but there's only some underwear and socks and a pair of old trainers. Aside from that it's empty. Then she notices the zip. There's an inside pocket.

All it contains are their passports. No big surprise really. It's what you'd expect to find packed if someone was planning to go on the run. Only a couple of problems. Firstly, she's never had a passport. She used to complain that all her friends were heading off to France and Italy and other sunny destinations while they never went anywhere but her dad claimed he was afraid of flying. Secondly, she's never had any passport photos taken. She'd definitely have remembered that.

They're brand new, dark blue and in pristine condition. She remembers some fuss about this around the time the nation lost its collective mind and voted for Brexit. Her and her pals had been furious they weren't allowed to vote and even madder when people started to bang on about changing the colour of the passports, as if anyone gave a shit about that.

She flips the first passport open. There's her dad's smiling face. And there, to the right of the photo is a name: Rick Nelson. Who the hell is Rick Nelson? She picks up the other passport and opens it, strangely excited to see what's inside the cover. Her photo is an old one, from at least a couple of years ago. She's pretty sure it's one of the ones she had taken for her bus pass. By contrast the name to the right is brand new: Karen Nelson. Is that her real name? Ruby mulls it over, trying it on for size to see if it fits. It doesn't. Karen is no gem.

After remembering to leave some food for Pluto, Ruby reluctantly drags herself along the back path towards Margaret's house, keeping away from the main street. She suddenly feels very alone in the world. Her dad has not only been shot but also taken away by someone. It seems like he's got some kind of secret past – why else would he have taken shooting lessons from Danny? She isn't even sure what his real name is. Or hers! It's something she would have loved to talk to her best friend Liv about but she is still on holiday with her family as far as she knows. And anyway, she lives miles away and with all the phones out of action she has no way of contacting her. She certainly wasn't going to try and walk there on the off chance that Liv was back – especially now she knows they are patrolling the outskirts on quad bikes.

How the hell had people done anything before the internet and mobile phones existed? The only people she could really talk to about this were Lucas and Margaret. And how much does she know about either of them? She's particularly reluctant to confide in Margaret after what old man Baldwin said about her. But then she doesn't trust him either so who knows what the truth about any of this is?

She'll talk to Lucas first, see what he thinks. He hasn't let her down so far and knows Baldwin better than she does – she could see whether he takes the man's gossip seriously. Would Margaret really dob them in? She had seemed keen to help them this morning. But maybe if she thought Ruby's dad wasn't what he seemed she'd be more suspicious. But then if she tells Lucas about the passports he'll probably start banging on about witness protection again and she'll end up punching him. She really doesn't have a clue who to trust, including her dad. If he isn't Alex Winter then who is she? Is she actually Karen Nelson? Or is that another made-up name?

All these questions are thrashing around in her mind as she walks slowly towards Margaret's back door. She's never been inside before. Margaret's scrotty little dog is sitting in the windowsill barking his head off as she approaches the house and she worries that he'll go for her if she just walks in so she holds back. As she hesitates the back door flies open.

'I thought Lucas was coming next,' Margaret says, looking over Ruby's shoulder as if she thinks he'll be wandering down the path behind her.

'He was,' Ruby says. 'He left at least twenty minutes ago.'

'Then where the hell has he got to?' Margaret says. 'Because he sure as shit hasn't turned up here.'

39

The manor house used to be the home of some favoured servant of the crown, harking all the way back to the days of William the Conqueror.

Danny's never been one for forelock-tugging but when he was a bairn he remembers being terrified of the lord of the manor, who owned everything in the village and ran the place with an iron rod. Thankfully those days were long gone. Apart from a brief interlude the house has been empty for years – ever since the estate had to sell up everything to pay for death duties when the last proper lord died and his feckless son found himself on the bones of his arse.

The only other owner in that period was some young whizz-kid entrepreneur who found that you could just as easily lose a fortune as gain one. Like everyone else Danny had heard rumours of wild parties in the short space of time the upstart lived there – orgies, according to some of the villagers who loved that sort of gossip. He'd put good money on Margaret being the one to have started the rumours – she loves throwing a curve ball in – but Danny has never really believed them. It's too cold for that sort of thing up here.

Word has it that the place has been sold again recently – no doubt to yet another outsider wanting to lord it over the villagers – but there'd been no sign of anyone moving in. Danny loved living in the middle of nowhere but maybe the remoteness was giving the buyers second thoughts. However, if the soldiers wanted a base big enough to house them and their prisoner it was just about the only other option after the farm, which clearly hadn't been touched in recent days.

Danny had managed to grab a couple of hours' kip on some hay bales in the empty barn at the farm, reluctant to return home as he was pretty damn sure they'd be keeping a watch on the place after he shot down that drone. It was surprisingly comfortable, though his back is, as usual, a little stiff this morning. What with that and his gammy leg it has taken him longer than he would have liked to reach the edge of the estate.

He knows this place like the back of his hand as it's always been a good spot to find rabbits or even the odd deer. There is a fence around the perimeter but it's got so many holes in it after the last owner neglected his duties that it's not a problem to gain access. He's reluctant to get too close though – if the soldiers have moved in they might well have tightened up security, with patrols or even cameras.

Danny settles down with a pair of binoculars about fifty yards from the fence at the rear of the property to recce the place. There are no obvious signs of life and he's just about to start moving around the area to get a better view of the front when Scout growls and there's a crack behind him. He freezes, waiting for a shot, or at the very least a verbal warning, but there's nothing. He slowly turns around, his hands in the air, not wanting to provoke any kind of attack. Standing ten yards behind him is Lucas, looking like he's been in a mud fight.

'What the fuck d'you think you're doing sneaking up on an armed man like that? You're lucky I didn't blow your brains out.' He's actually furious with himself for letting it happen. How could some hapless teenage kid sneak up on him? He's definitely losing it. He really should have heard something. As well as all his other ailments, maybe he's even going a little deaf? Getting old is a fucking nightmare. But he's not the only one. In the past Scout would have heard Lucas from a mile off. There wasn't much point keeping a dog and listening out yourself.

'I'm sorry,' Lucas says, holding his hands up in apology. 'I was heading home to change my manky clothes and saw you heading off in the distance. Thought it would be more fun than going to Margaret's house so I followed you. Which was pretty easy, what with footprints and paw prints in the snow.'

'Margaret's house?' Danny asks. 'Why would you be going there?'

'She found Ruby and me hiding in one of the holiday homes this morning, offered to let us use her computer to find out what's on that memory stick.'

'Did she now?' Danny smiles. That woman can't keep her

nose out of anything, he thinks, almost admiringly. At least it means that young Ruby is safely out of harm's way for the time being.

He pats the ground beside him.

'Get over here, lad, and don't trample around like a baby elephant like you were just now.'

Lucas looks at him as if he knows he's taking the piss but he doesn't call him out on it; instead he cautiously makes his way over to Danny's side and settles down next to him.

'What happened with you and that soldier who nearly caught us?' the boy asks.

'Don't worry about him,' Danny says. 'He's out of the picture.'

He sees the kid go a little pale but has no intention of going into any more detail and turns his focus back onto the house. Lucas is very quiet for several minutes and when he speaks it's obvious he's decided to let it go.

'Is this where you think they're based?' he asks, looking over towards the house. 'The people who have Ruby's dad.'

'Good a place as any,' Danny says. 'They'd want somewhere that was large enough to accommodate them and close enough for a rapid response to any problems. And I've already checked Milburn Farm. Though there's no sign of them here so far. Before you blundered in I was just about to move around the outside, get a better view of the front of the building.'

'Don't let me stop you.'

'I won't. Just making sure the coast is clear.'

'Can I come with you?'

'D'you think you can be quiet? And I mean *quiet*.'

'Course.'

'No talking unless I ask you something. Follow me as precisely as you can but even then watch where you're walking – keep your eye out for hunting traps in particular. The last bloke who owned this place was too cheap to get proper security so he just threw a lot of traps all over the place, hidden in the undergrowth. They'll be hard to spot in the snow and I don't want you to lose a leg – it'll slow me down – so tread very carefully. Don't get too close and if I put my hand up, stop immediately. Got it?'

Lucas nods. Danny gets to his feet, tells Scout to stay put, and moves off slowly, not bothering to check if the boy is behind him. The lad might like to piss about a bit too much but ultimately he's got a good head on his shoulders and can follow instructions. He'll be fine. As they edge around the perimeter, keeping a good distance away from the fence, the front of the house gradually comes into view. Danny stops. Parked outside the house is an ambulance, a green jeep and a quad bike. He's just about to say something to Lucas when two soldiers come into view a few feet inside the fence and stop. He raises his hand and he and Lucas freeze. Luckily they're mostly hidden by the trees and both of them are in dark clothes which would make them difficult to spot from that distance.

One of the soldiers leans his rifle against an old sundial that's covered in ivy, pulls out a packet of cigarettes and offers his partner one. The pair light up, completely oblivious to anything outside the fence. No way are these the real thing,

Danny thinks, watching the second man discard his weapon too before taking a cigarette. Sure enough there are some wasters in the regular army but these guys are consistently careless. If he had to guess he'd say they were mercenary wannabes who either got rejected in the recruiting process or got thrown out for being shit. Or being batshit crazy, which would be his least favourite option. Crazy people were more dangerous and harder to predict. He motions to Lucas to get down and stay down while he moves nearer to them.

He edges through the trees, keeping well out of the soldiers' line of sight, to try and get close enough to see if he can gather some intelligence. Information is power, as a girlfriend of his used to say.

It's easier than it should be as the two men have now turned their backs on the fence, paying no attention whatsoever to what's behind them. He quickly gets close enough to hear them talking.

'I'm done with this shit, White,' the nearest guy says in a broad Scottish accent. 'Gold is clueless, we should just go in guns blazing, grab the girl and get the hell out of here.'

'It's a clusterfuck, Red, that's for sure. But I'm not sure it's Gold's fault. Green screwed up.'

'Bollocks, man, we're at least four men short of what we need. There's only one guy on each barricade and no one's had more than a couple of hours' sleep.'

'Aye, but if Green hadn't bollocksed it up we'd have been in and out of here in a heartbeat, like we planned,' the other soldier says. He's the taller of the two. And a local lad too, by the sounds of it.

Danny makes a mental note of the coloured names. Using false names was further confirmation that these guys weren't on the straight and narrow. They didn't want to be traceable when this was over.

'He won't do that again,' Red says.

'Went to pieces, I heard.'

They both laugh.

'Stupid git. Running before he could walk,' White adds.

'Aye, but who sent Green in to start with? Green by name and green by nature, that lad, barely out of nappies.'

'He'll never get out of them now, will he?' the other soldier laughs. Clearly the need to joke in the face of horrors is one thing that stays the same, regular army or not.

'Gold's fault again.'

'You'd do a better job then, would you?'

'Too right. Just because the prick was an officer for ten minutes doesn't make him any better than us. I mean, why haven't we cut their power off yet?'

'You don't know this area very well, do you?'

'No, thank fuck, it's like something from the Middle Ages.'

'Aye, that's the point. Quite a few of the houses have their own generators cos the links to the national grid are reliant on overhead lines which are pretty shaky given the weather up here. So cutting the power off is kinda redundant. Anyway, people are more likely to stay indoors if they've still got all their heating. If you take that away they might start making a fuss – coming outside to chop trees down and that. Best to save it as a last resort.'

'OK, smartarse, but why wait until today to carry out a house-to-house search to find the girl?'

'It's all supposed to be on the down-low, isn't it? Gold doesn't want to draw too much attention to what's happening. Discretion is the watchword, he said. Leave No Trace and that.'

'Bollocks to that. We've already lost Green and now Brown has gone missing. There's only seven of us left, including Gold, and he may as well be a non-com for all the use he is.'

'Brown's probably done a runner,' the tall one says. 'No great loss. His heart wasn't in it and he was never the sharpest tool in the box.'

'Tool's the right word, mind.' Red laughs and throws his cigarette to the ground, making no attempt to stub it out. Good job it's been snowing, Danny thinks, otherwise these twats would have the whole village up in flames.

The tall guy is a little more careful, taking a last drag before dropping the dog-end by his feet and stamping it out as the two men move off again. Danny waits for a moment before turning, startled to see Lucas standing right behind him.

'Was Brown the guy you were shooting at?' he asks quietly.

'How did you hear that from over there?'

'Young ears,' Lucas says. 'We're not all deaf.'

The kid waits for a moment and Danny hopes he's going to let it go but this time he doesn't.

'Well? Was he?'

'How would I know? We didn't exchange names.'

Lucas clearly knows he's avoiding the question.

'What happened to him?'

Danny is about to tell him but has a quick flashback of the soldier's head disappearing into the sinkhole for the final time. He's not sure the kid is ready for the reality of the situation they're in. Losing your innocence is a bastard because you can never get it back again. He doesn't like lying to the lad though.

'I let him go,' he says.

40

Lucas has been captured by the soldiers. Ruby's sure of it. It's been well over an hour since he left that holiday home and there's been no sign of him. Maybe the reckless sod tried to get out of the village again and got caught this time. She had been desperate to see what was on the memory stick but that's on the back burner for now. She's too worried about him. First her dad, now her . . . friend.

How could he have been so careless? Or maybe he wasn't. Maybe, like her, he just bumped into Baldwin and got distracted? But that makes no sense as he was ahead of her and the man would have said something if he'd seen Lucas – particularly as the old alky seemed to think they had a thing going on. As if. She likes him, but only as a mate. And not the kind of mate they talk about in biology. Maybe she should go back out and see if she can find him?

'I'm sure he'll be here soon,' Margaret says, sensing her concern. 'Head in the clouds, that lad, he's probably just daydreaming and gone back to his own house by mistake. His mother is just the same, all over the place.'

'You shouldn't talk about her like that,' Ruby snaps. 'She's ill.'

'Is she? What's wrong with her? I thought I hadn't seen her about for a while.'

Ruby regrets saying anything. She's pretty sure that Lucas wouldn't want anyone knowing his family's business. Especially someone like Margaret. If Baldwin's right it will be all over the village in no time.

'I don't know, do I, I'm not her doctor.'

'No need to be rude, missy, I was only asking.'

Ruby ignores her. She's not going to take any shit from someone like Margaret. Just because you're old doesn't mean you can say what you like.

'I should go and look for him,' she says.

'I don't think that's a good idea. You were lucky to avoid that jeep as it was.'

Ruby knows she's right. Margaret had told her about being stopped by those two men. It was surely only a matter of time before her luck ran out and they stopped her as well. And she still didn't have the faintest idea what they wanted her for. Maybe it was time to look at the memory stick after all. Lucas was a big boy. He could take care of himself.

'You're probably right,' Ruby says, taking the memory stick out of her pocket. 'Where's your computer?'

It takes ages for the computer to warm up. It's like something from the steam age, whizzing and whirring as Ruby waits impatiently for the desktop options to appear. It's so old that she's amazed it's even got a slot for a memory stick.

Unusually, Margaret is being discreet, leaving her to it while she makes yet another cup of tea downstairs, so while she's waiting Ruby has a little nose around the small study that's at the back of the house. The first thing she notices is that there are no family pictures on the desk or any of the shelves. She's seen the photo of Margaret's late husband in the hallway downstairs but that was taken years ago, when he was a young soldier, there's nothing at all in here. She wonders if they had any children – the woman's never mentioned them so it's unlikely and she doesn't seem particularly maternal, quite the opposite really. Though what would Ruby know, she never even knew her own mum. The only one she's spent any time with is Liv's mum, who's young, fun and lovely, nothing like Margaret at all.

The second thing she notices is the binoculars on one of the shelves. She's pretty certain the woman's not a bird-watcher, just a nosy cow. She must use them to spy on people. People like her. She picks them up and looks out of the window, focusing on her house. You can even read the door number on the front. Ruby wonders how many times Margaret watched her as she snuck around the village with Liv. All that time they thought they were going unnoticed when there were eyes on them. She's going to need to be a bit more aware of that in the future. If there is a future.

She glances at the computer and realises that it's fully up and running now. It's a simple Windows system so she clicks on File and then the USB drive. There's only one folder on there. It's called 'Your Story'. When it opens she sees there is just one document in it. A letter from her dad.

Dearest Ruby

If you're reading this you're either 16 (Happy Birthday!) and old enough to know the truth about how we ended up here, or something has happened to me. I really hope it's the former but if it's the latter I pray that you have found a place of safety. Don't trust anyone.

Please believe me that everything I've done has been to protect you. I'm sure I've made many mistakes along the way but please understand that whatever I've done has come from a good place. I've loved you with all of my heart from the first time I set eyes on you and keeping you safe has always been my number one priority.

I'm sorry that I haven't prepared you for any of this but had always intended to give you this on your birthday, when you would hopefully be mature enough to cope and could make your own decisions about how to move on. If events have conspired to stop me doing that at least you've found this letter. Once you've read it I hope you'll understand why I've kept our real story – and your mother's – from you.

I've laid this out in chronological order so that you may get a clearer understanding of how our lives became so complicated, so quickly. I hope that you have the time and patience to read it in that sequence as it may help you understand why I did what I did at every point.

I'm certain that whatever happens – and whatever you decide to do once you read this – you will prosper. You're the image of your mother and have the same warmth, bravery, spirit and optimism that she had. She wanted you to have a better life than she did and would be incredibly proud of the woman you've become, as am I.

Take great care who you share this with. Stay safe. And again: Trust no one.

Your ever-loving father

Alex

Ruby can feel the tears pouring down her face. This sounds so final. She will not believe that her father is dead. Even though she has always wanted to know more about her mother there is a part of her that doesn't want to read on as she knows that this will change everything she thought she knew about her dad and herself. And probably who she will become. She takes a deep breath and presses on.

The first surprise is that her mum's real name was Emma. She had always been told it was Sylvie, which is weird but not exactly disturbing. Hopefully the reason for that will become clear later. The second is that she was in foster care and ran away from home. Her dad has told her none of this before. He always said that he didn't know much about her background – that her mum didn't like to talk about it. That's about it, apart from her meeting a mysterious businessman called Simon in London. Ruby races through the first few pages of the letter, a little bemused, to be honest, as she'd expected something a bit more dramatic.

She wonders if her mum, who would only have been about seventeen at the time – not much older than she is now – had an affair with the businessman. Maybe Alex is hinting at that to justify something bad that he did before she was born? She hopes to God he didn't kill the man in some kind of jealous rage. She speeds onto the next section.

That's the real shocker.

41

Months went by and still no news from Emma. I sent her a ton of emails but didn't get a single reply and after a while they began to bounce back with the same response: 'Undeliverable. Your message did not reach some or all of the intended recipients.'

I had just about given up when out of the blue I got an email from her flatmate, Rosie, asking me to contact her. It was the first time I even knew Emma was in London, almost a year after she had run away from home.

Rosie was worried about your mum and had found my email address on the computer they shared in the flat. I rang her immediately but she wouldn't talk about it over the phone. Said she was scared 'people' might be listening. So the next day I was off to London on the train.

The flat was a poky, semi-derelict hovel, almost a squat really. I could see why Emma hadn't wanted me to see her there and hoped she wouldn't be too unhappy that I'd just turned up on the doorstep. I was more than a little disappointed when Rosie opened the door. Worse still, the first thing she told me was that Emma had moved out.

Rosie was a quiet Irish girl, a little anxious, though that could have been the circumstances. Before she would let me in she checked my driving licence. Even then she appeared to look around outside to make sure I wasn't followed. At the time I thought she was being way too paranoid but I was wrong.

To cut a long story short, Rosie told me what I mentioned earlier: that Emma had been really struggling to make ends meet with only a few waitressing jobs to keep her head above water when she met Simon, the rich businessman that I've already told you about.

After a few dates Emma announced that she was moving in with him. Rosie claimed she tried to dissuade her, said it was too soon, but Emma was adamant: it was her life and she knew what she was doing. As I said, the flat was tiny and the pair of them must have been living right on top of each other, so a little bit of me wondered if Rosie was really as disappointed as she claimed. She soon put me right.

Emma hadn't been telling her the whole story. She kept a diary and the day before she moved out, Rosie, worried about what your mum was letting herself in for, stole a look at it. She couldn't believe what she read. Sadly, it took her several months to summon up the courage to contact me.

You might want to be sitting down at this point. As Emma suggested in her final email to me, this man, Simon, had made her an offer she couldn't refuse.

Twenty thousand pounds to have his baby.

What the fuck! Ruby rereads that bit of the letter in case she's misunderstood. She hasn't. She stares at the screen, hoping the words might change. Some random paid her mum to have a baby? Is that baby her? Or does she have a half-sister or brother she knows nothing about? She's always wanted a sister. She glances at the bottom of the page. There are only half a dozen pages left to read – they'd better answer all of those questions or she'll go off it. She's about to press on when she hears a strange noise from outside, a metallic clang followed by a creak. She gets up from the chair to look out of the window and sees someone creeping into Margaret's back garden. At first she hopes it might be Lucas but it's clearly someone bigger and older than him.

Ruby looks back at the screen, reluctant to stop reading but Margaret should be warned. She can be down and back in a heartbeat. Ruby dashes down the stairs, charging straight into Margaret who is just coming out of the kitchen with a mug in her hand. The mug goes flying across the hallway into the wall, sending hot liquid everywhere.

'What in holy hell?' Margaret cries. 'Where's the fire?'

'There's a man in your back garden,' Ruby says, grabbing Margaret's arm and steering her into the kitchen.

She can see the man more clearly now as he edges carefully along the fence at the side of the garden towards the back door. She's seen him before. He's the older guy who was arguing with the guard at the roadblock she nearly ran into the day before.

'There, look,' she says, pointing out of the window. But Margaret has already seen him and is heading towards the door.

'What are you doing?' Ruby says. 'You're not going to let him in, are you? He might be dangerous.'

Margaret turns back to her, looking even fiercer than she normally does.

'That's no man,' she says. 'It's Nigel.'

42

Ruby stares at the woman, who, now she thinks about it, does look like she's seen a ghost.

'I thought he was dead,' she says.

'He is to me.'

Margaret throws open the door and marches out into the garden leaving a trail of footprints on the snow behind her.

'What the fuck are you doing here?' she shouts.

Ruby watches as Nigel stops in his tracks, looking around as if wondering what the neighbours will think.

'Language!' he says.

'Fuck off,' Margaret replies. 'Answer the question.'

'I was worried about you,' he says.

'Bit late for that.'

He looks hurt. 'That's unfair. I always worry about you.'

'Didn't stop you running off to that organist tart from the church though, did it?'

Nigel looks down at his shoes, which Ruby notices are what's wrong with this picture. Nobody in their right mind would wear smart leather shoes to walk in this weather.

He's also got a suit and tie on. Even if she hadn't seen the picture in the hallway she would have guessed he had once been a soldier but he's one that wouldn't pass closer inspection. His clothes look like he's been sleeping in them. When he looks up again he sees her standing in the doorway.

'Who's your friend?' he asks.

Margaret turns around and glances at Ruby.

'Aren't you going to introduce me?' he adds.

'No. The poor girl's got enough problems. Now, either tell me why you're here or turn around and take your sorry backside back to that slapper.'

He moves towards Margaret who steps back.

'Don't come any further,' she says.

Nigel stops. He smiles but it doesn't reach his eyes.

'Don't be like that. I tried to come and see you yesterday but got stopped by some TA type wielding a gun. He wouldn't let me into the village. There was something off about him so I decided to try again today. But this time I walked here through the woods on one of the footpaths. They can't stop me coming to my own home.'

'This is not your home any more. You threw away the privilege to call it that.'

Nigel blinks but presses on. He's clearly not easily put off his stride. Or he doesn't care what Margaret says. Ruby reckons it's the latter.

'If they were doing their job properly and keeping the place locked down they'd have patrols out but obviously they're not because here I am.'

He's clearly misjudged his wife.

'That's more of a "how" than a "why",' she says. 'Try again, and make it a better explanation or turn around and piss off. Up to you.'

Margaret's giving the poor guy such a hard time that Ruby's almost starting to feel sorry for him. Almost.

'Can we talk inside?' he asks, glancing at Ruby. 'In private.'

'No,' Margaret says, not giving an inch. 'You can say what you've got to say in front of the girl.'

'We shouldn't wash our dirty linen in public, Margaret.'

Ruby can see Margaret's shoulders tensing up. She's ready to kick off.

'I haven't got any dirty linen, Nigel,' she hisses. 'If anyone's got any nasty skidmarks to hide it's you. You never did wipe that well. She's thrown you out, hasn't she?'

He looks sheepish but doesn't say anything.

'Hasn't she?' Margaret presses. This time he nods and gives her a weak smile.

'You've always been able to read me, Margaret.'

'I'm not reading anything, Nigel. It's just that you look like you've slept in a bush.'

'My car, actually,' he says, rubbing his arms for warmth. 'It was very cold. And I didn't really plan for snow. Any chance of a brew?'

Margaret's not big on sympathy. 'Has anyone seen you?'

'I don't think so. Why?'

'They'd have been a little surprised. I told everyone you were dead.'

Suddenly there's a noise above them and Margaret

grabs Nigel's arm and pulls him towards the door. Ruby backs inside the kitchen to give her room as she drags her bemused ex-husband into the house, slamming the door behind them.

'There's no need for that, Margaret,' he protests.

'There's every need.' She's already looking out of the window and glances back at Ruby.

'I think they've got themselves a new drone.'

43

Alex's body is spasming. He groans loudly, grimaces and grinds his teeth so hard that he can hear them crunching.

Red must hear his moans from the corridor as he comes into the room to check it out, though he doesn't exactly rush.

'Fuck's up with you?' he grumbles.

Alex rolls his head to face him, screwing up his features.

'My guts are killing me. Really need the bog.'

'Tough titty. I'm not your fuckin' babysitter.'

'It's you who'll have to' – he stops to moan again – 'clean the shit up.'

Red stares at him, trying to work out if he's faking it. Alex groans again, arching his body to its limit, pushing hard against the bonds that are still keeping him tied down to the bed.

'Fuck's sake,' the soldier says, turning around and sticking his head out of the door.

'Boss!' he shouts before coming back to the bedside. 'You'd better not be pissing me about.'

Gold strides through the door. 'What is it?'

'Says he needs the bog again. Looks legit.'

Alex makes a straining sound, another spasm contorting his body. Gold looks concerned.

'OK, give me your rifle and untie him. You can take him. I've seen enough of his hairy arse for a lifetime.'

Unusually Red does as he's asked without complaint, loosening Alex's leg bonds first before moving to his upper body and arms. All the time Gold keeps the rifle pointed at the bed. There's no need for him to bother, Alex has no intention of trying to escape. Yet.

Once he's loose he slowly moves his legs off the bed and struggles to his feet, bending double as he stands and clutching his stomach with both hands.

'Quick,' he says.

Red has taken his rifle back and pokes him in the back with it.

'Get going. I'm right behind you. One wrong move and I'll put a bullet in your spine.'

Gold actually leads the way out of the room but veers off in the opposite direction as Alex staggers towards the toilet. He barges through the door and flings the lid down, frantically dropping his trousers before hurling himself onto the seat.

Red laughs, keeping the door open with his foot.

'Better out than in,' he says.

Alex strains desperately and lowers his head down towards his knees. He stays like that before suddenly jerking back up, howling with frustration and lowering his head again.

'Jesus,' Red says, 'you really have got it bad. You ate the same field rations as us. You got an allergy to dehydrated chicken or something?'

Alex says nothing, just continues to groan. He can see Red's feet edging closer. He slumps ever further and stops groaning. Then waits. And waits.

'You still awake?'

Red nudges his shoulder with the end of his rifle.

Still nothing from Alex.

The soldier moves closer and Alex flies off the seat, the back of his head smacking into the underside of the other man's jaw. Red's head jerks back and crashes into the door frame as Alex moves towards him, grabbing at the rifle with his good arm. The Scot is stunned but hangs tough, clinging on as he shakes his head to try and clear it. It doesn't take him long. He snarls at Alex, a smile suddenly crossing his lips.

'I've been looking forward to fucking you up.'

He's much stronger than Alex and wrenches the rifle towards him until the pair of them are close enough to kiss. The kiss that comes is of the Glasgow variety as Red's head thuds into Alex's nose and he flies back towards the toilet. He's not letting go of the rifle though, despite the pain in his shoulder, and his momentum drags Red forward too, something the man clearly wasn't expecting as he stumbles into Alex, the weapon trapped between them. The sound of it going off is ear-shattering in the small cubicle. Alex collapses onto the toilet seat, blood flowing down his chest into his lap. Red's blood. The man himself slumps to the floor, the top of his head blown away.

Alex can feel himself starting to shake from shock but he grips the edge of the toilet to try and control it, knowing that Gold and anyone else in the building will be there in moments. He gathers himself, stands, pulls his trousers up and smashes out the bathroom window with the rifle butt, getting as much of the glass out as he can before climbing onto the toilet seat and throwing himself out of the window. Thankfully there's grass below and a thick covering of snow so the fall isn't too horrendous, though he lands on his wounded arm and yelps in pain. He leaps to his feet and sprints across the grass towards the fence, hoping that there's an easy way out somewhere. If not he'll shoot his way through. The nearer he gets to the fence the harder it gets as the snow is getting deeper. The good news is that he can see holes in the fence. Another few seconds and he'll be away and gone.

Suddenly his foot hits something hard, there's a loud snap and a searing pain in his leg that stops him in his tracks. He screams like he never has before and his momentum carries him to the ground but his leg stays where it is, his rifle flying out of his hands, well out of reach. The pain is so bad he almost blacks out but he bites down hard on his teeth to ride out the initial agony. He turns his head and claws away at the snow around his foot. He's caught in a small animal trap, the jaws of which have sliced deep into his calf on both sides of his right leg. He sees Gold run out of the front door of the house – which he now recognises as the abandoned manor house just outside the village – and far behind him he can see another soldier sprinting across the grounds. He can still get away if he can get the trap off. He sits up, ignoring the brutal pain, and grips the two sides of the trap, trying to pull them apart. But it's no use. His damaged shoulder means he just doesn't have the strength. It won't budge. And trying to move the jaws not only makes the pain worse but something else tears in his arm too. Despite a dizziness that threatens to overwhelm him he's making one last attempt to free himself when he feels the pistol against the side of his head. It's over. He's failed. His final thought before he passes out is that he will never have the chance to tell Ruby how sorry he is and she will probably hate him for the rest of her life.

Danny and Lucas are back on the edge of the village when they hear a gunshot. They stop and look back towards the house, which is no longer visible through the trees. A few moments later they hear a loud scream.

'Was that an animal? A fox maybe?' Lucas says, though he looks like he already knows the answer.

'No chance,' Danny says.

'Christ. Ruby's dad then, d'you think?'

Danny nods. 'Probably.'

'Should we go back?' the kid says.

'And do what? We've got one rifle between two of us. There are at least four armed men there, I reckon. No point getting ourselves killed. What's done is done. If we're going in we need to be prepared.' Danny turns back towards the village. 'You have to choose your battles, son.'

Danny can feel Lucas staring at his back, caught in two

minds. The kid's got a big heart but he's out of his depth here. Whoever got shot just now is shot, they can't put the bullet back in the rifle.

'You'll not make it back without me, son, all the paths are covered in snow now,' he shouts over his shoulder.

Danny carries on walking, knowing that the kid will see sense, and moments later he hears him hustling along to catch up.

'D'you think they'll have heard that shot and scream at Margaret's house?' Lucas asks when he catches up.

'No chance,' the older man says, 'too far away.'

'Don't tell Ruby then,' Lucas says. 'Hope is the only thing keeping her going.'

44

Margaret stares out of the window as the drone hovers above her garden, wondering if she should take a leaf out of Danny's book and shoot the damn thing out of the sky. She glances at Nigel who's also watching the drone, clearly astonished at what is happening in the village. The vain bastard probably thinks that it's all gone downhill since he left. They watch until it suddenly lurches off over the gardens towards the north end of the village.

'I think you'd better tell me what's been going on,' he says, as if he's somehow come to save them. She nearly tells him to boil his head but despite her reservations – and they're huge – it will feel good to talk it through with someone and she's a bit short of grown-up allies at the moment.

'I'll make some tea,' she says. 'And then I'll bring you up to speed. But you're not staying.'

'No coffee?' he asks, ignoring her last remark.

She shakes her head.

'Three tea bags then, don't forget,' he says. 'And leave it

to brew for at least ten minutes. No sugar.' Margaret remembers one of the many reasons she's been happier since he left her.

As she potters around, Nigel sits down at the kitchen table as if he still owns the place.

'I know who you are now. You're the Winter girl,' he says, pointing at Ruby. 'From just up the road. I'm Mr Carr. I expect you remember me from the parish council events on the village green. I used to be the chairman and MC.'

He does look familiar now she thinks about it but Ruby shakes her head just to piss him off.

''fraid not,' she says. 'Never heard of you.'

Behind his back Margaret smiles. She's beginning to like Ruby. The girl has the right attitude. She'll be all right if they can keep her out of harm's way.

'Well you were very young then,' Nigel says. 'Your dad would certainly know who I am. I had to speak to him about the state of your garden on several occasions. How is he?'

She hesitates. Suddenly all Ruby wants to do is tell someone what she's just read – and maybe if it was just Margaret here she might do that – but she's not explaining any of that to this prick.

'Not great,' Ruby says. 'One of those soldiers shot him yesterday.'

Nigel laughs nervously. 'That's not funny, young lady.'

'It wasn't meant to be.'

Nigel glances around at Margaret, clearly looking for some kind of support. 'I'm sure that's not the case,' he begins but Margaret cuts him off.

'It's true, I think,' she says. 'I saw a military-style ambulance take him away. We've been under siege ever since.'

'But why would they shoot a civilian? He's an artist, isn't he?'

'A graphic designer,' Ruby says. Although now she's even having doubts about that. Maybe Lucas's idea about witness protection wasn't as crazy as she'd first thought.

'Strange sort of job,' Nigel mutters.

'Says the man who delivers groceries,' Margaret fires back.

'I run a food distribution company!' She's clearly touched a nerve but doesn't poke it any further.

'The truth is we have no idea what's going on,' Margaret says. 'But we think it's because they're trying to get their hands on Ruby.'

'Who's Ruby?'

'That would be me,' Ruby says.

Nigel's face is a picture. He hates it when things are out of his control and Margaret can see him struggling to come to terms with what he's hearing. He's an old soldier through and through and the idea that some of his ilk would try and take over the village, shoot one of the residents and chase after a young girl is difficult for him to conceive. She knows that he has a very black and white idea of who the good and bad guys are. Quite literally, as he's always been a massive racist. Another reason she was glad to be shot of him. There are a lot of things Margaret doesn't like about most people but their skin colour isn't one of them.

'I'm sure there must be a simple explanation. They wouldn't do all this just for a girl.'

Ruby's too busy thinking about going back to the memory stick to respond to the misogynistic twat.

'The soldier on the barricade told me they were looking for an escaped prisoner,' he continues.

Margaret snorts her disbelief at that one. 'If you believe that you'll believe anything.'

'I'm not completely naive, Margaret. When I couldn't get into the village I went to the police office in Rothbury to make sure they were aware of the situation. They checked with their regional headquarters and assured me that it was an official operation and everything was under control.'

'Yet you still came to see for yourself?'

'Belt and braces, Margaret. Belt and braces.'

'You still think there's something wrong though, don't you? They're not even real soldiers.'

Nigel looks a little uneasy, as if that's something only he could have worked out.

'Why do you say that?'

Margaret lists a number of things on her fingers.

'No insignia. No rank badges. No markings on their transport – apart from a red cross on their so-called ambulance. No names. No ID cards. Shall I go on?'

'No, you're right,' he says. 'I'd noticed all of that myself, obviously. I just didn't want to worry you.'

The man's as insufferable as ever. Margaret passes Ruby a cup and then plonks his tea in front of him, splashing some of it onto the surface. She's made it the way she likes it. If he dares mention it she'll probably kill him. He takes a sip and goes to say something but sees the look on her face and closes his mouth. Instead he gets up and finds a cloth and wipes up the spillage himself. He looks around for a coaster but she threw them all away the day after he left. They were all military crests of one kind or another and she realised that she didn't give a hoot about a few stains on the table. After a few moments he concedes defeat and just holds the cup in his hands.

'Do you know who's in charge?' Nigel asks. 'Or how many of them there are?'

'No idea,' Margaret says. 'I've only spoken to one soldier, who's been driven around in a jeep by another man, though I don't think it's always been the same driver. There were three soldiers in the ambulance which might have included those two but I only saw them from a distance and I haven't seen anyone who looks like a leader.'

'Me neither,' Ruby says. 'Lucas and I saw a couple of soldiers patrolling the village and I saw the man who sent you packing at the barricade but that's it.'

'He didn't send me packing, young lady, I made a strategic retreat. He who lives to fight another day and all that.'

'Whatever.'

Nigel ignores Ruby and Margaret laughs when the girl gives him the finger behind his back.

'Who's Lucas?' he asks.

'Young lad, lives with his mam at the south end of the village. He's been helping Ruby keep out of the hands of these people,' Margaret says.

'The one who set fire to the school? Mother's a drunk?'

'She's had some issues, yes.'

'Explains a lot.'

Ruby considers dumping her tea on the judgey old bas-tard's head but he really isn't worth it.

'Have you spoken to Brian Masters?' he continues. 'He'll probably know what's going on.'

'I doubt it,' Margaret says. 'He's been living in Spain for the last year.'

'Really? What about Alastair?'

'He's gone too. Most of the people who were here before have taken the tourist shilling, sold up and moved away. It's all second homes now, Airbnb central. Apparently there's some kind of scam where you can claim it as a small busi-ness and don't have to pay any council tax. Probably why the roads in the village are full of potholes. I was thinking about doing it myself. Make a few bob.' That's palpably not true but she knows it'll wind him up. Nigel harrumphs.

'Over my dead body.'

'If you insist,' she says, smiling sweetly. 'I've killed you off once, I can happily do it again.'

Ruby laughs and gets up, having had enough of the cou-ple's back-and-forth. It's time to get back to something a lot more important. Nigel seems about to say something to her but she ignores him and is heading for the stairs when there's loud banging at the front door. She stops but no one else reacts. The banging starts up again.

Ruby glances at Margaret who moves past her and into the front room to check who it is though she has no doubts that it's the soldiers again. No one else would bang the door quite so fiercely. That bloody drone must have caught them standing in the garden. A quick glance through the net curtains confirms it – the same two men as before, only this time the driver is also on her doorstep and he, in particular, looks like he's ready to do some damage to someone. She heads back to the kitchen.

'It's the soldiers from the jeep. They don't look happy.'

Ruby immediately turns for the back door.

'Wait,' Margaret says. 'You can't just run out the gate, they might be watching the back. Let me talk to them. I'm sure I can put them off. You two keep out of the way.'

'I don't see why I need to "keep out of the way",' Nigel says. 'I'm the ex-army man, surely it should be me who—' Margaret's glare silences him.

'For once in your life do as you're told. If you do anything that puts Ruby here in danger I'll get Danny to chop your balls off – and don't think he wouldn't do it.'

Nigel's face reddens but he clearly knows what's good for him and keeps his mouth shut.

'Hide her,' she says. 'You know where.'

45

Margaret waits until the banging starts again then opens the door, once again catching her visitor in mid-knock. He stumbles slightly. Works every time. The driver, who is standing a yard behind the first man, looks like his head might explode.

'Good morning, Silver,' she says, ostentatiously checking her watch. 'It's a little early for a gentleman caller. I haven't had time to put my Agent Provocateur pants on yet.'

The soldier blushes slightly but steels himself.

'We need to come in,' he says.

'I'm sorry?'

'We've had reports of a young girl being seen in the vicinity so we're doing a house-to-house search.'

'Reports? D'you mean you've been spying on everyone with that floating camera thing?'

'Where we get our information is confidential.'

'Really? Fine. Tell me about the young girl then. Is she the escaped prisoner you said you were looking for? Or are you after two people now? Or do you not have the first clue what you're doing here?'

The big man behind him is getting increasingly restless and opens his mouth to say something but Silver draws himself up to his full height – about five foot six in boots, Margaret thinks, no wonder he didn't make it into the real army – and steps forward.

'We're worried about her. Think she might be hurt.'

'And you can help with that how?'

'I'm a medic.'

'Good to know. You haven't got anything that'll fix my gout, have you?'

'Don't take the piss, Mrs Carr, I don't want to have to take you into custody.'

'I don't blame you, young man, I'll scratch your eyes out if you try.' She steps back to give herself more room. 'For the record, I haven't seen any young girls – they tend to keep away from me. I frighten them. I frighten most people, apparently.'

There's a short stand-off, neither budging. Those two should have had plenty of time to hide themselves by now but she's not letting these buggers in without a fight. She's about to close the door on them when there's a voice from behind her.

'What's going on?'

She sighs. It's Nigel. Wrong time, wrong place, as usual. Why can't the man ever keep his big nose out? Silver looks a little surprised.

'Who are you, sir?'

'Nigel Carr. Coldstream Guards. I'm the man of the house.'

Margaret closes her eyes and takes a breath, trying hard

not to react, not wanting to help the soldier divide and conquer. When she opens them she sees Silver looking from the photo of Nigel on the wall to the man himself then back to her.

'I thought you said he was dead?'

She smiles. 'You must have misheard me. I said I wished he was dead. Sadly, they are two different things.'

Silver looks straight past her, clearly deciding that Nigel will be easier to deal with than the argumentative woman in front of him.

'We need to search your house, sir.'

'I don't think so,' Margaret says at the same time that Nigel says 'Of course,' and brushes past her. 'Anything to help a fellow serviceman. I heard you say you're looking for a girl though,' he adds. 'What do you want her for?'

'I'm afraid I can't go into details, sir, but suffice to say that we believe she is in possession of something that can damage national security.'

Nigel glances at Margaret and nods as if that was what he'd suspected all along.

'She's not hurt at all then,' Margaret says, but both men ignore her. Nigel turns back to the soldier.

'In that case I'm at your disposal. You'd better go right ahead.'

'Thank you. And you should know that we're offering a reward for any information that helps us find the girl. So if you know anything, now would be a good time.'

'A reward?' Nigel says. 'How much?'

'Five thousand pounds,' Silver says.

Nigel turns to Margaret, his eyes wide.

'Did you hear that, Margaret? Think what we could do with that kind of money.'

She glares at him, willing him to shut up.

'If we knew anything. Which we don't,' she says, bitterly rueing her decision to invite this man back into her house. She almost adds *And there is no 'we' any more* but knows he would react badly.

Surprisingly, Nigel keeps his lip buttoned though Silver clearly notices the tension between them.

'Spread the word though, won't you, I'm sure someone must know something,' he says, brushing past Nigel and looking pointedly at Margaret.

'Have you got a warrant?' she says, stepping in front of him.

'They don't need a warrant, dear, it's clearly a national emergency,' Nigel says, laughing and patting her on her shoulder. She flinches slightly and is tempted to slap his hand away but she doesn't want to provoke him. Instead she reluctantly stands aside and Silver and his colleague march into her hallway.

'You take the ground floor, Black, and I'll go up top,' Silver says, heading up the stairs.

'Keep an eye on him,' Margaret mutters, brushing past Nigel and following the other guy who has headed straight for the kitchen. Beyond that is the garden and that's what worries her most. If Nigel has taken her seriously that's where he'll have hidden Ruby.

46

Ruby is sitting in the dark in what seems to be an old air-raid shelter hidden under the Carrs' back lawn, keeping as quiet as she can. Nigel made it very clear the place wasn't soundproofed.

What kind of conspiracy theory loons have one of these in their garden? She couldn't believe it when Nigel pulled up the camouflaged trapdoor and told her to head down there. She almost refused but she knew Margaret couldn't keep the soldiers at the front door for much longer and it was as good a place as any to hide. She hopes she hasn't put her trust in the wrong people cos there's no escape if the soldiers find it. Maybe they already know it's there?

Although there is some lighting in the shelter Nigel was also insistent that she shouldn't turn it on as he reckoned it could be seen from above. She wonders if that's true, suspecting he's the kind of man who obsesses over the electricity bill, even though she doubts he still pays it. Even her dad, who otherwise is nothing like Nigel, used to complain about her leaving all the lights on. She wishes that was all he had to complain about now and for the millionth time that day hopes to hell he's OK, regardless of how much he's lied to her in the past.

Maybe Danny has managed to find out where they're keeping him. Thinking of Danny reminds her that Lucas is still missing. Have they caught him too? She can feel a net closing in on all of them.

Ruby may not be able to risk putting the lights on but she does have a torch that she found placed perfectly near the bottom step. She switches it on, keeping its beam as low to the floor as she can, and looks around the space. There's enough canned food down there to feed an army for weeks. Beans mostly, though, so the smell would get pretty bad. She's not sure what they'd cook it on but would bet that Nigel has a portable stove tucked away somewhere. There's some cushioned seating along one wall so she plonks herself down and waits.

She thinks again about the stuff she read on the memory stick. What's it got to do with all this? Is she a fucking surrogate baby? Did her mum take the money and do a runner? If she did, what the hell happened next? And where does Alex fit into all that? As soon as she's out of here she's going to read everything on there, even though she's scared about what she might find out.

It isn't long before she hears voices. She can't make out what they're saying yet but they're definitely getting closer. If they're going to give her up – and if they are she reckons it'll be the not-dead husband who does it rather than Margaret – then it's going to happen soon. Ruby curses herself for leaving her rucksack upstairs and hopes the soldiers don't find it – the last thing she wants is to get Margaret in trouble. The woman may be rude and nosy but now she's got to know her a little Ruby has to admit she quite likes her. She casts the torch around to see if there's anything she can use to defend herself if the worst should happen. To her astonishment she finds the perfect thing. Leaning against the right-hand wall, its sharp blade gleaming in the torch light, is a samurai sword.

Margaret catches up with the other soldier in the kitchen. He's throwing things around in the pantry which is a fruitless task, there's not enough room in there for a small cat to hide. He heaves out a bucket and a mop and some brushes but eventually figures out that he's wasting his time. Instead he doubles back to check out the front room.

'I hope you're going to tidy that mess up,' she says, following him.

There's nothing to find in that room either, or in the back room – the parlour as Nigel pompously calls it – apart from Boris who must have slept through Nigel's return; he growls at the strange man in his presence but is too lazy to do anything else. The soldier is beginning to toss things around randomly, showing his frustration. There really are no hiding places here. Not in the house anyway.

'Maybe it's because you didn't count to a hundred before you started looking,' Margaret says. 'Smacks of cheating.'

The soldier smirks. 'Silver said you were a gobby cow.'

Margaret nods. 'Can't argue with that. Shall I show you out now?'

She heads towards the front door but he steps in front of her.

'Just the garden to check,' he says, taking her shoulders and turning her to face the other way. She curses under her breath. 'How about you lead the way?' he adds.

'You don't fool me,' she says. 'I know what you soldiers are like. You just want to check out my backside.'

When she glances behind her she realises that she's making a mistake taking the mickey out of this one. He has the coldest eyes she's ever seen. She makes a mental note to tread a little more carefully and slows down, hoping that his friendlier colleague might come back down and call a halt to the search but there's no sound from upstairs. Nigel's probably regaling the man with tales of his past glories – defending Queen and country, tedious stories she's heard a thousand times. She almost feels sorry for the poor man.

When they hit the garden she tries to steer him towards the back gate – leading him up the garden path in more ways than one – but when she turns around he's stopped just outside the door and is surveying the area like a man who knows there's something to find there. That's when she sees the footsteps in the snow heading right into the middle of the lawn. Nigel has done his best to disguise them, clearly having kicked over them a little. It looks like he's also tried walking over to the large bushes along the right-hand side of the garden to add more footsteps to the mix but they're unlikely hiding places. The man searches them anyway, brutally kicking through the bushes, but the only thing he damages are a few snapped branches.

She moves to the middle of the lawn, making sure that she creates a fresh trail over the old one, and stands on the trapdoor to the underground shelter. Nigel's pride and joy. It's been there since the sixties – his dad was a volunteer with the Royal Observer Corps and he persuaded them to build one of their monitoring stations in his back garden during the Cold War. Margaret and Nigel had just used it as a kind of underground shed when they first inherited the house back in the mid-eighties after they were married. But when the pandemic started a few years back the silly man decided to modernise it. He removed the hatch at the top and covered the trapdoor with turf to keep it hidden too. She thinks he expected some kind of zombie apocalypse and was even a bit disappointed when it didn't materialise. Maybe that's why he then decided to get some excitement elsewhere.

The soldier gives up looking in the bushes and strides over to where she's standing. Way too close for comfort.

'Where is she?' he says.

'Who's "she"? The cat's mother?'

Margaret regrets forgetting her pledge to think before she speaks with this one when he moves firmly into her personal space. Her too-sharp tongue was another fault Nigel listed when he told her he was leaving. A smell of stale sweat wafts over her and she can feel the heat of his breath on her face.

'Don't piss around with me, I'm not like Silver,' he says, their noses practically touching. She tries hard not to blink. 'I won't take any shit from you.' He eyes her up and down. 'I've fucked worse while their husbands watched.'

Margaret can feel herself starting to tremble. She can tell from his empty eyes that he's not just talking, he's remembering the terrible things he's actually done. Things he enjoyed, by the look of him. He reaches out and puts his hand on her jaw, holding her head up so firmly that she can barely keep her feet on the ground. His huge biceps bulge underneath his T-shirt.

'You've got a smart mouth. I could start with that.'

She can barely stand, her legs are shaking so much. He moves his grip down to her throat, squeezing hard, forcing her down.

'On your knees.' He's so strong she has little choice but to do as he says. He reaches for his belt and undoes the buckle. She thinks she's going to be sick.

Then his radio goes off.

'This is base. Come in, Black. Over.'

He frowns and pulls the radio from his belt, glancing down at her.

'To be continued.'

He backs away and answers the call.

'Black.'

'You're needed here. Man down. I need Silver. Return immediately.'

'Roger. On our way.'

He turns back to Margaret and winks.

'Laters, love,' he says and runs back through the house shouting for Silver.

Margaret sinks to the grass, gasping for air, hyperventilating almost. She has her back to the door and when she hears it swing open again she screams. He's come back to finish what he started. But it's not him. It's Nigel. She never thought she'd ever be glad to see him again.

47

'That girl is in there somewhere, I could smell it! If I'd had five more minutes with that old bitch I'd have her now.'

Silver is staring at Black, wondering where the silent but scary-as-shit guy has gone. This version of Black is equally frightening but positively buzzing with energy, oozing equal parts mania and frustration as he races the jeep back to the manor house.

Something obviously set him off while Silver was upstairs, having to listen to hackneyed war stories from that tedious husband of hers. He can see why the old woman wished him dead. If he'd had to spend much longer in there he'd have put a bullet in the man himself. Still, it wasn't entirely a lost cause. He may not have found the girl but he'd come away with something almost as useful: information. Not that he was going to share it with Black, the bastard would be sure to take the credit.

He's recovered his mojo a bit after grabbing a couple of hours' sleep the night before and is more focused on the task in hand now. If he wants that holiday he needs the money a successful op will bring him. Though if he has to spend much more time with Black he could well change his mind again.

'She was just about to tell me what was going on.' Black takes one hand off the wheel and slaps the dash in frustration. He's not looking at Silver, barely even seems to know he's there. It's like he's giving himself a pep talk. 'If we'd done the house-to-house right at the start, we'd have found her in no time. As soon as this is sorted I'm going back there, finish what I started.'

Silver doesn't want to think about what Black started, about what he did to the poor woman to try to get her to talk. He's heard enough stories about soldiers like Black and turned a deaf ear to all of them. What you don't see, didn't happen.

He picks up the radio to try and find out what has happened back at base.

'Base, this is Silver, over.'

Nothing. Just dead air.

'Base, this is Silver, over.'

He's about to try once more when there's a response.

'Where are you?'

Gold has clearly decided to dispense with protocol. Silver doesn't approve. It's sloppy. It's no surprise that things are going downhill quickly if they can't get the basics right. And it all starts at the top. But if you can't beat 'em . . .

'Two minutes away. What's the problem?'

'Two casualties. Red's been shot and the prisoner is badly injured.'

What the fuck? Silver isn't surprised that someone would want to shoot Red, just that it's happened now. How in hell did he manage to get himself shot?

'I don't understand.'

'You don't need to understand. Just get back here and do your fucking job. Pronto.'

'Why do you need me? Can't Silver cope on his own?' Black shouts, impatience burning in his eyes.

There's a silence from the other end but then a crackle and a clearly exasperated Gold speaks again.

'No one flies solo in this company any more, Black. You two are meant to be a team. Look it up in the fucking dictionary. We've lost enough people who thought they could go it alone already. You'd think we were up against the fucking Taliban rather than some country bumpkins.'

The radio goes dead. Silver glances across at Black who grins at him.

'Gold's lost the plot. Why don't you drop me off and go back on your own? I can end this.'

Silver shakes his head and the man's grin vanishes instantly. Black seems like a man who revels in chaos but Silver prefers order. And this is about as far from order as it gets. His doubts about the mission come flooding back. He was shocked when he heard that Brown had done a runner but maybe the man had his head screwed on. It isn't just rats that leave a sinking ship, it's survivors.

48

When the trapdoor opens Ruby is hiding behind the steps, sword in hand. As daylight floods into the shelter she watches as feet descend the steps, ready to do whatever's necessary to get out. Thankfully, the feet are clad in leather shoes, not army boots.

'You can come out now,' Nigel says. 'It's safe. They're gone.'

She exhales loudly and steps out into the light cast from outside. He sees the sword in her hand and smiles.

'Margaret said you were tough.'

'How is she? I heard what that soldier said to her. I nearly came out to help her but then he got called away.'

He gives her a puzzled look. 'What do you mean?'

'Didn't she say anything?'

'No. She did seem a little upset but she's always been prone to overreaction. No real-world experience, you know. Doesn't know how to deal with the lower ranks. I've made her a cup of tea. That should calm her down.'

The poor woman would need more than tea, Ruby thinks.

Vodka might work. Clearly Margaret didn't want Nigel to know what had just happened though so she changes the subject.

'You used to be in the army, didn't you?'

'Of course.'

'When they say "man down" what do they mean?'

'Where did you hear that?'

'On their radio. That's why they left so quickly.'

'It depends. Someone is hurt probably.'

'Or dead?'

He nods.

'It's possible.'

Ruby can feel herself go cold all over.

'They've got my dad. It must be him.'

Ruby's back in the kitchen, holding Margaret's hand for comfort. Something that both of them need. The older woman seems to have physically shrunk, all that sparky energy has disappeared and she's really looking her age. More than her age even. The man must have terrified her. He terrified Ruby too and she wasn't the one he was threatening. If they'd do that to an old age pensioner what would they do to her if they caught her?

Nigel could clearly tell that something bad had happened out there but when nobody answered his questions he'd taken the hump and disappeared upstairs. He's been gone a while now. Ruby imagines he's the kind of man who spends a long time on the toilet reading the paper, and then tries to shake the image from her head.

'I'm not sure my dad's who he says he is,' she suddenly blurts out. She hadn't intended to say anything but the idea's been lodged in the front of her head so long that she had to relieve the pressure.

'What do you mean?' Margaret says.

'Something weird he wrote on that USB got me wondering.'

'Maybe you just misunderstood. D'you want to show me? See if I can make sense of it?'

Ruby nods. That's exactly what she wants. They get up to head upstairs but a loud tap on the window startles them both. Margaret freezes and Ruby jumps back from the table, her chair scraping on the stone floor. Lucas grins at Ruby through the glass, Danny behind him. She runs to the door and unlocks it to let them in.

'Where the hell have you been?' she says.

'Is that all the thanks I get for finding your dad?' Lucas says.

The words don't sink in immediately. She'd almost given up hope. Whether Alex has been lying to her suddenly doesn't seem so important.

'You've found him!'

Lucas nods. 'We think so. The soldiers are based at the old manor house. Pretty sure he's in there somewhere.'

She looks at Danny, who nods in confirmation, then she wraps Lucas in a huge hug, not caring that he smells pretty gross.

'Thank you,' she says. Behind him she can see Scout and Boris sniffing each other's arses in the garden and wonders if that's the dog equivalent of a hug. Lucas starts to squirm a little and she lets him go.

'Sorry, but I need a wee,' he says apologetically.

'Upstairs, first on the left,' Margaret says. Once he's gone she turns to Danny.

'Hello, stranger,' Margaret says. 'Been a while.'

'Too long,' Danny says.

There's a strange vibe in the kitchen and Ruby thinks there might be another hug in the offing when the silence is suddenly broken.

'Get the hell out of my house!'

The sudden shout startles them all. Have the soldiers come back already? Ruby turns around to see Nigel standing in the doorway, purple-faced with anger and pointing at Danny.

49

Danny's first instinct is to punch the man's lights out. It's something he's longed to do for years. But he doesn't want to be the villain here. Not in front of Margaret. Though maybe if Nigel throws the first punch he can demolish the self-satisfied prick with a clear conscience.

'Didn't you hear me? Get out!'

Danny glances at Margaret but it's like she's not there. Her eyes have glazed over. If he didn't know better he'd think she was scared.

'Now!' Nigel adds, striding towards him and gesturing towards the back door.

Enough is enough. Danny meets the blustering old fool halfway and goes toe to toe.

'Make me,' he says.

He smiles as Nigel clenches his fists.

'Don't think I won't,' the man says.

'Give it your best shot, Nige.'

He knows from years of winding him up that Margaret's husband – how he hates thinking of him as that – dislikes his name being shortened, which is why it's what he always calls him.

Danny grins as the old man takes a backward step, fear in his eyes. They both know he hasn't got what it takes. The grin disappears when he's suddenly drenched with water, him and Nige. Danny turn around furiously to see Ruby holding an empty bucket which, for some reason, had been on the floor when he came into the kitchen.

'What the hell?'

'Stop swinging your dicks around and grow up,' she says quietly. It's somehow more forceful that she doesn't shout. He can only just hear her over the sound of water dripping onto the floor from both men. 'My dad's life is in danger, he's probably getting medical attention right now, some psycho just threatened to rape Margaret and you two are butting heads like two ancient stags.'

'What!' It's like there's an echo. Nige's identical exclamation just a beat behind his own. Someone tried to rape Margaret? They almost race to the chair opposite her to comfort her. Danny has a sudden memory of a game of musical chairs the three of them took part in at a birthday party a gazillion years ago. He's tempted to brush the man aside again, as he did back then, but some sense of propriety holds him back and he lets the other man take the seat. Nigel, who drips more water onto the table top from his sleeve, goes to take Margaret's hand but she pulls it away.

'Why didn't you say anything, love?' he says.

Margaret doesn't move and for a moment Danny thinks

she's not going to react at all but then she looks up and starts speaking. Quietly but firmly.

'I'm not your "love". And I don't want to talk about it. Not to you, anyway,' she says. Before Danny can get too smug she glances at him. 'Or you, for that matter.' She sighs. 'In fact, why don't you both get out of *my* house? Go and join your fucking dogs.'

Danny looks out of the window and sees that Margaret's terrier is trying his best to mount Scout, who just looks bemused, turning in circles to try and shake the small dog off. He heads to the door, closely followed by Nige, and goes to separate them. When they're both outside he hears the lock click behind them.

Once they're gone Margaret turns to Ruby, and gives her a scathing glare.

'You had no right. It was up to me if I wanted to tell them that.'

Ruby nods. The woman's got a point. She hadn't planned to but just blurted it out when those two started with their macho crap. Behind Margaret's shoulder Lucas comes back into the kitchen.

'I'm sorry. You're right. I didn't mean to say anything but they just pissed me off. Boys are shit, aren't they?'

Lucas blushes but Margaret smiles weakly. 'I wish I'd figured that out when I was your age. Life would have been much simpler.'

Lucas is pretending to read something that looks like a shopping list which is pinned to a noticeboard on the wall. He clearly feels her watching him and looks around sheepishly.

'Not all boys,' she says. He nods but has the good sense to make himself scarce again so they can talk.

'I think I'll just go for another wee,' he says. 'Must be the cold.'

Once he's gone, Ruby sits down and takes the older woman's hand.

'You should probably get out of here,' Margaret says. 'Those men will be back again soon, I'm sure.'

'And leave you with those knobheads?' Ruby says, glancing out of the window where the two men are still prowling around each other. 'No chance.'

Margaret squeezes her hand in thanks. They sit in silence until the older woman is ready to talk. Ruby doesn't mind the quiet – she has quite enough to think about.

Despite the soaking things haven't cooled off in the garden. Danny knows he shouldn't have dragged the smaller dog off quite so firmly but the rutting little bastard wouldn't leave Scout alone.

'You really are the lowest of the low, aren't you,' Nigel sneers. 'Taking it out on an animal. But I suppose you are a poacher, no respect for other people's things.'

The way he says 'poacher', as if it's something akin to 'paedophile', sets Danny off again.

'Other people's things! You think you own everything, don't you? Including the rivers and the fish in them. Just because your old man was a paid lackey for his lordship doesn't make you part of the fucking aristocracy. He was a steward, that was all. Poaching was made a crime by people who can never get enough, people who wanted to find yet another way to take what should belong to everyone and make it their own.'

'Bollocks.'

'You capitalist pricks know fine well that if people round here can't feed themselves from the wild then they have no choice but to get a job in a shitty warehouse – one like yours – so they can earn enough to buy expensive pre-packaged food off the shelves in a supermarket instead of just catching it in the river that runs past their back garden. It's a stitch-up.'

'You can't just decide which laws to follow and which to ignore. That's anarchy. The rule of law is sacrosanct.'

'Really? Where's the law now then? Who's the sheriff in this town? Is it you?'

'I was a magistrate!'

'Of course you were.'

'What does that even mean?'

'You just love passing judgement on those less fortunate than you, don't you? Those who didn't inherit a nice house and a shedload of cash from their dead daddy.'

'Leave my father out of this. You're nothing but a common thief. You even tried to steal my wife. And it seems to me that you still are. I can see the way you look at her.'

Margaret glances out of the window and sees the two men arguing still. At least they're not actually fighting yet. She's not surprised it hasn't gone that far. Nigel might have a quick temper but he's not stupid enough to take on Danny in a physical contest.

'They've always hated each other,' she says.

'How long have you all known one another?' Ruby asks.

'Since school. Nigel was my first boyfriend. All very innocent back then though. But he went and joined the army and I took up with Danny.'

Ruby laughs. 'You don't hang about. How old were you?'

'About the same age as you are now, I think. My parents were horrified. Danny was younger than the rest of us, mature for his age but always a bit of a wild one. He would never take any shit.'

'How did you end up back with Nigel then?'

'When he came back on leave about nine months later he asked my father for permission to marry me. That's how things were back then. My father said yes without even asking me what I thought. Nigel's parents were quite well off at the time and he thought it was the best I could do.'

'Sounds like an arranged marriage.'

Margaret laughs bitterly. 'I never really thought of it like that but yes, exactly the bloody same. Though I'm sure both sets of parents would have been horrified at the comparison. Anyway, I said no. I was in love with Danny by then.'

'So what happened?'

'My mother went ballistic. Threatened to disown me. Or worse, send me off to a nunnery. I was weak, hadn't learnt how to stand up for myself. Not like now. Danny was heartbroken. Went off to join the army himself a year or two later, ironically. There weren't many other options for a lad from round here back then – especially one who didn't take to school that well, like Danny. He was good at other things.'

She winks at Ruby who can't hide her shock.

'You young 'uns think that we came out of the womb as pensioners. Sex wasn't invented by you lot, we've known about it for ages. I could teach you and that lad of yours a thing or two, I reckon.'

Now the girl is blushing.

'We're not, um, you know, he's not my boyfriend, if that's what you think. I don't have a boyfriend. I don't want a boyfriend.'

'Methinks the girl doth protest too much. You're obviously soft on him.'

Ruby looks mortified and now it's Margaret's turn to feel guilty.

'I mean there's no need to rush, pet,' she adds. 'You'll know when you're ready. When you meet the right lad.' She glances up at the ceiling. 'Though I'm not sure I'd climb over Lucas to get to Nigel.'

Ruby snorts and the pair of them are still laughing when there's a loud pounding at the front door which kills the laughter stone dead.

50

Margaret starts to tremble, the cup in her hand rattling against the saucer on the table. She tries to stop it but it's hopeless. Ruby legs it into the front room to look outside, then runs back to Margaret.

'It's the huge one, scary eyes. Was he the one threatening you?'

Margaret nods.

'Can you get Nigel?' she says quietly. 'I can't face that brute again.'

Ruby jumps up and unlocks the back door. The two men stop snarling at each other and turn to look at her.

'The big soldier is back again. The one who . . . you know,' she says, glancing around at Margaret who's gone back into zombie mode, before turning again to Nigel. 'You need to deal with it this time. Get rid of him.'

Nigel nods.

'You need to hide,' he says.

'I'm not going back down there again,' Ruby says.

'You don't have any choice.'

Danny steps between them.

'Down where? What are you talking about?' he says.

Margaret is still staring at the kitchen table when Nigel comes into the kitchen. The banging on the front door is threatening to smash through it. He puts his hand on her shoulder as he passes but she shrugs it off. She watches as he walks slowly down the hallway, composes himself, and opens the front door.

'You devious bastard,' the soldier shouts. 'You've got a fucking underground shelter back there.'

'I don't know what you mean—'

'Bollocks. We've got a thermal imager on the drone and I've just checked the footage. Out of my way.'

'You can't just barge—'

There's the sound of a scuffle and a shout of pain, then the psycho is in the kitchen, heading straight to the back door. He glances back at Margaret.

'Once I've sorted the girl out it'll be your turn.'

Nigel stumbles in after him, holding his nose. Blood is pouring through his fingers.

'I tried to stop him. He hit me with his rifle,' he says.

A part of her wishes he'd hit him harder. She reluctantly drags herself from the table and they follow the soldier out of the door. He stops suddenly.

'Whose is that other dog?'

Margaret sees Boris and Scout both sleeping on an old garden seat parked against the back fence.

'They're, um, both, ours,' Nigel says.

'The big one wasn't here before.'

'Of course he was. He must have been upstairs.'

The man looks unconvinced but eventually he shrugs and moves into the middle of the lawn.

Margaret can clearly see footsteps in the snow leading to the trapdoor. She's not the only one. Black turns to them and smiles. 'Boom!' he whispers.

He drops to one knee and feels around on the grass, searching for the entrance to the shelter. It doesn't take him long to find it beneath the turf. He pulls up on the handle and throws the trapdoor open, getting to his feet and pointing his rifle into the gap.

'I know you're down there. You've got three seconds to come out or I'll come down and get you. One. Two. Three.'

Behind him Ruby sprints out of the bushes, barrels past Margaret and charges into the back of the giant soldier, sending him flying down the steep steps. There's a shout of surprise, an audible crack then silence. Margaret really hopes that crack was the bastard's neck.

Ruby seems frozen to the spot but Danny runs out of the same bushes and slams the trapdoor shut.

'Fuck me,' Margaret says, turning to Danny. 'Was that your idea?'

'Sort of. Though it was supposed to be me taking him out. Ruby here jumped the gun and was gone before I could stop her.'

Nigel seems less impressed. Margaret guesses he's just annoyed that he didn't think of it. But it's not that.

'Just one problem,' he says.

Danny sighs. 'There's always a problem with you, isn't there, Nige? Never a solution. Go on then, I'll bite, what is it?'

'He's got a radio. And a rifle.'

'What the fuck does a catering officer know about signal transmission? I doubt he'll get a signal down there.'

'Do you really want to take that chance?'

Danny's protesting but Margaret can see he's got doubts now. For once in his life Nigel might be right.

'I suppose one of us should go down there and check,' she says.

Nigel takes a step backwards, away from the trapdoor.

'Looks like it's me then,' Danny says.

'I'll do it,' Ruby says.

'You're all right, pet, you've done your bit. Be a shame to have got this far and have you take a bullet when you open that door, wouldn't it?'

Margaret takes the girl's hand.

'He's right. Time to take a back seat, love.'

Danny makes them all move back to the kitchen just in case the drone makes a reappearance and sees what they're up to. No need to bring yet more soldiers to the house. He crouches down by the trapdoor and listens carefully. Not a sound. He steps to one side and grabs hold of the handle, flipping it open but keeping well out of the way. Nothing happens. No shots. Either the soldier is biding his time or he's out cold. He waits for several minutes but knows he can't wait forever. He edges closer, leans over and takes a look down the hole. It's too dark in there to see clearly but the man is lying, face down, at the foot of the ladder, his rifle on the floor behind him just out of reach. Bizarrely there's a samurai sword leaning up against the wall near the rifle. God knows where that came from.

The soldier isn't moving. He could be faking it though. Danny looks around the garden and sees a small rockery at the back. He grabs a large stone and throws it underarm down into the hole, striking the prone soldier on the back. He doesn't react at all. Relaxing slightly Danny takes a first tentative step on the ladder and when there's still no movement below rushes down as quickly as he can. He flicks a light switch at the bottom. The soldier's neck is at an angle that doesn't bode well for him. It looks like he landed on his head. He steps around the man and pulls the rifle further away, registering the EWMN tattoo he has across his knuckles. He's seen that on so-called hard men before. The man may well have been Evil, Wicked, Mean and Nasty but now he's dead. Simple as. Just to be sure he kneels down to check the man's pulse. Nothing. He reaches down to the radio and snaps it off the soldier's belt, grabs the rifle and heads back up, closing the trapdoor behind him.

The others have gone back inside but Ruby is still standing by the back door watching him carefully. He considers lying to her, knowing how hard it can be to know you've taken a man's life. He's never forgotten his first time. She tilts her head to one side, asking the question without saying a word.

'He's dead,' he says. 'Broke his neck, I think.' She nods and turns away, walking back into the house.

Ruby heads straight up the stairs, not even a smidgen of remorse, she's even more determined to learn what this is all about. Who are these men working for and why do they want her so badly?

Lucas pokes his head out of the toilet where he's obviously been hiding.

'Has he gone?' he says.

'No.'

He looks worried.

'He's dead,' she adds.

'What? How?'

'He fell down the steps of the underground shelter.'

Lucas looks bemused, like she's speaking in a foreign language, and she realises he wasn't there when the soldiers came the first time. He knows nothing about the secret hideaway.

'Crazy Nigel has one underneath his lawn.'

Lucas shakes his head. She's not sure whether his disbelief is over the dead soldier or the shelter. They're both equally unlikely, she supposes, and worries that she's getting used to this madness. He eventually comes up with a question.

'When you say "fell"?'

She hesitates but realises that she wants to be honest with him. She is beginning to suspect that lies are what have led her to this situation.

'I pushed him.'

He looks a little shocked.

'I'm not sorry.' Ruby realises how much she's changed since that first soldier appeared on the scene. She's no longer the girl who won the debate against reintroducing capital punishment that they held at school, or the one who thought eating meat was the worst crime ever. She hopes it's only temporary, as she's not sure she likes this version of herself. From the look on his face she's not sure that Lucas does either. It hurts her to admit that she actually gives a toss what he thinks but she does.

'In my defence, he threatened to rape Margaret,' she says.

He exhales. It's a lot to take in.

'D'you think we can ever be kids again?' he asks.

Ruby shakes her head. That ship has sailed.

'You know what you said about witness protection?' she asks.

He edges away from her, wary.

'I'm not going there again. I remember what happened last time.'

'It's just that I've been thinking about it. Maybe you were right. But maybe it was me who needed protecting. What if I saw something when I was younger? Something I've forgotten completely.'

'It's possible, I guess.'

'D'you want to find out? I'm going to finish reading what's on that memory stick.'

He shakes his head.

'I think you should get first look at that,' he says. 'But I'll wait out here in case you need someone to talk to.'

'Thank you,' she says. Ruby hesitates, considers giving him a brief kiss on the cheek to thank him for his kindness, then rejects the thought, she needs to stay focused. She opens the study door and is glad to see her rucksack is still there by the side of the desk. But then she stops dead.

The computer screen is blank; the memory stick gone.

51

Ruby's hair is streaming in the wind as Lucas drives the jeep down the back lane. She's still raging that the medic took her memory stick before she could finish reading the contents but the fresh air is working its magic on her anger. She looks across at Lucas, who's smiling back at her.

'Keep your eyes on the road,' she says.

He holds her glance, waits for a millisecond, then does as he's told. Is he flirting with her? She's read the signals wrong before, and it's awfully embarrassing when you get it wrong.

'How did you learn to drive, anyway?'

'Danny taught me on the back roads.'

'Still illegal, like.'

'I've got my licence.'

'Provisional!'

He laughs, caught bang to rights.

'Where are we going?'

'Baldwin's place. We can hide this in his garage.'

When Ruby realised the memory stick was missing she'd

punched the wall so hard that Lucas had run into the little bedroom to see what the problem was. That's when he'd seen the soldier's jeep sitting outside the house. It was a dead giveaway that the man hadn't left so he suggested hiding it. They should probably have got Danny to do it – he wasn't the one they were looking for. But she needed a bit of space from the oldies – to give her time to think about what she'd read earlier and what to do next – so she'd just nodded without thinking it through. It was only a short drive but if they were seen all hell would break loose.

'Are you sure he'll help us?'

'Course.'

She wonders how Lucas can maintain his positive outlook with all the crap that's happened in the last twenty-four hours. He's been chased and shot at, forced to hide from at least two psychotic soldiers and almost set two different houses on fire yet he still seems as happy as a pig in shit. It could be irritating but it's exactly what she needs. Not that she'd tell him that, he thinks enough of himself already.

There's a part of her that would like him to put his foot down, fly through whatever barricades the soldiers have put up, while giving them the finger, before disappearing into the distance and leaving all this crap in their rear-view mirror. But Lucas's attempt to get out of the village the night before had shown that it isn't as easy as that. Even in a vehicle they'd be easy to catch before they got to the next village, especially with those fucking drones spying on them. And these monsters have still got her dad and while there's a chance he's still alive she's not going anywhere without him.

She's brought out of her dream world by the sound of a shot and a squeal of tyres as the jeep skids towards the pavement. Lucas wrenches the wheel one way then the other, somehow wrestling control of the vehicle as it veers across the road then straightens up again. Ruby looks ahead and there's a soldier standing in the middle of the road pointing his rifle right at them.

'Did he shoot one of the tyres out?' she shouts.

Lucas just nods, focused on keeping the jeep moving. It's obvious he's seen the soldier right in front of them but he's stopping for no one. She stares daggers at the man and sees the moment he realises they're not slowing down. He dives out of the way but the car clips his leg as they pass and he crashes head first into the wall, his rifle going flying too. It's probably not fatal but the guy's going to have one hell of a headache when he comes to. Lucas keeps his foot down.

Baldwin's garage is just two turns away and with the lead they have and the soldier's injury it's possible they could hide the vehicle before he catches up with them, if he can still walk at all, that is. Ruby looks back and the man hasn't moved. She's still got her head turned when Lucas careers around the first bend and she's thrown across the seat almost into his lap. He immediately swings the jeep the other way and she's thrown back again, hitting the door with her shoulder. Lucas accelerates towards Baldwin's garage doors, which fortunately are wide open, and hits the brakes just before the entrance, pulling to a halt about a foot from the back wall. Ruby shakes her head to clear the sudden dizziness but Lucas is already out of the vehicle and pulling the doors to the large workshop shut. If the soldier follows their tracks he'll know exactly where they are but there's not much they can do about that now. If they're lucky the injury will slow him down enough that the still-falling snow will cover them.

She looks around and sees Baldwin fast asleep on an old sofa which looks like it has been dragged off a tip. It's on the other side of another car that has the bonnet up as if he was working on it before he gave up and crashed out. There's an empty whisky bottle lying on the floor by his feet and a pool of liquid on the floor. She hopes it's come from the bottle.

'Jesus, he's disgusting.'

Lucas frowns at her. 'Give him a break, his wife killed herself a few years back. She hung herself from a tree in the woods, never settled down here, they say, had no friends, suffered from depression. It's not just you who hates this place.'

Now she feels like shit. It's awful how little she used to know or care about the people in the village – people who all have their own troubles that she's now relying on to help her. As she climbs out of the jeep Lucas runs over and gives the old man a shake. It takes a moment or two but eventually he stirs, blinking at the sudden light in his eyes. He goes to speak but Lucas shushes him, putting his finger to his lips. The old man might be sleepy, still a bit pissed even, but he takes the hint.

'There's a soldier after us,' Lucas says, keeping his voice

as low as possible. 'He'll probably be here any second. Can you get rid of him? Tell him you haven't seen us.'

Baldwin rubs his eyes and stands up slowly.

'What have you done, lad?'

'Nothing, honest. We were just driving and he shot out one of the tyres.'

Baldwin glances at the jeep.

'Did you nick that?'

Lucas hesitates and the old man laughs and pats him on the shoulder.

'I was young myself once, you know, used to get up to all sorts.' He glances around the garage. 'You might want to cover it up though, otherwise he might not believe me.'

Ruby sees a tarpaulin rolled up on the ground just to the left of the doors. She runs over and gets there just before Lucas. Between them they manage to throw it over the jeep.

'We should get out of here,' she says but almost immediately there's a loud bang on the door.

'Open up,' a voice shouts. It has to be the soldier. Clearly the man's injuries weren't anywhere near as bad as she'd hoped.

'That'll be your friend, I guess,' Baldwin says quietly. 'Maybe you should get under there yourselves.' They crawl under the tarpaulin at the back of the vehicle. When Baldwin's satisfied they're out of sight he turns to the door.

'Give us just a moment. You caught me having a crafty wank,' he shouts.

Lucas sniggers and Ruby puts her hand across his mouth. She can feel the light stubble on his jaw. Eventually Baldwin pushes the doors open, letting in more light. Ruby scrunches up into the smallest shape she can manage.

'Have you seen two kids?' the soldier asks.

'Haven't seen anyone, man. There's a curfew in place. Didn't anyone tell you?'

'They were driving a jeep, heading this way. The tracks lead right to your door.'

'That was probably my car made those,' Baldwin says, nodding at the other vehicle in the garage. The soldier looks dubious. Baldwin barely pauses for breath, clearly hoping to distract him from the tracks.

'How old are these kids? What do they look like? I might know 'em. I could tell you where they live.'

'I dunno. About sixteen, I guess. The girl's short, skinny, longish brown hair, the boy's taller, maybe five ten.'

'Doesn't mean anything to me,' Baldwin says.

'What's that smell?' the soldier says.

'Sorry about that,' Baldwin says, 'personal hygiene's gone to pot recently.'

'No. The other smell. Like exhaust fumes. What's under the tarpaulin?'

'Nothing.'

'Doesn't look like nothing.'

'Well, not nothing. Just a mate's car that I'm checking out for him.'

'Show me.'

'Have you got a warrant?'

'This is my warrant.'

There's a grunt and a thudding sound. Ruby takes the

chance of sneaking a look. Baldwin is on the floor, clutching his stomach, the soldier holding the rifle the wrong way around. It's pretty obvious he's hit the old man with his rifle butt. Baldwin tries to kneel up but as he does he vomits all over the soldier's boots.

'Ah, bollocks,' the armed man says, backing away slightly.

'Sorry,' Baldwin says, 'but you shouldn't hit a man who's been drinking whisky all day. Asking for trouble, isn't it?'

'Out the way.' The soldier limps past the kneeling man and grabs the corner of the tarpaulin, heaving it off the jeep in one movement. Although Ruby and Lucas are behind the tailgate they're still clearly visible in the small space.

'Up,' the soldier says, pointing the rifle at them.

Behind him, Baldwin is on his feet now, still looking groggy. He stumbles against the wall and looks like he's going to throw up again. The soldier glances around but doesn't see anything to concern him so turns back just as they're getting to their feet.

'Hands in the air,' he says. They do as they're told. Lucas is twitching slightly, edgy, looking around as if he still thinks they can get away. In contrast, Ruby can feel all her energy ebbing away. It's the end of the road.

'Well, haven't I hit the jackpot,' the soldier says, grinning from ear to ear. 'Nice little bonus heading my way, I reckon.'

With his spare hand he picks up his radio. 'Come in, base, it's White, over.'

There's a brief pause then a crackle before:

'Base here. What is it, White? Over.'

'I've got the girl,' he says. 'I'm bringing her in now. Over.'

Baldwin coughs loudly behind him and the man turns around sharply, clearly aiming to give him another crack with the rifle butt. Ruby sees the soldier step back a fraction, like he's seen something he shouldn't have but before he says anything there's a loud hiss and the man's hit full in the face by a rapid stream of oil from the can that Baldwin now has in his hand. The soldier's hands go straight to his face, his rifle falling to the floor, and he staggers back against the bonnet of the jeep. Baldwin steps forward and kicks him viciously in the balls. The man groans and falls to his knees, waving his arms around frantically, clearly torn between trying to clear the thick black liquid out of his eyes and blocking another blow to his balls. It doesn't really matter which he tries as Baldwin follows up his kick with a knee to the guy's head which smashes back against the bonnet. The crack echoes around the garage and he falls face first against the concrete floor, out like a light.

Ruby laughs, almost hysterically, not quite believing what she's just seen. Lucas whoops and runs across to Baldwin, high-fiving the old man as if he's just won an Olympic medal or something. The garage owner is grinning manically, definitely still a bit pissed. Ruby wonders if he'd have even tried all that if he'd been sober; probably not, she reckons, whispering a quiet thank you to the powers of alcohol.

'Give us a hand, lad,' Baldwin says, grabbing the soldier's feet. Lucas takes his arms and they pull him across the floor towards an inspection pit on the other side of the garage.

'You serious?' Lucas says.

'Aye, lad. He'll not be out for long. We need to put him

somewhere he can't get out from and this is as good a place as any. Serves the bastard right for twatting me with that rifle.'

They drag the man to the edge of the pit.

'Wait one,' Lucas says and reaches down to unclip the radio from his belt.

'Smart move,' Baldwin says and Lucas grins broadly until he sees Ruby giving him a look.

'Someone else's idea really,' he says.

Baldwin gives the unconscious man a final nudge with his boot to send him rolling into the hole and crashing to the floor. He might still be alive but it's really not his day, Ruby thinks; first he's nearly run over by two kids and then a fat drunk gets the better of him.

'What now?' Lucas says.

'You reverse that jeep out. I'll put the cover on the pit and then you park on top of it. He'll not get out of there in a hurry.' He looks at Ruby. 'Nip down to the end of the road and make sure no one's around to see us. Toot sweet, there's a love.'

Ruby does as she's told, practically skipping down the track, so relieved to still be free that she's feeling a little giddy. For the first time since she walked into the kitchen at home and saw the wounded soldier she's starting to think there might be some kind of an end to all this.

She hears an engine roar and glances back to see Lucas manoeuvring the jeep over the inspection pit cover. The two men then put the tarpaulin back on the vehicle. Job done. Glancing around to make sure there's nobody else about she runs back to join them. Baldwin's holding the soldier's discarded rifle like a souvenir – as if he's going to fire into the air in celebration – and there's a lot of back-slapping. They're a bit too pleased with themselves.

'Will he be able to breathe in there?' she asks.

'Probably,' Baldwin says, but it's clear he couldn't care less. 'Now, which one of you is going to tell me what the hell's going on?'

'Come back to Margaret's with us and we'll tell you on the way,' Lucas says.

'Margaret's? I don't think so. I'd be as welcome as a fart in a lift.'

'She has a bottle of whisky in her cupboard.'

Ruby thinks Lucas is making that up but she sees Baldwin glance at the empty bottle on the floor.

'Why didn't you say so before?' he says.

52

'And then I sprayed oil in his face and knocked the bastard into the middle of next week,' Baldwin says, laughing. He's already halfway through a packet of chocolate digestives Ruby found in Margaret's pantry.

Danny is leaning back against the cooker, looking slightly uncomfortable but Lucas is lapping up the man's retelling of the story like he's some kind of returning war hero.

They'd brought Baldwin up to speed on their way back to the house. Ruby hadn't been so sure it was a good idea to include him, and once he'd heard their story even Baldwin seemed to have doubts, not really wanting to get involved. But Lucas had pointed out he was already involved. The unconscious soldier in his inspection pit was testament to that.

It seemed like it was going to be OK though and Ruby was feeling that things were changing in her favour – the garage fight felt like a tipping point. But then she saw a red-faced Margaret standing in the kitchen doorway.

'Mr B was awesome,' an oblivious Lucas says to Danny. 'We were this close to being caught.' He holds his right hand up and puts his index finger and thumb about a millimetre apart.

There's a minor explosion behind him. Margaret completely loses it.

'What the fuck is Archie Baldwin doing sitting at *my* table, wolfing down *my* biscuits with a big shit-eating grin on his fat face?'

Ruby feels the temperature in the room drop to zero. Everyone can tell she's steaming. Almost everyone.

'Mr Baldwin saved us,' Lucas says, turning around. 'We were this close to—'

The look on Margaret's face stops him mid-sentence.

'I heard you the first time.' She holds up her own hand mimicking Lucas's earlier demonstration. 'And now you're this close to getting my boot up your arse. Get him out of here.'

Baldwin laughs. 'Didn't take you long to spoil things, did it, you old witch. I didn't want to come here in the first place. But these kids said they needed my help. And I was promised whisky.'

'You'll not be getting a drink here. You reek like a barmaid's apron already,' Margaret says.

'I needed a drink to put up with you. And I can clean myself up later whereas you'll always have a face like a slapped monkey's arse,' Baldwin fires back.

'Steady,' Danny says, putting a hand on Baldwin's shoulder, who immediately shrugs it off.

'Don't fucking touch me,' the big man says. 'You're just as bad as she is.'

Ruby's had enough.

'Stop it,' she shouts, banging her hand on the table. 'I thought you people wanted to help me.' She turns to Margaret. 'Weren't you the one who said that you might not like everyone in the village but you hate outsiders even more?'

'He's the exception to the rule,' Margaret says, pointing at Baldwin. 'He's a useless old drunk who's done nothing for this place but cause it trouble. Just look what he drove his poor wife to.'

There's silence. Ruby can tell that Margaret knows she's gone too far this time. Baldwin's on his feet now.

'How fucking dare you! She had depression. She was lonely.'

Instead of apologising, Margaret doubles down. Ruby puts her head in her hands and watches through her fingers like a rubbernecker at a car crash.

'Maybe that's because her husband was always in the pub.'

Baldwin holds his hands up.

'I never said I was perfect. But what about you two?' He turns to Danny. 'Lilian was worried about all the debt we were building up and most of that was down to you. We were on the bones of our arse because you kept working on people's cars for next to nowt. You literally took my livelihood away, stole the food from our mouths.'

'And yet you still had money for beer,' Margaret says.

Baldwin spins back to face her, jabbing his finger in her face.

'And you completely ignored her. Until you blackballed her application to join the Neighbourhood Watch. She just wanted to make some friends. But Mrs high-and-mighty Carr didn't think she was good enough.'

Margaret takes a step back.

'That's not what happened. We just didn't want the wife of a local villain getting involved in the group.'

'Villain! What the fuck does that mean?'

'You were always breaking the by-laws, burning tyres, fly-tipping, drinking in the street.'

'Hanging offences, eh! Strange that you never had a problem with lover-boy's poaching!' Baldwin turns and heads towards the back door. Danny tries to stop him.

'Look, let's sit down and—'

'I told you not to fucking touch me.' Baldwin brushes his arm away in anger, flings the door open and storms out into the back garden.

Ruby glares across the table at Lucas who is looking around, open-mouthed, like a kid who's just discovered there's no Father Christmas.

'Well, that went well,' she says.

Margaret stays in the doorway for a minute or two, staring across the kitchen to the garden where a clearly incandescent Baldwin is raging around, cigarette in hand, the two dogs keeping well out of his way for fear of feeling his boot. The two kids are still sitting dumbstruck, both obviously bemused at how quickly that all blew up. They'll realise one day that the longer you hold on to resentments the bigger the shock waves when you release them. Best to get things out early. Eventually Danny breaks the silence.

'He does have a point, you know. We've never exactly welcomed incomers with open arms.'

Margaret's first instinct is to argue but, for once, she bites her tongue. Was Baldwin right? His poor late wife was from down south somewhere – Yorkshire maybe? Coldburn had a distinct lack of eligible single women then – it was even worse now – and she thinks he first met her on some kind of online dating site. She probably did get treated with the standard mistrust that faced everyone who moved there from elsewhere – even if they came from another Northumberland village – but surely it wasn't that bad? Though now she thinks about it she can't remember a single conversation she had with the woman. And the fact that she has no real idea where she came from speaks volumes.

'I can vouch for that,' Ruby says.

'Me too,' Lucas says. 'No one spoke to me or my mam for ages when we first moved here. And when they did it was usually to complain about me.'

'You were a little twat, to be fair,' Danny says, which lightens the atmosphere a little.

'Are we really that bad?' Margaret says, already knowing what the answer is before everyone else in the room starts nodding.

Margaret opens the back door and approaches Baldwin – who's now sitting on the bench – with extreme caution, like he's a rabid dog who might try to bite her.

'Fuck do you want?'

'To apologise.'

'You're about ten years too late for that.'

'I have a peace offering.'

She holds up a bottle of Laphroaig that she'd been saving for a special occasion. Her apologising to someone definitely counts as that, it doesn't come naturally.

'I thought I'd had enough?'

'You can never have enough of this, surely?'

Baldwin laughs.

'I never had you pegged as a secret drinker.'

'We've all got secrets,' she says.

'True enough. Got a glass? Even I draw the line at necking the good stuff from the bottle.'

She holds up a pair of plastic beakers she'd taken from the draining board.

'They're not exactly crystal,' she says.

'They'll do.'

Baldwin shuffles along the bench to make room for her. She sits down and hands him both beakers, pouring a small measure into both. He looks at her questioningly and she tops one of them up a little more before putting the bottle on the ground. He hands her the beaker with the least in and they both raise a glass.

'To Lilian,' he says.

'To Lilian,' she repeats.

They drink, her savouring a small mouthful while he knocks it back in one and holds the beaker out for a refill. She quickly tops him up again.

'Now let's hear this apology,' he says. 'And it better be good.'

53

The first proper meeting of the war committee is convened back at the kitchen table with Ruby dearly hoping that the uneasy peace can be maintained.

To help that happen, Danny and Nigel, who had apparently been having a nap in the spare room upstairs, are sitting at opposite ends of the table, carefully placed there by Ruby, just in case their temporary truce comes to a sudden end. There's been enough fighting for one day.

Lucas and Ruby sit on one side and Margaret and Baldwin the other, the bottle of whisky and two beakers in front of them. Baldwin's beaker is noticeably fuller than Margaret's. Ruby has no idea what she said to the man in the garden but whatever it was it worked.

'Maybe we should have an agenda,' Nigel says. Danny laughs then frowns as he realises it's not a joke.

'Who made you the chairman?' he says. Ruby's glad they kept them apart otherwise things would be going downhill even faster than they did before.

'I think Ruby should lead,' Margaret says, patting her

hand in encouragement. A couple of days ago Ruby would have found that laughable but she's a different animal now. And the resurfacing of old rivalries has pushed her patience to breaking point.

'Everybody happy with that?' she says.

'Of course they are, love,' Margaret says. 'You're a natural.'

Nigel doesn't look convinced but Lucas nods.

'You don't normally have a problem being bossy,' he says. Ruby kicks him under the table and then starts.

'I think we should try and rescue my dad.' She's conscious that she still doesn't know the full story of her dad's past but isn't willing to share her doubts with anyone other than Margaret just yet.

Danny laughs. 'Talking my language. Go hard or go home! I hope you're taking minutes, Nige.'

Ruby ignores the petty squabbling, it's a minor irritation in comparison to the earlier explosion, and presses on.

'Since this started I've spent most of the time hiding but I'm done with that.'

'I'm not quite sure what you expect us to do,' Nigel says.

'Fight back?' she replies with a glare.

'Don't you think it would be good to know what this is all about first?'

'Yes, but now they've taken my memory stick I don't see how that's possible.'

Nigel hesitates, glancing around for some kind of support but not getting any. He isn't giving up though. Ruby now understands why Margaret was happy to see the back of him. He's a dick.

'Fools rush in, remember. Perhaps there's more at stake than you realise. What if there's a rational explanation for all this?'

Danny sighs and she notices that Lucas is also giving Nigel the evils. She's not sure what's got him all riled up – maybe, like her, he just doesn't like the guy.

'You think there's a rational explanation for someone shooting my dad? And threatening to rape your wife?'

'Ex-wife,' Margaret corrects.

'Steady on, we're still marr—' Margaret's glare stops Nigel in his tracks and before he can restart Ruby stands up, making sure she looks at everyone in the room while she speaks. It's something she learnt at the debate practices at school – eye contact helps to convince people that they share the same beliefs as you, even when they might not.

'The one thing I do know is that my dad has always been there for me and now it's my turn to be there for him. But I can't do it on my own.'

'I'm in,' Lucas says immediately. She nods her thanks at him and can see a little grin at the edges of his mouth.

'Me too,' Margaret says. 'I'm not sure how much use I'll be but I do know one end of a rifle from the other. And unlike my ex-husband I'm not willing to lie down and take it up the arse.'

'Margaret!' Nigel protests. 'You can't be saying things like that. And anyway that's not what I'm doing. I'm just trying to stop us going off half-cocked.'

Margaret ignores him, addressing Ruby directly.

'Like I told you before, love, we've seen off the Romans

and the Vikings and even the bloody Picts so we can see off these buggers too.'

Danny takes a more pragmatic approach.

'Let's slow down a moment before grabbing the pitchforks and heading off to the manor house and look at what we know. The seven Ps.'

'What are they?' Ruby asks.

'Proper Planning and Preparation Prevents Piss Poor Performance.'

Baldwin sniggers. Danny winks at him and continues. Ruby smiles, maybe this is going to work. Perhaps the two men have more in common than they think.

'I heard two of their men talking up at the house and it's pretty obvious they expected to come in and get out quickly, taking Ruby with them. So they haven't got the numbers they would have wanted to do this for very long – and if they were going to bring in any more reinforcements they'd have done it by now. They probably don't want to draw any more attention to themselves than they already have. I heard them say there were only nine of them to start with. That's why there's only one guy on each barricade rather than two – they haven't got enough people to do it in shifts so they're probably out on their feet by now. How many soldiers have we seen in the village altogether?'

'There were four at the start,' Ruby says. 'The first guy, who came to the house, but he's . . . out of the picture. Then three more in the ambulance.'

'And have you seen any of those three again?'

'I'm not sure.'

'I think the dead guy in the shelter is the one who chased us,' Lucas says.

'I saw him before,' Margaret says. 'Could be. Same size, built like a brick shithouse.'

Ruby nods but doesn't say anything, letting Danny lead this bit, he's the expert after all. She's keeping an eye on Nigel. He's way too passive. There's something wrong there but she can't quite put her finger on it.

'What about the other guy who was here earlier? Silver, was it?' Danny says.

'I'm sure he was one of the four,' Ruby says. 'I think he's the medical guy, so he was probably in the ambulance.'

'That's right,' Margaret chips in. 'He said he was a medic the last time he was here.'

'So that could be five different guys, but four if we're lucky,' Danny says. 'I saw two guards on patrol at the house, one had longer hair, Red, I think his name was. The other one was called White.'

'Red could have been in the ambulance too,' Margaret chips in. 'One of the stretcher bearers had longish hair.'

'And White was the name of the guy who came after us in the garage. I heard him say his name on the radio,' Ruby adds.

'OK, that's good. He's out of the equation then. The two of them were also talking about a leader called, um . . .'

'Gold,' Lucas adds.

Danny snaps his fingers. 'That's right. Gold. I doubt he's been getting his hands dirty.' He glances at Nigel. 'Officers tend to stick to desk work if they can get away with it.'

The older man mumbles something but no one really hears or cares.

'And Brown was the one shooting at us in the trees yesterday,' Lucas says, excitedly. He turns to Danny. 'You said he'd run away.'

Ruby notices Danny's hesitation and wonders what really happened to Brown.

'He won't be coming back,' Danny says eventually. She has a pretty good idea what he means. He changes the subject before anyone else asks. 'They have a guard at either end of the village and I reckon there's probably at least one extra back at the manor house to help this Gold guy watch your dad – assuming that he's being held there.'

'How many is that altogether?' Margaret asks.

'Nine minimum. Twelve, max,' Baldwin says.

Danny looks at him, a glint of humour in his eyes. Ruby's equally surprised. The man has knocked back two big measures of whisky since they sat down, but still seems lucid. Years of practice, she guesses.

'What?' Baldwin says, lifting his head up. 'I'm an engineer. Counting's my thing. Didn't even use my fingers. It's nine if you're right about the three in the ambulance being seen twice.'

'Nine confirms what I overheard from the patrol so let's work on that. How many do we think are out of action now?' Danny asks.

'Well there's one under our garden for starters,' Margaret says.

'And that White fella is in my pit,' adds Baldwin.

'Plus the guy you said "ran off",' Lucas adds, using his fingers to indicate inverted commas. Contrary to what Ruby thought before, it's clear he hasn't bought Danny's story either.

'And the one my dad stabbed,' Ruby says quietly.

'So four down,' Danny says, 'which leaves five.'

Baldwin nods, clearly happy with the maths.

'What about the gunshot we heard?' Lucas says. 'Could that be another one?'

Ruby sees Danny's eyes flicker a warning to him but it's too late.

'When was this?' she asks.

Lucas closes his eyes, puts his hand to his head.

'Back at the manor house,' Danny says.

Ruby feels like she's been hurled into a cold shower, her earlier ebullience disappearing instantly. She shivers.

'D'you think they shot my dad?' she says, quietly. 'Is that why they radioed for medical help?'

Lucas still isn't looking at her so she keeps focused on Danny, knowing he won't soften things because she's a girl. 'Maybe,' he says. 'Though whether they'd waste time treating him is hard to say. What would be the point? If we're really lucky, he managed to shoot one of them.'

She nods. He could be right. If they're using her dad as bait then they'll want him alive until they've got their hands on her.

'Is there anyone we haven't accounted for?' Danny asks.

Everyone shakes their head.

'Maximum of five then,' Baldwin says. 'Could even be four if one of them has just been shot.'

'And there are six of us,' Ruby says, feeling a little more optimistic.

'Only two of whom have any combat experience,' Nigel says. She's beginning to truly despise him.

'I'm not sure "logistics" counts as combat experience,' Danny says. 'Unless we need someone to do some stock-taking.' Nigel glares at him but says nothing. Ruby's not sure what that all means but can tell it's Danny's way of saying that he's not counting the old man as an asset.

'I've been in a few fights,' Baldwin says. 'Fists mostly, but I think I can hold my own.'

Having seen him in action in the garage Ruby has no doubt that it's more than a few, he actually seemed to be enjoying himself. They just need to hide the whisky.

'And we've got guns,' Margaret says. 'Enough for everyone.' Nigel doesn't exactly look happy that she's put that out there but Ruby is. This could actually work.

'I'm fine,' Danny says, holding up his own rifle.

'Me too,' Ruby adds, taking her dad's pistol out of the rucksack.

Everyone except Lucas looks a little startled but she can't be bothered to explain. With everything that's happened it doesn't seem so crazy any more.

'You got ammo too?' Danny asks. Margaret looks at Nigel who eventually nods.

'D'you think we have a chance?' Ruby asks.

'Realistically? Not really,' Danny says and her heart sinks. 'But if we change the odds a bit more then maybe.'

'How do you propose we do that?' Nigel asks. 'No one else in the village will help you. Seems to me they've all gone into hiding.'

'We take out the guys on the barricades,' Danny says.

54

Danny sits in the garden on his own, thankful for the peace and quiet, completely unused to having other people invading his space and his thoughts. The row with Baldwin was bad but at least it blew over as quickly as it started; Nige's heavy presence is a different thing entirely and the constant bickering with Margaret is getting on his tits. He smiles, self-aware enough to know that he's not been entirely innocent of chipping away at the old fart.

He's wondering if they're biting off more than they can chew. He didn't want to piss on Ruby's bonfire in front of the others but there's basically him and a bunch of well-meaning amateurs, including two pensioners and two kids, taking on a group of heavily armed, highly trained mercenaries. Though having seen some of them in action the training may not have been all that.

Lucas is a good kid, he can shoot and follow instructions, but he's sixteen years old. Baldwin's a scrapper but he's also a drunk, no stamina and even less judgement. Nige can talk the talk but he's no fighter; a desk jockey to his boots, always has been, always will be.

Which leaves the two women. Well one woman and a girl. Margaret's as tough as old boots but she's no spring chicken and he can tell she's still pretty shaken up from what happened earlier with that soldier. Ruby's spirited and willing but she froze when the guard confronted them on the street and probably would again. Scout gets off the garden sofa and, sensing his owner's worries, trots over to join Danny, who thinks that the dog might actually be more use than most of the rest of them. All in all it's not much of a hand they've got.

And with that thought the germ of a plan begins to take seed. He checks that nobody's watching and goes back over to the hatch.

Baldwin is fast asleep in the front room and Margaret and Nigel are in the kitchen arguing about making something to eat. Ruby wonders if her mum and dad would have ended up like that if they'd had the chance. It's getting a little tedious so she taps Lucas on the hand.

'Let's go upstairs,' she says. His eyes light up but she rolls hers. 'To talk,' she adds. He fakes disappointment so badly that she can't decide whether he's messing with her or flirting. She really is a novice at this stuff. If only Liv were around – her friend understands boys a lot better than Ruby does. She worries that he's not taking the situation seriously enough – if there's anything he takes seriously. And then she remembers his mum's issues and gives herself a mental slap for thinking that.

Once they're upstairs they head for the small bedroom where the computer is. She's half-hoping she made a mistake earlier and the memory stick will have magically returned. It hasn't. She even gets down on her hands and knees and checks under the desk and around the edges of the carpet but it's no use. She slumps back against the wall, defeated.

'Will you promise not to go ballistic if I tell you something?' Lucas says. 'I don't want any more fights.'

'What is it?'

He looks at her quizzically, not missing the fact that she ignored his question.

'How can I promise when I don't know what you're going to say?' she protests.

Lucas closes the door and sits with his back against it. He may not be getting the promise he wanted but he's clearly not letting her get out of there without going through him. She reckons she could do that if she had to – she once knocked her karate coach off his feet when she attacked before he was quite ready for her and he was way bigger and stronger than Lucas.

'Are you sure the soldier took the memory stick?' he asks.

'Yes. Of course.' But is she? No one actually saw him, did they? 'Why are you asking me that?'

'When I came up for a piss earlier I bumped into Nigel coming out of here.'

'And?'

'Look, I'm not sure, and I don't want you to go crackers . . . but I think he might have had a memory stick in his hand.'

'What? Are you sure?'

'No. That's why I wasn't gonna say anything. He didn't realise I was there and put something in his pocket really quickly. But it might have been the stick. And he was behaving a bit oddly just now. Like he knew more than he was letting on.'

'Did you notice that too?' Ruby said. 'I thought I was just imagining things. He was definitely distracted. And he barely said a word when we were discussing our options.'

'Where was he when the memory stick disappeared?'

'How do I know? I was in the shelter.'

'You must have some idea?'

Ruby thinks back. As far as she knows, Margaret stuck close to the psychopath downstairs so Nigel must have been watching the other guy, the medic.

'I think he was up here,' she says quietly.

Lucas nods. They sit in silence for a moment while she thinks it through.

'He probably had a chance to look at it when we took the jeep to Baldwin's,' Lucas says eventually.

'Maybe even before that,' Ruby says, remembering sitting with Margaret at the kitchen table before Danny and Lucas turned up. Nigel was upstairs for ages. And what about just now when he said he was having a nap?

'The bastard,' she mutters, getting to her feet.

'We don't know anything,' Lucas warns her. 'Why don't I talk to him first?'

'Get out of my way.'

Ruby is raging. She runs downstairs, strides into the kitchen and shoves Nigel in the chest with both hands. He bounces back against the kitchen table, shouting in protest.

'Hey!'

'What happened to the memory stick?'

'What?'

'The memory stick that was in the computer. What have you done with it?'

'I thought that soldier took it,' Margaret says. She has tears streaming down her face and for a moment Ruby wonders if Nigel has hurt her. She suspects it wouldn't be the first time. Then she notices that she has been chopping onions on a wooden board on the table.

'We only have Nigel's word for that, don't we?'

Margaret looks puzzled.

'But that soldier, Silver, searched upstairs when you were in the bunker.'

'That's right,' Nigel says.

'And did anyone actually see him take it?' Ruby asks.

'I was down here being threatened by that psychopath,' Margaret says. 'Nigel was supposed to be keeping an eye on the other one.'

Ruby turns back to the old man, who sighs, clearly having thought he was off the hook.

'Well,' she says. 'Did he take it or not?'

The back door opens and Danny comes in.

'Can you keep the shouting down, girl? You're supposed to be in hiding and you're waking up half the neighbourhood.'

Ruby takes a deep breath, trying to find some control. It used to be her strong point but not any more. She pokes Nigel in the chest again.

'You haven't answered my question.'

'I think you should calm down, young lady.'

'I don't give a rat's arse what you think, *old man*. Why don't you empty out your pockets?'

'I'll do no such thing.'

She turns to Danny.

'Will you help me search him?'

Danny's expression makes it obvious that he'd like nothing better.

'Keep your hands off me,' Nigel says, backing away towards the wall, while keeping a close eye on Danny and Ruby who both close the gap towards him. He holds his hands up to stop them.

'OK. OK. It wasn't the soldier who took the memory stick,' he says. 'It was me.'

Ruby hears Margaret gasp and for a moment she's lost for words. But only for a moment.

'It's mine. Give it back.'

'She's right,' Danny says. 'Her dad left it for her. You should let her have it.'

Nigel turns to look at the other man.

'You were in the army. They said that she had something in her possession that was a threat to national security. It might be dangerous for the girl if she sees something she shouldn't!'

'I don't need your protection,' Ruby says. She looks to

Danny for support but he doesn't seem certain which way to go. Maybe his old army allegiance is a problem. It doesn't matter though as Margaret's clearly outraged.

'Have you been looking at it?' she says, standing up and moving alongside Ruby. There's no doubt whose side she's on.

Nigel hesitates. It's pretty clear he has.

'You had no right!' Ruby says. 'That's private. That's my life on there.'

'If you didn't want anyone else to read it you shouldn't have left it open on the screen.'

She grabs for his pockets and the old man backs away in alarm, taking the memory stick out and holding it up in the air so Ruby can't reach it.

'National security is a serious matter.'

'And did you see anything on it that was a threat when you were snooping around upstairs?' his wife says.

'Possibly. I need to have a further look to be sure.'

'You'd better not be doing this for the reward!'

'No one said anything about a reward!' Baldwin appears in the kitchen doorway, rubbing his eyes. 'You kept that quiet.'

With everyone but her distracted by Baldwin's appearance Ruby makes another lunge for the memory stick but Nigel spins around to avoid her grasp. As he does Margaret plucks the stick from his hand. He turns furiously and back-hands her viciously across the face, knocking her back into the cooker. Everyone freezes in shock except Baldwin who strides across the room and punches Nige full in the face.

'We don't hit women round here,' he says as Nigel staggers backwards into Danny, blood pouring from his nose for the second time that afternoon. The impact seems to bring Danny to life. He grabs Nigel around the throat, picks up the knife from the table, and presses it against his neck.

'Give me one reason I shouldn't kill you now,' he says.

Nigel's face is turning red and he's clearly struggling to breathe but no one cares.

'You OK?' Danny says to Margaret. She nods but there's a bright red mark on her cheek and tears in her eyes.

'He done that before?' Danny asks. She nods again and he tightens his grip on Nigel's neck. Ruby can see a small line of blood trickling from the edge of the blade.

'Please,' Nigel croaks.

'Let him go,' Margaret says quietly. Danny looks like he might protest but then does as he's told. Nigel sinks onto a chair, sucking in air. Margaret hands the stick back to Ruby. 'Go and see what your dad wanted you to know,' she says.

Danny kicks the back of Nigel's chair and waves the knife at him.

'And you need to get the fuck out of here before I cut your head off and feed it to Scout.'

'It's my house,' Nigel says quietly.

'Not any more,' Margaret says. 'And Danny's right. You should leave. Now.'

55

Alex winces as the medic – who claims his name is Silver – stitches his calf back together again. He's back on the same bed. No straps on this time, for the moment anyway, though one of his wrists is handcuffed to the bed frame. Not that he could do much running away with the state his leg's in.

'You're lucky you didn't snap it,' Silver says. 'Those traps are brutal.'

'I don't feel lucky.'

The medic smiles and continues his work.

The trap's jaws cut deeply into the subcutaneous fat of Alex's calf which was a weird yellow colour. He had almost fainted after Gold pulled the trap apart to release his leg and he'd seen how bad the injury was. Not as bad as that shithead Red's, obviously. At least he'd managed to take another one of them out.

'Are you the guy who treated my shoulder too?'

Silver nods.

'You were lucky again there, the bullet went straight

through. It could have ricocheted all over the place, done all sorts of damage.'

'Living a charmed life, aren't I?'

'Not as charmed as the girl and her boyfriend. Not sure how they've kept out of sight. Though we know who he is now so it won't be long.'

Alex doesn't want to show his ignorance but curiosity gets the better of him.

'Enlighten me.'

'Kid named Lucas. Troublemaker apparently.'

Alex pictures a tall gangly lad he's heard vague stories about. First time he's heard his name mentioned in the same breath as Ruby's though.

'Looks like it's news to you,' Silver says. 'You wouldn't be the first dad who didn't know what his kids were up to.'

The medic seems a little bit out of place compared to the other soldiers Alex has seen so far, i.e., not actually a sociopath.

'How did you end up doing this?'

'Medicine?' the guy says.

'Working for these mercenary bastards,' Alex clarifies.

Silver sighs. 'Didn't quite make it through medical school. Got to earn a living and they pay well. I have a family to look after.'

'Me too.'

The medic reaches into his bag and unpacks a field dressing to cover the stitches. As he does the door bursts open and Gold enters the room.

'Where's Black?'

'He went to look at the drone footage.'

'The jeep's gone. I thought I made it clear, I don't want people going solo.'

'We don't have much choice, do we, we're spread pretty thinly. Anyway, he's a big boy, he can take care of himself.'

'It's not his health I'm worried about. It's what he's capable of. He's not exactly the poster boy for "leave no trace". You're supposed to be keeping him on a leash.'

Silver holds up the field dressing.

'I can't be in two places at once.'

Gold grumbles something, turns on his heel and walks off. It's clear there's no love lost there. Alex wonders if he can plant a few more doubts in Silver's head.

'He seems a little stressed,' Alex says.

'It's a stressful business.'

'Not a great sign in a leader.'

Silver smiles. 'I know what you're doing. Don't bother. It won't work.'

'You do seem to be a bit short on manpower, though,' Alex says.

'No thanks to you,' Silver says. 'Did you really kill Red?'

Alex nods. 'It was an accident but I can't say I'm sorry.'

'No great loss,' the man mutters.

'Not a friend of yours then?'

'You could say that. Man was off his box. And he's not the only one. But I'm not doing this to make friends.'

'Why are you doing it?'

'I'm a medic. It's what I do.'

'But your friends are going to kill me anyway. As far as

I can tell they're only keeping me alive to lure Ruby here. Isn't that right?'

Silver frowns. 'That's above my pay grade. These guys operate on a need-to-know basis and all I need to know is that this time next week I'll be lying on a beach in the Med with my wife and kids.'

'Kids?'

'Two girls.'

'Imagine how you'd feel if someone tried to take one of your daughters.'

The medic puts the final piece of tape on the bandage and gives Alex a long look.

'But Ruby's not *your* daughter, is she?'

56

*Your mum's millionaire boyfriend gave her a basement apart-
ment in his swanky house in Kensington. The one he lived in
with his wife.*

*Apparently he'd promised Emma that she and the future
baby would get the best medical care money could buy. The
man's wife couldn't have children and they didn't want to
adopt so his other half was delighted with the arrangement.
Don't get me wrong, I don't have a problem with surrogacy, it's
brilliant for couples who can't have a child, but this whole thing
seemed dodgy and moving at a frantic pace and I hoped I was
in time to talk her out of it. Not least because back then it was
against the law. Luckily she'd given Rosie a forwarding address.*

*The first time I went to the house I got lucky. There were
large wrought iron gates on the entrance and an intercom off
to one side. The man of the house was at work but I persuaded
the guy who answered that I was a relative of Emma's and,
astonishingly, he let me in. I don't know if he was having a
bad day or just not very competent but I doubt he still had a
job the next day.*

He pointed me to a door at the side of the house where I was met by a frumpy middle-aged woman, who showed me where to go. I wouldn't normally be quite so judgemental about someone's looks but you will see why I mention this later.

The woman led me to a suite – a large living area with a separate bedroom and bathroom – and opened the door for me. I was puzzled why she would do that but when I walked in I understood. Your mum was lying in bed. She was clearly shocked but almost immediately gave me a huge beaming smile. She looked radiant. And heavily pregnant.

It's official. Ruby knows that this baby is her – it has to be, given the timing and everything. She was a fucking surrogate baby. And Alex is not her father. It's not possible – he says himself that he hadn't seen her mum for almost a year. Her heart is racing and she wonders if she's going to have a panic attack.

A few days ago she was looking forward to celebrating her sixteenth birthday and now she knows that her whole life has been a lie. She'd obviously suspected it from the earlier bit of the letter but having it confirmed is a real hammer blow. She closes her eyes and takes a deep breath, exhaling slowly, trying desperately to keep a lid on things, while simultaneously watching a highlights reel of all her previous birthdays on the back of her eyelids; the cakes, the presents, the candles growing in number each time. Always just the two of them celebrating. Her 'dad' the only ever-present presence in the images. And the only ever-present liar in her life. She opens her eyes, calmer but somehow angrier too. How could he do this to her? She has to know the answer so she turns back to the screen.

I know this is all a shock to you and maybe I should have started with the headline news but it felt like it would be too much to throw the big stuff in early. I didn't want to freak you out straight away. Or maybe I'm justifying it to myself for being cowardly. You pay your money and you take your choice.

Despite herself Ruby smiles. That's another of her dad's favourite sayings. Alex's favourite sayings. What the hell is she supposed to call him now? If she ever gets the chance to call him anything again. She presses on.

You're a smart cookie so I'm sure you've done the maths and worked out that I'm not your father – not biologically anyway. I'm your uncle. Emma was my sister. For the record: it's important for you to know that almost from the start I have considered myself your dad and always will but I understand if you choose to disregard that. I've done the best I could but if you're reading this alone it means I have let you down badly. To be fair, I have had to learn on the job, not having had the best tutors.

Some background – all true this time, I promise.

Emma and I were both put into foster care when we were in our early teens. Our mum, your grandma, was killed in a car accident – our so-called dad had abandoned us years before. Thankfully we were placed in the same town. I got lucky – my foster parents were a little too old to bring up a teenage boy

*but they were fundamentally decent. Emma's weren't. The rest
you know now. Hopefully we can talk more about this in person
soon – you must have a thousand questions. I've imagined every
circumstance in which you would have to read this without me
around and few of them have ended happily. For now, I'll move
on. Back to the apartment. Emma seemed shocked but pleased
to see me. The woman who'd shown me to the suite left us for a
while – turned out she was Emma's nurse. I've tried to recreate
some of our conversation; I wanted you to get a flavour of your
mum – to see how much she wanted you. It may not be one
hundred per cent verbatim but the sense of it is right.*

'What are you doing, Emma?'

'Pretty obvious, isn't it? Look at the size of my belly.'

'How are you feeling?'

'Fine. Blood pressure's a bit up and down but apart from
that . . .'

'It's great to see you.'

'Vicky verky. Why don't you sit down?'

I sat on the edge of the bed and took Emma's hand and we
stared at each other for a while, like we were trying to see if
anything had changed much. She was obviously carrying a
little more weight – most of it you! But apart from that she
was the same Emma I'd last seen some eleven months earlier.
Despite that I still wanted to get her out of there. The whole
set-up creeped me out.

'How did you find me?' she asked.

'Rosie contacted me. She was worried about you.'

'No need. Like I said, I'm fine.'

'Why didn't you tell me about your foster dad?'

'Wasn't your problem. I knew how you'd react. Didn't want you to get in bother.'

'I wish you'd told me.'

'Water under the bridge.'

'I suppose. How are they treating you?'

'Grand. I can eat what I want. They've got a chef here who can turn his hand to anything. Though he does like to serve spinach with pretty much everything. Simon says it's bursting with good stuff though, so that's OK.'

'Where is this Simon?'

'At work, I suppose. He's hardly ever here. Just pops down late at night to check on me. It's mainly Laura and Janet keeping an eye on me.'

'The nurses?'

'Janet's a midwife. She'll be in soon.'

'Right.'

'Don't look so judgey, Jonathan, I know what I'm doing. I really want to have this baby. Look, feel her.'

'Her?'

'I know it's a girl. I just know it.'

She took my hand and placed it on her extended belly.

'Your hand's freezing.'

'I'm sorry.'

'Can you feel her?'

'I'm not sure. I don't think so . . . oh, God, yes, she just kicked me.'

'She does that a lot. I think she's going to be feisty.'

'Like her mum.'

'I guess.'

'So how can you bear to give her up?'

Emma frowned and looked over to the door, clearly checking that the nurse wasn't listening in. Thankfully she'd closed it on her way out. She leant over towards me.

'I'm not going to,' she said, quietly.

A door slams downstairs. Ruby comes up for air again. She closes down the document to give her time to think. She can't get her head around this at all. How could her mum be so naive to think that this Simon would let her keep a baby that he's paid twenty thousand pounds for? And where's the man's wife in all this? Was she really happy that her husband had moved a pregnant girl into the house? Maybe he kept his wife in the attic! Except for the pregnancy it's all sounding a bit Jane Eyre-ish.

She's just delaying the inevitable so she opens up the file again but as it loads she catches a glimpse of a photo embedded at the end. She knows her dad – Alex, she corrects herself – asked her to read everything in chronological order but her curiosity gets the better of her. Maybe it's a photo of her mum? She's only ever seen one or two of those in her life. She scrolls down only to find it's an image of a middle-aged man. It's clearly a posed photo, a bit too polished, certainly not a selfie. The man is handsome, or at least would have been when he was a bit younger. He looks like he's in his early fifties in the photo, short dark hair going slightly grey at the sides. He's smiling but like Nigel's attempt earlier, it doesn't suit him. Ruby doesn't like the look of him though he's very well-dressed, a sharp grey suit and blue tie – every inch the businessman but there's a nagging familiarity there, like she's seen him before somewhere.

Someone knocks on the door.

'Come in.' Ruby swivels her chair around.

Margaret sticks her head in the room. The dark red mark on her cheek looks even worse now.

'I just thought you should know that Nigel's gone.'

'Good. You OK?'

Margaret nods and glances at the computer. 'How's it going?'

Ruby goes to say 'fine' – her default answer to the question – but this time the word sticks in her throat. It's very fucking far from fine. She can feel herself starting to tear up. She's not sure she can handle all this on her own. Margaret senses her confusion and steps into the room.

'Maybe you should wait until you see your dad again rather than read all that. It might be better to hear it from the horse's mouth, so to speak.'

'I'm not sure that I want to see him again. And maybe it's not even possible. What if we're too late?'

'Danny's got a plan. I could see it in his eyes. He's gone out too.'

'You sure he's not gone after Nigel? I thought he was going to kill him earlier.'

'Positive. He went out the back way first, to take Scout for a walk. Told me he'd be a little while, that he was going back to his place to get some clean clothes on. Though he did have a shifty look about him. I'm pretty sure it'll be something to do with rescuing your dad.'

At the word *dad* Ruby's tears start to fall. She tries to hold them back but it's no use.

As Margaret moves to comfort her she gets a glimpse of the screen. She looks puzzled.

'Why have you got that photo up?'

'I don't know yet. My dad put it on the memory stick. Right at the end.'

Margaret's puzzled look changes to one of real concern. She actually looks scared. Which means Ruby is too.

'You know who it is, don't you?'

Margaret nods.

'That's Simon De Vere.'

The name sounds familiar but Ruby can't pin it down. She shakes her head.

'Who's he, when he's at home? The Prime Minister?'

She laughs at her own joke but Margaret is stony-faced.

'Close, but no cigar,' she says. 'He's the Secretary of State for Defence.'

57

Danny watches the armed guard from behind a parked van. The man looks out on his feet. He's perched on the edge of the first barrier staring into space, his rifle across his lap. By Danny's estimate the soldier's been there for more than twenty-four hours without a break. He should be an easy target.

Scout is sitting at his feet, happy to be out and about after being cooped up in the garden with that scuddy little terrier of Margaret's. Like his master, Scout generally prefers his own company. Danny reaches into his bag and pulls out his trump card, leaving it at Scout's feet. The dog starts to stand but Danny holds his hand up.

'Stay,' he says, moving out from behind the van and strolling towards the soldier. He's halfway there before the man even sees him. Danny almost feels sorry for the guy but the man has clearly made some bad life choices and now he's going to pay for them.

'Halt,' the soldier shouts, reaching for his rifle and clambering slowly to his feet. Danny keeps on moving but puts his hands up in the air to show that he's no threat. Even though he most definitely is.

'Final warning. Stop or I'll shoot,' the soldier says as Danny gets within ten yards of him. This time Danny does as he's told. Tiredness can lead to mistakes and the man's finger is too close to the trigger to piss about.

'You need to turn around and go back home.' The soldier jerks his rifle back towards the houses as if Danny doesn't know where he lives.

'I've got some information about the girl,' he says.

The soldier moves towards him, too far away for Danny to pounce but give it time.

'What information? If you know where she is you'd better tell me now.'

'What's in it for me?'

'I won't fucking shoot you.'

'Can't talk if I'm dead.'

The soldier studies him for a moment and reaches for his radio but then changes his mind.

'What do you want in return?'

'If I tell you where she is I want you to let me leave the village.'

'No chance.'

'No one will need to know and you'll be the hero of the hour. Probably a nice bonus in it for you too. All you have to do is turn your back for a second and I'll be gone, just like that.' Danny clicks his fingers to indicate how quickly he'd disappear.

Out of the corner of his eye Danny can see that Scout

hears his cue and comes out from behind the van, moving silently towards them. As he nears them the soldier senses movement to the side and sees the dog approaching.

'That yours?' he says, nodding at Scout.

Danny turns his head fully now and flicks it towards the soldier, a signal Scout knows well.

'Never seen him before.'

Scout is nearing the soldier now and the man sees that he's holding something in his mouth.

'Jesus Christ,' he says. 'Is that what I think it is?'

The dog stops right in front of the armed man and drops his trophy at his feet. It's a severed hand.

The soldier crouches down to examine the hand and sees the letters tattooed across the knuckles. E, W, M and N.

'What the fuck? Is that Black's hand? Where the hell did he get that from?'

He looks up but he's far too late. Danny smashes him in the head with the tyre lever he had concealed down the back of his pants and he's out like a light. Man should be grateful it wasn't the samurai sword treatment that his pal Black got.

Scout barks as the man hits the ground and Danny pats the dog on the head.

'Good boy,' he says.

Within minutes the soldier's legs and arms are cable-tied and he's been dragged into the woods and roped to a tree, masking tape covering his entire face apart from a small gap for his nose. Minimum force hasn't always been

Danny's approach but the guy's had a shitty day and probably doesn't deserve to die just yet.

He stands back to inspect his work, satisfied that the odds have improved again.

It's time to make their move.

58

'You think he's your real dad?'

Lucas's wavering finger is pointing at the photo of the Secretary of State for Defence, the Right Honourable Simon De Vere MP.

Ruby nods. In a normal world she would have googled the shit out of him by now but she doesn't live in that world any more. Maybe she never will again.

'Don't you think he looks like me?'

Lucas examines the image more closely.

'I guess. And so that would make Alex . . .?'

'My uncle. He was my mum's brother.'

'Fuuuuck!' Lucas mutters, drawing it out appropriately.

She can't think of anything else to say. She's always been one of those driven kids who prepares like crazy for every eventuality. She once sat up reading *Hamlet* all night to prepare for a mock exam. But how do you prepare for a hand grenade suddenly being tossed into your quiet little life? She just has to hope that the scars aren't too deep so she can clear up the damage and head towards something a bit more normal. But who with? This guy in the photo? She really can't imagine it. But Alex may not even still be alive. And if he is, how can she forgive him for all the lies?

Lucas sits down beside her, edges his chair as close as he can get it and puts his arm around her, somehow knowing that's exactly what she needs at this precise moment. She leans her head into his shoulder and closes her eyes.

After Margaret's revelation about Simon De Vere she had just sat there, staring at the screen, hoping that she might soon wake up from this insane nightmare. She was so quiet that Margaret had fetched Lucas in the hope he could get through to her. She'd obviously briefed him on the headline news.

'Take your time,' Lucas whispers. 'I'll still be here when you're ready to talk.'

'I'm a surrogate baby.'

There's a long silence, like he can't deal with that or something. Maybe he thinks she's weird now. After what seems an age he finally speaks.

'I have no clue what that means,' he says.

Ruby snorts with laughter, she can't help it, it's the release she needs.

'What?' he says. 'I can't know everything.'

Now she's started laughing she can't seem to stop. This whole thing is off the scale batshit crazy. If she wasn't laughing she'd be crying and fuck that, she's all cried out. She points at the screen.

'It means that this man paid my mum to have me. Like he could just buy anything.'

Lucas blinks a couple of times, like a slow computer considering a calculation.

'So she was gonna give you away?'

Ruby thinks back to the last thing Alex had written in the letter: *I'm not going to.*

'I'm not sure. Maybe at first but then she changed her mind. I guess I'll never know, given she died having me – assuming that wasn't another lie.'

Lucas holds her a little tighter.

'How did you end up with your dad?' he asks.

'I have no idea,' she says, reaching for the mouse. 'D'you want to find out?'

He nods, then goes to speak again but hesitates.

'What?' she says.

'Are we still calling Alex "your dad"?'

To be my dad or not to be my dad, that is the real question, she thinks. Bollocks to whatever Hamlet thought it was.

'For now,' she says, scrolling back up to where she left off and hoping that the rest of this wouldn't force her to change her mind.

59

Silver knows that the mission is coming to an end one way or another and he's beginning to wonder whether he's on the wrong team again. It was bad enough back in Rojava where you had no idea who you were fighting with or for half the time. One day you'd be alongside guys from the States battling the Russians, the next it would be the other way around. And sometimes you couldn't remember whether you were fighting for the Syrian government or the Kurds – not that most people cared. A job is a job. However, the story that Alex just told him is preying on his mind. He's worked for some bad men in the past but De Vere might well take the shitty biscuit.

And it's not just that. Gold's decision to copy the stupid colour-naming trick from *Reservoir Dogs* has unsurprisingly proved a curse, as it did in the film. Green and Red are dead, Brown and White have vanished off the face of the earth and Black's gone AWOL The colours are fading, he thinks, then laughs. His wife is always telling him that he doesn't have a sense of humour but that wasn't bad.

He knows he has to get a grip. That trip to the Med with the wife and kids will be even further off if he messes this job up. And she's not the forgiving type. On the plus side, the fewer of them left, the bigger his share of the money. Maybe he can upgrade to the Windies to keep her happy.

He stops the ambulance at the barrier and waits for Grey, the guard there, to move it so he can get through. It's slow progress, the poor guy must be out on his feet – he's been there for way more than a day without a rest. Gold might not be the idiot that Red believed but he severely underestimated the numbers they needed to get the job done this time – though it would have been hard to anticipate Green's premature attempt to be a hero.

Eventually the barriers and the stinger are pulled to one side so he can drive into the village but Grey is clearly bored out of his skull and signals to him to stop. He winds the window down.

'How much longer d'you think we're going to be here?' he asks.

'Not long now. We can't keep this place locked down forever. If we don't find her soon we're going to have to call it quits. Did you see Black come through here earlier?'

'Aye, he was driving like a maniac, didn't wait for me to move anything, just careered around the barriers like Lewis fucking Hamilton. Nearly hit the wall on his way through. He was lucky I recognised him cos I was ready to shoot the bastard.'

Close up the man looks exhausted. Silver doubts he could hit an elephant's backside with a banjo but he just nods to acknowledge the shit the poor guy's having to put up with.

'Don't suppose you know where he was heading, do you?'

'Not a Scooby, didn't get the chance to ask him, the speed he was going. Wouldn't be surprised if you find he's turned the thing upside down somewhere.'

Silver thanks the guy and moves off, slowly driving the ambulance down the main village street looking for a sign of the jeep. How he's ended up baby-sitting a psychopath like Black is beyond his comprehension. He must have done something very bad in a previous life. Oh, yeah, that's right, he did. When he eventually gets to those pearly gates he's going to have to get his story straight or he's heading downstairs. Might be easier to buy some asbestos underwear.

He scans the streets as he drives, desperately searching for something; the girl would be the dream ticket, the jeep useful, one of his fellow soldiers a consolation prize, but the place is deserted. Clearly the villagers have taken their warning about the escaped prisoner seriously though half the houses seem empty anyway. Second home syndrome, Gold calls it.

He drives all the way to the end of the village to check with the guard there but as he turns the corner to get sight of the barricades it's pretty obvious that it's another fruitless task. There's no one there. He stops the ambulance and gets out, rifle in hand. The barriers are all in place, the stinger in between them but no other sign of life. Not another fucking deserter. He thinks about calling it in but what's the point? There's only Gold back at base and he's not going to leave the prisoner unguarded. And unless he can find Black there's pretty much no one else to ask for help.

Silver checks the area. The snow looks like it's been kicked around a bit just in front of the first barrier and there are a few fag ends scattered around but that's it. He trudges back to the ambulance, turns it around and heads back through the village to the boy's house, Lucas, the old man back at the house had called him.

He knows it's probably a wild goose chase, the old man was just showing off, telling him who the kid was and where he lived, but it's just around the corner so he may as well check it out. Predictably, the house is deserted. These kids aren't stupid or they'd have found them before now. He decides to do one more tour of Coldburn before heading back to base.

When he reaches the village green in the centre he stops and puts the handbrake on. It's a ghost town. There's a huge cat sitting on a wall at the side of the road looking like he owns the place but no other sign of life. He turns the engine off and takes out a cigarette. His wife thinks he's given up – and he will – it's just another promise he's failed to stick to in a long line of them.

He might have to renege on this being his last mission if they don't find the girl. There's no way the head honcho will pay the big bucks he promised – if he'll pay them at all. It's a total shitshow all round. He closes his eyes, imagining a sandy beach, his wife lying in the blazing sun while his daughters paddle in the crystal clear waters. He's sitting in a nearby beach bar, in his cool shades, smiling as he watches them. Then he imagines what he'd do if someone tried to take one of them. He'd scorch the fucking earth to get them back. He opens his eyes again, stubs out the cigarette and drives on.

Almost immediately he sees a man standing on the corner of one of the side roads, waving his arms at the approaching vehicle. As he gets closer he recognises the guy. It's the old man from the house who told him about the boy. The one who came back from the dead, well, temporarily at least. He wonders what bullshit story he's got to tell him this time.

60

I don't know why Emma thought she could just walk away from the deal she'd struck with this Simon. I think she'd been fooled by his smart clothes and fancy wines into thinking he was a reasonable man.

I wish now I'd pushed her more but before I got a proper chance the midwife, Janet Moore, turned up demanding I leave and within minutes I'd been rather brusquely escorted from the building and thrown off the premises.

I sat outside the main gates for hours, hoping that he or his wife would come back but they never did. The first time they opened again was to let Janet Moore back out. As she waited inside her car for the gates to swing slowly open she stared at me through the bars and I could see she was nervous. She wound down her window, reached into her bag and took out something.

When she pulled out of the gateway she quietly urged me not to move or even look at her and dropped a card out of the open window before pulling away. I waited until she had gone and the gates were closed before moving. There was a CCTV camera pointing at the gates but she had pulled out of its range so no one could see me. I picked up the card. On it she had scribbled 'Holland Park. Café. 3pm.'

It was a cold day and the park was empty which was probably why she'd chosen it. Despite the weather she was sitting outside, clearly not wanting anyone inside the café to overhear us. She even made me sit on a separate table so no one watching would think we were together.

The first words she spoke were 'You need to get your sister out of there.' I've never forgotten them and not a day goes by that I don't think about how things might have been different if I'd managed to do just that. God knows I tried.

First of all she gave me the lowdown on Simon De Vere – it was the first time I heard his full name but it didn't mean anything to me then. Janet Moore hated him. She had desperately needed a job; she'd been sacked from her last one for stealing from the pharmacy. Her sister needed life-saving drugs which were insanely expensive and it was a last resort but she got caught. She was on the verge of losing her house when De Vere offered her a way out – to help look after a pregnant girl – which she gladly accepted. She had no idea how he had found her but it had seemed like a gift from heaven. Although surrogacy was technically illegal she had no moral objections to it so talked herself into believing she was doing a good thing.

She'd been working for him for almost two months before your mum showed up, preparing the suite at first and hiring a nurse to do the day-to-day care. Clearly De Vere had no doubts that his grooming of your mother would lead her to accept his offer. Or maybe he had other young women on the go and just hoped that one of them would succumb. Regardless, in that brief time she had lost two young nurses who both left because of the man's predatory behaviour towards them. In the end she'd hired the oldest and plainest nurse she could find – the one who had showed me into the suite that day. All of that was bad enough but there was worse to come. Much worse.

Firstly your mum let slip to Janet that she hadn't been artificially inseminated as the midwife had believed. De Vere had insisted that they actually had sex to conceive you, more than once, apparently. It was either that or the deal was off. Whatever you think of her decision to go ahead with that please remember that he was a rich, influential 44-year-old man with all the power and she had just turned 18. Janet Moore believed he was as near to a paedophile as made no difference.

I urged her to come to the police with me but she refused, insisting that I didn't know what he was capable of. She had really done her research, and obviously I've done a lot more since. De Vere had been in the army but made his name in the security industry and now ran a company called Claustra, which provided services to both private enterprise and the military. He married into money and was extremely well connected with friends in high places, including the Prime Minister. She was terrified of the man. It was already sounding ominous but then she dropped the real bomb.

She had been worried about your mother's health and had persuaded De Vere to bring a doctor in to examine her. She was right. Emma was suffering from pre-eclampsia, which basically means her blood pressure was so high that there was a risk that either she, the baby or both could die if the pregnancy *went to full term. De Vere had screamed at the midwife and the doctor that his child (you) would not be delivered prematurely and that she could not be moved to a hospital for the birth no matter what the risks. He told them to fix it. And he refused to give your mum any say in the matter or even tell her about the diagnosis – he even got his security people to put listening devices in the rooms to make sure no one else told her. I wonder now if he knew that Emma was planning on reneging on their deal and thought this was the easiest way to resolve that problem. Regardless of his motivation, Janet Moore firmly believed that Emma might die giving birth. I tried again to get her to tell the police what she'd told me but she practically ran away from me.*

Ruby stops reading and rolls her chair away from the screen. Alex has never hidden the reality of her mum's death from her – it looks like he wasn't lying about that – but reading that her real father had known she was in danger and done nothing about it is heartbreaking.

She glances across at Lucas who hardly seems to be breathing, anger coming off him in waves.

'This is hard-core, Rubes,' he says. 'It's difficult for me to read. I can't imagine how it's making you feel.'

'It's making me feel that my real dad's a fucking monster.'

'D'you think that he's behind what's been happening here?' he says. 'Is he the one who's after you?'

She's been thinking of nothing else since she found out who 'Simon' was. And now she's read about his past involvement in a so-called security company she's absolutely certain.

'Who else could get away with holding an entire village captive? Remember what Nigel said, that the police confirmed it was an "official situation" and everything was under control. The old man might be a twat but I don't think he was lying about that.'

Lucas nods at the screen. 'How did Alex get you away from him?'

'Your guess is as good as mine,' she says, rolling back to the screen.

The next day I went to the police station but was practically laughed out of the place. What evidence did I have? My sister was a grown-up and if she wanted to complain they were all ears but where was she? I should be careful, making such baseless accusations about a pillar of the community.

I had given Janet Moore my phone number and to be fair she did what she could. She kept me in the picture and even managed to tell Emma about the risk to her life when she was helping her take a shower – hoping the noise would drown out what she was saying if De Vere was listening in. Your mum told her that you were her only consideration – that she would gladly sacrifice herself if it meant you would be healthy but that she didn't believe it would come to that. She felt 'fine'.

Over the next few weeks I tried everything. I was threatened with being locked up for wasting police time the third time I went to the station. I tried every newspaper I could but they laughed in my face. Didn't I know how litigious Simon De Vere was? I tried to get back in to see Emma but security had been beefed up and there was no way I was getting in without a fight. So that was what I gave them. They beat me up so badly I was in hospital for three days. My attempt to press charges was also laughed off – several witnesses said I was trespassing on private property and had assaulted a security guard. The police reckoned I should be thankful that Mr De Vere wasn't pressing charges against me. The fact that I ended up with three broken ribs, a broken nose and two dislocated fingers was just 'unfortunate'. It was becoming obvious that Simon De Vere was untouchable.

I have to be honest, Ruby, I had just about given up at this stage. I couldn't get near your mum and no one in authority would listen to me. Janet Moore hadn't called for days. When I was discharged from the hospital I rented a small flat as close to De Vere's house as I could afford. I knew I wouldn't have to stay there for long, one way or another. I left several messages on the midwife's phone, telling her where she could find me, but all to no avail.

Then, about a week after I'd come out of hospital, I was woken up by loud banging on my front door. It was Janet Moore. When I opened the door she thrust a bundle into my arms. You.

She turned to go but I managed to grab her arm.

'What about Emma?' I said.

'I'm sorry. She's dead,' the midwife said.

I couldn't breathe. I hoped I'd misheard her but knew I hadn't. I think I would have collapsed if I hadn't had you in my arms. It was like I instinctively knew my job now was to protect you.

'She fought so hard but lost too much blood in the end. De

Vere never even blinked,' the midwife continued. 'I wouldn't be surprised if they put your poor sister's body in a skip. I couldn't let him anywhere near that child.'

She practically sprinted away. I shouted my thanks but I don't think she even heard me. Within a week she was dead. Beaten to death during an attempted mugging in the street. Or so it said in the papers. I didn't believe that story for a second but you and I were long gone by then.

Suddenly the screen goes blank. Ruby taps on the mouse but nothing happens.

'You've got to be fucking joking me,' she says, clicking again, then checking the lead hasn't fallen out. There are footsteps pounding up the stairs and she worries that the soldiers are back but it's Danny who bursts into the room.

'I think they've taken down the power,' he says.

'Haven't they got a generator here?' Ruby asks. Her dad had put one in years ago.

'Margaret says no. Apparently Nigel was too tight-fisted to pay for one,' Danny explains. 'Regardless, we need to get out of here. I think this means they're coming for us.'

61

Danny is busy cleaning a shotgun barrel on the kitchen table. He knows full well that, normally, once the power is taken out an attack is imminent – been there, done that – and he's anxious that they should get their retaliation in first. It's classic *Art of War* stuff – attack when least expected.

He's already given Ruby a simple lesson in using her gun – which she apparently found in her dad's safe. It was in surprisingly good nick. Danny had shown Alex how to maintain it after he'd sourced it for him but hadn't really thought that the man would do it. Now it's obvious that, given who he was up against, Alex was very highly motivated.

Lucas has Danny's own rifle to hand and Margaret has produced the shotgun from somewhere in the house. Baldwin, who seems to have finally sobered up a little, has claimed the one he took from the soldier in his garage. Danny will still make sure the man is in front of him when they set off. This will be hard enough without any friendly fire incidents.

The others are waiting patiently for him to finish his

checks, apart from Ruby, who's clearly itching to go. She's brought them all up to speed on what she's found out about her past but is frustrated that the power was taken out before she could finish reading and is desperate to talk to Alex to find out what happened next. Danny wasn't entirely surprised to be told that Simon De Vere was behind this. The man had previous.

'Never met the man but I nearly ended working for his company once,' he says, immediately getting everyone's attention.

'When I left the army in 2005 I was approached by one of his recruitment people who said they were looking for people with my qualifications. They were putting together a team of men to support military operations in the Middle East and needed someone to lead it. I have to admit I was tempted, I'd been thrown out of the army for punching a senior officer and knew that there wouldn't exactly be a queue of prospective employers waiting for me. I was surprised they wanted me, to be honest.

'But after I'd had a chat with a few old comrades I realised that I was exactly the kind of man that Claustra came looking for. They had a history of recruiting army rejects, men with a chip on their shoulder or a reputation for extreme violence – mainly because they knew they'd be desperate for work and they could pay them well below the going rate for trained professionals. And then they could go in low for government contracts – under-bidding companies that were paying proper wages and recruiting men who were at the top of their game. And they could compete internationally against the firms who were recruiting hardened soldiers from Latin America at a much cheaper price than Brits.

'Everyone knew that De Vere – who wasn't a politician then – had the ear of the government, a real insider. He was one of the first businessmen to realise that the government didn't care about doing the job properly, it cared about making its friends and supporters money – and handing out contracts to them is the easy way to do it. Look at what happened with PPE at the start of the pandemic – exactly the same thing, giving contracts to their friends regardless of who was best placed to provide the service they needed. One guy they contracted ran a fucking pub, for God's sake.

'And then there were the war stories I heard about atrocities in the Middle East and Afghanistan, the cold-blooded murder of women and children. Some of them, sadly, were carried out by the regular army but the vast majority of the offenders were contractors, mercenaries basically, and many of those were people working for Claustra. It was mostly hushed up but real army people knew the truth and that was enough for me. I told them I wasn't interested.'

Lucas puts his hand up.

'You're not at school, lad, if you've got something to say just say it.'

'If this man's so powerful why wouldn't he have sent more soldiers? And you said they weren't any good. Wouldn't he have sent in his best?'

'Plausible deniability, I reckon. A larger team would raise all kinds of red flags – it would be too obvious that something big was going down. And I doubt he expected much resistance. He was sure it would be a quick in and out and hoped no one would notice. And as to those he has used here, if it all went to shit that would be his defence if it came back to bite him on the arse. "I'm the Secretary of State for Defence. If I wanted to hire a private army I could afford a better one than these jokers."

'From what I've seen of these guys in the village, it's got Claustra written all over it. A group of gung-ho individuals, undisciplined and out of control with no leadership in sight. De Vere was supposed to have severed his links with the company when he became a minister but people like him always want to have their cake and eat it. He'll still have his fingers in the pie and be collecting his dividends, you can bet on that. So when he needed someone to carry out his dirty work, he's gone back to the place he knows best, probably hired them via some shell company based in the Caymans to keep his name out of it.'

He looks around the room, making sure to catch their eyes.

'The good news is that we outnumber them now. We can take these bastards down,' he says.

Ruby straps her rucksack to her back, her newly cleaned gun safely tucked away in the front pocket. She grins at Lucas then puts on her game face. She's ready to go. The group make their final checks in the hallway. They're going on foot to avoid attracting too much attention. Danny has told them how he took out the guard at the nearest end of the village and is planning to do much the same with the one who stands between them and the manor house. If it ain't broke, don't fix it. If they're lucky – and they've counted correctly – there might then only be two men between them and Alex.

One thing is still bothering her though. She turns to Danny.

'How did De Vere think this was going to work out? Did he really think I would be happy to be taken back to him after all this time? Why do all this?'

'Because he can,' Danny says. She's about to ask him what he means but then realises it may seem too simple but he's right. It's nothing to do with her. It's all about exercising power. She nods, which he clearly takes as permission to carry on.

'Everyone ready?' Danny says and the others nod too, smiles gone now, just a grim acceptance that this will all be over soon and they'll have their village back. Or be dead. There's no middle ground.

Ruby opens the front door and stops in her tracks. She is face to face with the wrong end of a gun which Silver, the medic, is pointing at her. Behind him, in the street outside the house, Nigel is sitting in the passenger seat of the ambulance.

'Gotcha,' Silver says.

62

'Everyone slowly lower your weapons to the floor,' Silver says. 'Then kneel down and put your hands on your head.'

Danny can see the rest of them glance at him, looking for a lead. He knows that everyone else is thinking the same thing: it's five against one. But the one has beaten them to the punch and they're trapped in the narrow confines of Margaret's hallway. It's a bottleneck and there's no escape. If the soldier started shooting they'd all be dead in a moment.

'Do as he says.' He slowly lowers his rifle to the floor and gets on his knees, reluctantly obeying the command. The rest follow suit. All except Ruby, who remains standing.

'Did he bring you here?' She spits the words out, glaring across the street at Nigel, who is slowly climbing out of the ambulance.

'On your knees,' Silver says.

'Why should I? You're not going to shoot me.'

She can see him hesitating and knows it's true. He has to deliver her in one piece. De Vere really wouldn't want damaged goods – he wouldn't even let her be born prematurely so he definitely won't want a bullet hole in her.'

Silver nods slightly, acknowledging that she's right.

'Who would you like me to shoot instead? How about me laddo here?' he says, turning the gun on Lucas.

'No,' she shouts.

'Then kneel.'

This time she does as she's told.

'I thought you were the good one,' Margaret says from behind her. Silver blinks but doesn't respond. 'But you're not, are you, you're just as bad as the others. And as for you . . .'

Ruby glances back. Margaret is pointing at Nigel with a shaking hand. And it's very clear that it's not fear that's making her shake. It's fury.

'I used to pretend you were dead. Now I actually wish you were.'

Nigel has moved into the middle of the road now.

'You shouldn't have let those two gang up on me.'

Nigel points to Baldwin and Danny. The man couldn't seem more pathetic if he tried. Margaret shakes her head and Ruby almost wishes they'd let Danny finish him off earlier. Nigel goes to say something else but Silver's patience has clearly been exhausted. He fires a shot into the air.

'Everybody just shut up and listen. First things first, where's Black? The guy who was with me last time I was here.'

Ruby stares down at the ground, hoping everyone else is ignoring the question too.

'Have it your own way,' Silver says. 'One less mouth to feed.'

'It's for the best.'

Ruby looks up. Nigel is now close behind Silver, wringing his hands in anguish.

'I'm sorry, Ruby, but a girl should be with her father,' he adds plaintively.

'That wasn't your decision to make,' she says.

'Enough,' Silver shouts. 'You stand by the ambulance,' he tells Nigel, who does as he's told. 'And you,' Silver adds, pointing. 'Get up slowly, collect all the weapons, and bring them to me.'

Ruby realises he's talking to Lucas who doesn't react.

'Now!' Silver looks like he's about to blow up, the strain of keeping control of them beginning to show.

'Do it, Lucas,' she says and he finally starts moving. She can hear him shuffling between the others and a few moments later he edges past her towards Silver.

'Now put them in the front of the ambulance – on the passenger seat. Give him a hand!' The last instruction is for Nigel who seems almost catatonic. The old man eventually looks up and nods, taking some of the load from Lucas.

Silver steps away, clearly making sure he has both the hallway and the vehicle covered while the weapons are loaded into the ambulance.

'Now kneel down on the pavement by the front door,' he orders Lucas, who does as he's told. Nigel stays by the ambulance.

'Excellent. Carry on like this and no one's going to get hurt. Now listen up, everyone. Ruby is going to get to her feet in a moment and take her rucksack off and hand it to me.'

Ruby can't keep the disappointment from her face.

'I wasn't born yesterday, love,' Silver says. 'I didn't think you had your packed lunch in there. Then we're going to walk backwards over to the ambulance and she's going to stand facing it with her hands behind her back. That's stage one. For stage two Nigel here' – he glances behind him – 'is going to take these.' He holds up some handcuffs that he has unclipped from his belt. 'And cuff her hands. Ruby will then get in the back of the ambulance and we will drive away. If I see any of you move outside of those instructions I will shoot you. Understand?'

There are no dissenters.

'What about me?' Nigel says, quietly.

'What about you?'

'You can't leave me here.' The old man shuffles towards the soldier without him noticing.

'Says who?'

'But I helped you. And what about the reward?'

'I knew you'd be after your pieces of silver,' Margaret shouts. 'Fucking Judas.'

'Everyone be quiet,' Silver says. 'There is no money,' he says to the old man without looking back.

'But you promised,' Nigel says and touches Silver's shoulder. The soldier reacts instantly to the surprise contact, smashing his rifle butt back and catching Nigel full in the chest. He staggers back from the force of the blow and slips on the icy surface.

'Back away,' Silver shouts but the order's superfluous as Nigel falls back onto the road, clearly in pain. Margaret instinctively tries to get up to help him.

'Stay where you are,' Silver shouts.

'He needs help,' she says.

'He'll have to wait.'

He glances back at the old man who's now panting heavily on the ground. He's turned a funny grey colour and even Ruby can tell that it doesn't look good.

'He'll be OK,' the soldier says unconvincingly.

'Let me help him up,' Margaret says. 'He'll freeze to death lying there.'

'When we've gone.'

'I thought you were a medic,' Margaret says. 'Didn't you take an oath or something? You know that we can't call an ambulance with the phone lines down.'

Silver looks back at the old man, whose chest is still rising and falling. Just about.

'He's fine.'

'You don't know that. How can you be so callous?' Margaret says.

'Would you prefer it if I finished him off? Another word and I'll take that as a "yes".' No one speaks. The only sound is Nigel's laboured breathing.

'You,' he says to Ruby. 'Rucksack off and walk slowly over to the vehicle. Hands behind your back.'

She does as she's told. Silver throws the handcuffs at

Lucas. 'You're the new Nigel. Cuff her, throw the rucksack in the front of the ambulance and then get back over here and kneel down again.'

Lucas follows his instructions to the letter whispering an apology as he does. Once he's finished Ruby slowly climbs into the back of the ambulance. She can't risk anyone else getting hurt. Silver lets out a breath; he clearly feels he's finally ended this. He closes and locks the door behind her. She hears him talking to someone on the radio – she can tell by the crackle of the response – but can't make out what they're saying. She sits on a seat at the side but the cuffs prevent her from fastening the seat belt. Getting thrown around in the back is the least of her concerns and she's only just got her backside on the seat when the ambulance pulls off.

It feels like 'Ruby' is about to disappear and she has no idea who or what will replace her. The only bright light on the horizon is that she might get to see Alex again and maybe even find out how she ended up here. If he's still alive.

She's barely settled down when the van suddenly pulls to a halt and she's thrown sideways off the seat, crashing against the back doors. They can't be at the manor house yet, it's too soon. She can hear voices and moves along the middle of the ambulance to get closer to the front.

'I've got the girl,' she hears Silver say.

'You fucking legend,' a voice says. 'We're gonna be rich.'

'Jump in, Grey, let's get back to base. It'll all be over soon.'

'What about the barriers?'

'Just move them out the way. We can pick them up when

we leave. You might want to smarten yourself up when we get back though,' Silver adds.

'Why?'

'The minister's on his way in a chopper. He'll be here within the hour.'

63

The second the ambulance pulls away Margaret jumps to her feet and rushes to Nigel. Old habits die hard. Old soldiers even harder. He's barely conscious now, his breathing ragged. She takes his hand and checks his pulse. It's there but faint.

'Are you OK?' she asks. 'Can you speak?' He moans quietly but doesn't move or reply.

'We should get him inside,' Danny says, getting up and nudging Baldwin with his foot. 'Give us a hand, big man. He'll freeze to death out here.'

'Who gives a shit? What about Ruby?' Lucas says, clearly worried sick. He's already up and looks ready to chase down the road after the ambulance.

'One thing at a time,' Danny says, glancing back at the old man. 'Don't sink to their level, son. We can't just let him die in the street like a dog.'

Baldwin slowly clambers to his feet and helps Danny carry Nigel into the house.

'Put him on the sofa,' Danny says. 'Get some cushions to put under his head, lad.'

While Lucas grabs the cushions, Margaret runs into the kitchen, fills a bowl up with water and finds a clean cloth. She has no real idea why but maybe a cold compress will help. All the time she's hearing her wishing him dead over and over in her head, like a witch's curse on repeat.

When she gets back into the front room Nigel is on the sofa but he's still unconscious.

'Now can we go after Ruby?' Lucas asks anxiously.

'I suppose,' Danny says. 'Though it's not going to be easy without the weapons.'

'Go back out to the shelter,' Margaret says without looking back up. 'Mr Paranoid here was preparing for a zombie apocalypse. There are more rifles in a locked box in there, key's hanging up by the back door. There's even a samurai sword in there somewhere, though God knows what use that was meant to be.'

64

Silver's passenger is grinning all over his face. Grey's the very definition of demob happy – he knows he'll be done with all this shit soon. Silver wishes he felt the same.

It was the old man's fault for sneaking up on him but he regrets his reaction. It was just instinct, something he's been trained to do, but he's always thought he had more control than that. And maybe he should have taken a look at him before leaving. He's been fooling himself that he's a good man surrounded by psychopaths but perhaps he's no better than the rest of them. He listened to Alex's story and felt real sympathy then went and abducted the girl anyway. It's made up his mind that this is his last job. He's losing any shred of humanity he once had. He'll find something simpler and less morally dubious – window cleaners always seem happy; well, they whistle a lot at least. He can't remember the last time he whistled. He tries it but his mouth's too dry and it sounds like he's trying to blow something away from his face. Grey gives him a weird look so he packs it in.

'You doing anything nice when this is over?' Grey asks him.

'Going on holiday with my wife and daughters,' Silver says smiling.

'Must be great to have a family.'

'It is.'

Ruby feels the ambulance rumble over a cattle grid. She knows they're entering the driveway to the house. When she was younger and the house was empty some of the kids used to play hide and seek up there. She knows that whatever happens now she's never going to get that kind of innocence back again.

A minute or so later the vehicle pulls to a halt. Ruby thinks about rushing whoever opens the back door but with her hands cuffed behind her back there's not much point, especially now there's two of them. Even if she knocks the first one down she's not going to get very far before the other one catches her. When the door finally opens she gets quietly to her feet and climbs out of the ambulance, shrugging off Silver's attempt to help her down the steps. It's a bit too late for him to be a fucking gentleman now.

As she steps onto the gravel-laden driveway a grey-haired man comes out of the front door and strides towards her, smiling broadly. This must be Gold, the leader of this bunch of mercenary pricks.

'The elusive Miss Winter,' he says. 'You have no idea how happy I am to see you.'

She spits in his face.

He grimaces and backs out of her reach, wiping his face with his sleeve.

'I see my joy isn't reciprocated. I'm surprised. Normally hostages are much more grateful when they're rescued from their captors. Maybe we've got a Stockholm Syndrome situation here.'

'I wasn't a hostage.'

'You say potato,' Gold says. Ruby has no idea what he's talking about.

'Bring her into the house,' he tells the two other soldiers. 'Her father's on his way.'

'He's not my fucking father,' Ruby shouts but he's already heading back, ignoring her protests.

Silver nudges her in the back with his rifle.

'Follow him,' he says.

'What if I don't?'

The soldier hesitates, looks a little confused. 'Give me a break.'

'No, really, who are you going to shoot this time?'

He sighs. 'Have a guess,' he says and she immediately regrets the question. Now they've got her they don't need Alex.

'Can I see him?' she asks.

'That'll be up to Gold and given that you've just spat in his face I doubt he'll be inclined to do you a favour.'

After stopping at Danny's place to pick up some supplies, he, Lucas and Baldwin head for the latter's garage. Danny had planned on using his truck but the bastards have shot out all the tyres in his absence so they need some wheels – and it should ideally be something that won't look out of place. Danny hears banging as soon as they turn the corner at the bottom of the road.

As they open the garage door the radio that Lucas took from the guy in the inspection pit crackles on his belt. The banging stops.

'Is that you, Black? Thank God,' the imprisoned soldier shouts. 'Get me out of here. Some fat wanker hit me when I wasn't looking and threw me in here.'

Lucas grins at Baldwin who wanders over to the pit and leans down. 'Fat wanker reporting for duty,' he says. 'If I hear another word from you I'll turn the jeep's engine on, leave it running and close the doors again. Should give you at least ten minutes to pray to whatever god will still listen to you before you suffocate.'

The anguished groan is almost as loud as the banging was but the prisoner knows better than to speak again.

Baldwin quickly sticks the spare on to replace the flat tyre and reverses the jeep out of the garage, before climbing out and joining Lucas in the back. Danny manoeuvres the other car already in there on to the board covering the pit to keep the soldier trapped before jumping in the driving seat. The pair in the back crouch down, keeping out of sight, as he drives through the deserted village.

Danny had been going to use Scout and the severed hand to get past the final guard but now that they have Ruby time is of the essence so he is hoping that using the jeep will distract the man until they're close enough to take him out.

However, as they turn the last bend, he sees that the barriers are now unmanned. Silver must have picked the guard up on the way to the house. Clearly they think their work is done. Danny hopes that means that they're a little complacent but he's concerned that the odds have changed since they decided to fight back. Half an hour ago he was hoping it would be five against two. Now, at best, it's three against three. They may not have been the strongest members of the team but the loss of Ruby and Margaret and the failure to take out the second guard has changed the odds considerably. He glances at his companions and wonders again if they're biting off a lot more than they can chew.

65

Alex is drifting off in bed, still sleeping off the effects of his latest morphine shot when he hears Ruby's voice.

Or does he? He's so disorientated it could have been a dream – or a nightmare, more like, as what he heard was, 'He's not my fucking father.' If it was real she's obviously read his letters. Worse still, she's in the company of men who are working for Simon De Vere. He wonders whether they found her or she gave herself in voluntarily when she realised who her real father was. That would explain the shout. She's always wanted a bigger, more exciting life than he was able to give her. Until this year he wouldn't even let her have a proper birthday party with friends.

'Ruby,' he croaks. It was meant to be a shout but it's a long time since he's been given any water and his mouth's as dry as a Quaker town. Maybe they're punishing him for killing Red and trying to escape but he thinks not, they're just short of numbers and his well-being isn't exactly a priority. Since Silver patched him up the second time, the only man he's seen is Gold. He assumes that everyone else in this rag-bag outfit has been in the village hunting down Ruby and now they've succeeded.

Alex tries to generate some saliva to loosen up his vocal chords and, to a degree, it works. The next shout is a little louder.

'Ruby!'

There's no reaction. Either she can't hear him or she doesn't care. He's starting to believe it's the latter as she must know that now they have her, he's expendable. In fact they have to kill him – if they don't he'll never stop trying to get her back. He tries once more, taking in a deep breath and giving it everything he has.

'Ruby!'

This time there's a reaction. It's a muffled shout but every bone in his body tells him it's her. She's really there! He smiles for the first time in days as what he heard this time was definitely 'Dad!'

Out in the main entrance of the house Ruby struggles to get out of Silver's grip but he's holding the back of her hoodie with an iron fist. She's sure that was Alex who shouted just now. He's very close.

'Let me go,' she screams, as if he's going to take any notice. She tries to kick back at him but he simply sweeps her feet from under her and she falls to her knees on the tiled floor, his hold on her never easing.

Gold comes through a door off to her left to see what the fuss is all about.

'Take charge of her, will you!' he shouts at Silver.

'Easier said than done,' the soldier says.

'I want to see my dad,' Ruby shouts.

'He should be landing in the next thirty minutes,' Gold says.

'Not De Vere,' she says. 'My real dad.'

'I think you'll find a DNA test will prove you wrong.'

He points to a door at the far end of the corridor.

'The man in there stole you. Your real father has spent nearly sixteen years looking for you. See the difference in that. Just because you've lived with him for all that time it doesn't make him your father.'

Silver flinches at that. He wonders if Gold knows that his own daughters are adopted. Almost certainly, he thinks, given the background checks that Claustra carry out on people. In which case he can go fuck himself.

'Would it do any harm?' he says.

'Would what do any harm?' Gold retorts, clearly unimpressed with the question.

'To let her talk to Alex.'

Ruby looks back at Silver, confused by his sudden interjection. Maybe the man has a heart after all.

'It's Alex now, is it? You become all buddy-buddy all of a sudden?'

'No. Just think she should get a last chance to speak to him before the main man gets here. Maybe she'll even get an apology.'

Gold leans his head slightly, clearly curious about where this came from. Ruby decides to keep out of the powerplay. If she says something the senior guy may go against her out of spite, he seems the type.

'On your head be it,' Gold says eventually, glancing at his watch. 'She can have ten minutes to say goodbye. But I want you in there the whole time and if there's any sign of a problem, fix it. Whatever it takes.'

66

Ruby walks slowly down the corridor, her heart in her mouth. She wasn't sure if she would ever see Alex again but now that she's about to she doesn't know how she'll react. In so many ways he's not the man she thought he was.

Before she can push the door open Silver grabs the back of her hoodie again.

'Don't piss about when you get in there. I'm doing you a favour here, this is on me.'

It's true. He may still be the enemy but there is a bit of decency in there somewhere. She nods, but when she tries to pull away, anxious to get inside, his grip stays firm.

'Hold your horses.' He reaches down behind her and, to her surprise, he unlocks her handcuffs and clips them back on his belt. 'Any nonsense and I'll drag you straight back out, OK?'

'Yes, OK. I'll be good.' Ruby is sure that he knows she'll still kick him in the balls at the first opportunity but he lets her go anyway. She bets it's because she's a girl. No way would he be so lax if it was Lucas. It's a small glimmer of opportunity which she vows he's going to regret – that macho superiority complex will be his downfall.

She pushes gently against the door and there he is, Alex, sitting up in a makeshift bed at the far end of the room. A drip running into one of his arms.

'It was you,' he says gently, reaching out for her with one arm. She can see that his other arm, the one with the drip in, is manacled to the bed frame. She stands still for a moment and he drops his hand, a look of concern on his face. He must have as many doubts as she does. It's a temporary stand-off. Then she's off, running towards the bed and hurling her arms around him. He holds her as tight as he can with his one available arm.

'You OK?' he says. Ruby just nods against his shoulder, unable to find any words that would make sense. It's like a lifetime has been crammed into the short space of time since she ran from the house. It's hard to believe it was only yesterday.

Silver watches them from the doorway, keeping a safe distance from the girl, knowing that despite her promise and her youth she'd have his eyes out if she got the chance.

He can't wait to get home.

Danny drives over the cattle grid then veers off the road into the trees, careering over the bumpy ground, missing branches left and right. He knows this place like the back of his hand.

'Jesus, man, you might have warned us,' Baldwin says from the back. 'This is playing havoc with my piles.'

'No point letting them know we're here,' Danny says. 'We'll go in the back way on foot just in case anyone is watching from the house'

He pulls up behind a dense thicket of brambles and turns the engine off, standing up and looking back to make sure it can't be seen from the road. It's a perfect spot.

'Out you get, the house is just the other side of those trees. Follow me carefully, there are still traps all over the place out here.'

Ruby finally lets go of Alex and steps back to take a closer look at him. His shoulder is strapped up but there's also a dressing on his leg now. He's paler than she remembers, apart from the recent-looking black eye, and has a salt and pepper stubble that she's never seen before. He's always been clean-shaven.

'You look like shit,' she says.

'You should see the other guy,' he says. He's not laughing so she's pretty sure he means it. She doesn't explore it, some things are best left unknown, for now. Eventually, if they can somehow get out of this, she'll want to know everything though – there have been enough secrets for one lifetime.

'What happened to your leg?'

'Got caught in an animal trap when I tried to escape.'

'Ouch.'

'It did sting a little.'

She smiles.

'I thought I told you to run,' he says.

'When was the last time I did as I was told?'

'Good point.' Alex cuts to the chase. 'I take it you found your birthday present.'

Ruby nods. She's biting her lip to stop herself jumping in, caught between desperately wanting to know the rest of the story and never wanting to talk about it again in the hope that it will all go away. If you don't talk about something it's like it never happened, isn't it?

'Is there anything else you want to know?'

'The computer went dead so I didn't get to the end.' She glances back at Silver who's stony-faced. 'I think they cut the power off.'

'Where did you get to?'

'The dead midwife. And I peeked at the photo.'

'Ah, right. So you know who and what your biological father is now?'

She nods again, unwilling to say his name.

'Shall I finish the story?'

Danny reaches the hole in the fence and holds up his hand. He waits until he hears Lucas and Baldwin freeze as instructed then steps through the gap, surveying the outside of the house, or at least as much of it as he can. It's the same gap he watched through last time so he can't see the front door. He waits for at least five minutes, counting slowly in elephants to make sure. There's no sign of any patrols. Maybe they're in luck and there's only Silver, his boss and the other guard to worry about.

He signals to the other two and they come through the fence to join him. There's about forty yards to go to the house but it's a completely open space, visible from any window on this side of the house. It's not perfect but there's no other way in and at least they're hidden from anyone guarding the front entrance. If there is a lone guard – and given their lack of numbers there's unlikely to be more than that – it's the most likely place he'll be keeping watch from. Unless he's on the roof.

There's a large set of doors and a small window towards the back of the house, the first covered with curtains, the latter frosted. He holds his hand up again, which tells the other two to hold their ground, and sets off, sprinting as fast as his gammy leg will allow him. If there is a sniper on the roof Danny will be dead before he even hears the shot. When he reaches the building he breathes a sigh of relief and stands with his back against the wall, points at Baldwin and beckons him to come. The man runs like a carthorse and is only about halfway there when he suddenly goes flying, yelping in both pain and surprise.

Danny doesn't move, waiting to see if there's any reaction from a guard or patrol but it remains quiet. He's about to move off when he sees Lucas running over to help the grounded man. The kid's a lot quicker than he is and is there way before him. Baldwin is sitting on the ground holding his ankle, his face contorted in pain.

'What happened?' Danny says when he eventually reaches them.

'There's something solid hidden in the snow back there. I tripped on it, went flying.'

Baldwin points back, about ten yards behind him. Danny wanders over carefully. There's a closed animal trap, mostly buried under the snow. Its teeth are stained with what looks like fresh blood, which probably explains the scream he and Lucas heard earlier. He limps back over to Baldwin who's now standing with the lad's help.

'You were lucky. There's a trap there but someone got there before you. If it had been open you could have lost your foot.'

'Still fucking hurts,' Baldwin says. 'I've knackered my ankle, can't put any weight on it.'

That's all they need, Danny thinks, they were already short-handed. They quite literally can't afford to carry a passenger. He looks back at the treeline, immediately seeing a spot where Baldwin can at least do something useful.

'Let's get you back over there,' he says, supporting Baldwin's other arm to help Lucas get the mechanic out of sight.

They leave him with a rifle in hand, sitting behind the overgrown ornamental sundial Danny saw on his last visit. It's not ideal but the man will be partially camouflaged by the ivy hanging off it.

'If anything moves that you don't recognise, shoot it,' is Danny's final instruction.

Danny and Lucas make their way back to the side of the house. He signals for the lad to wait while he sidles along the wall until he gets to the first window. Although there's a curtain drawn behind it he can see into the room through a small gap on the edge of the window frame.

The first person he sees is Silver. He looks tired but still alert. The second person he sees is Ruby. The third is Alex. They've found him.

67

Alex can see that Silver is pretending not to listen in to their conversation but he obviously is, even though he's already heard most of this. He had thought he was winning the soldier over earlier but given that he's clearly the one who dragged Ruby here maybe he was wrong. Or perhaps it's not too late? He takes a deep breath and begins:

'After the midwife handed you over I didn't stop to think, I just bundled up my stuff and ran. I knew it wouldn't take De Vere long to discover you were gone and when he did he'd use all his resources to find you. I had to get away.

'I had no idea what I was doing really, just acting on pure instinct. Two things I was pretty certain about. The first was that De Vere wouldn't go public – there was no way he'd want the whole story of what happened with your mother to get out – remember that surrogacy was still illegal then. The other was that I didn't want him to get his hands on you.

'I knew I was the first person he would suspect. Emma was bound to have mentioned me and even if she hadn't the nurse and the guard from the house would remember me. It wouldn't take a man in his business long to track me down either. I also had no doubts that he would quickly work out that Janet had brought you to me. And I was pretty sure that he'd find her and make her talk when he did.'

Ruby raises her hand as if she is in school just like Lucas did earlier. Both of them laugh nervously even though there's really nothing funny about this situation.

'You said in your letter that she was mugged. D'you really think he had her killed?'

Alex hesitates then nods. 'I'm sure of it.'

She drops her head, thinking of all the people who've been helping her in the last day. What will happen to them?

'D'you want a break?' Alex asks.

'No. I'm fine.' She's desperate to know the rest of the story despite her worries, so he continues.

'I admit I was panicking a little. I didn't have a car and I couldn't get a taxi from the house just in case they found out where I'd been living and checked with the local firms so I just legged it, carrying you in my arms and didn't stop until I was ready to drop. I took out as much money as I could from a cashpoint near the flat, terrified that they would have a way of finding out which ones I used in the future.

'There was no way I was heading home – Emma and I had both been living in Bristol before your mum did a runner – so I headed in the other direction. Thankfully there was a lot less CCTV around then. I jumped on a series of buses, eventually ending up in Stevenage where I finally felt it was safe to get on a train heading north. I'd never been further north than Leicester in my life before so I was hoping it would be the last place they would look.

'I guessed that De Vere, with his political contacts and his background in the security industry, would have men at his disposal whose job it was to search for people so I had to find a way to get off-grid. And, luckily, I knew just the man who could help me.

'My best friend on my graphic design course was a bit of a dodgy guy who had developed a sideline in high quality fake ID to help him pay his way. No one on the course, other than me, knew about it and while I lay low for a while in Newcastle he provided me with a driving licence and birth certificates for the pair of us.'

Ruby doesn't stick her hand up this time, just blurts her question out.

'Did he make you those passports I found in your bag?'

'He did.'

'But they were made-up names?'

'They were.'

'Good. I hate Karen.'

He laughs again.

'It's not like I could check with you.'

'Is your name really Jonathan?'

He smiles. 'I'm afraid so. But I think I prefer Alex now.'

'Me too. How did you pick my name?'

'When we got on the train heading north it was snowing – that's where Winter came from. And your mum's favourite film was the *Wizard of Oz*. I thought about Dorothy but it seemed a bit old-fashioned so I went for Ruby, after her ruby slippers. I think Emma would have liked it.'

'I like it.' Ruby takes Alex's free hand. 'I'm a gem.'

They both smile at the old joke though it's not a full-on smile for her as this whole conversation feels like a goodbye. And she hates goodbyes.

Alex takes her silence as a cue to continue.

'I'd heard that Northumberland was one of the least populated areas of the country so I stuck a pin in a map and headed up here, driving around in a clapped-out second-hand car that I bought for cash from a back-street garage in Newcastle. Eventually I found a place that I thought we could disappear to – Coldburn. It was miles from anywhere and the house was in a poor state so they let me have it for a peppercorn rent on the condition that I fixed it up. I was practically penniless so it was a great deal for me. And it's been our home ever since.'

'What did you think I would do when I read the letter on my birthday?'

'I had no idea. I knew it was only a matter of time before De Vere found you though. I'd obviously kept very close tabs on his career and watched in horror as he grew in power and influence throughout the years. I guess I was in denial really.

'Now it seems obvious I should have told you before but I decided it would be too much for you when you were younger and vowed to tell you on your sixteenth birthday. It's one of the reasons I agreed to you having a party, I wanted to do something fun before the shit hit the fan.

There are a thousand things I could probably have done differently but I was making it up as I went along, and looking over my shoulder as I did. Sadly, we didn't quite make it that far.

'I hadn't really planned on being a "dad" quite so early in life and had no idea of how to look after a baby so I'm sorry if I messed up but my main priority was always to keep you safe. I know De Vere's your biological dad and you probably want to meet him but I'm telling you he's poison, Ruby. Pure poison. If I had a gun I would shoot him the second he walked in here and fuck the consequences.'

Danny has moved along the building to the other side of the doors where he's now got one eye on Silver, whose attention seems fixed on Alex and Ruby. Whatever they're talking about, he's hooked. Unfortunately Danny hasn't caught a glimpse of anyone else so still has no real idea how many more of them there are.

He has sent Lucas around to the back of the house to see if he can find an unguarded entrance. If not, they're going to have to go in through the front door which is far riskier.

He hears a movement behind him, the lad is coming back so soon that it's clearly been a wasted recce. But when he turns around it's not Lucas.

'Drop your weapon,' the soldier says.

Alex blows his cheeks out. It's a while since he's talked for so long.

'Could you get me some water?' he asks Ruby. She grabs

a plastic cup from the bedside cabinet and hands it to him. He necks the lot.

'Any chance of a refill?' he says, looking at Silver.

'Nice try,' the soldier says, 'but I'm going nowhere.'

'Shy bairns,' Alex says, continuing to address Silver. 'You still think you're a good man working for De Vere?'

'I've got a job to do and a family to support. Simples.'

'Can I at least ask you not to mention my friend who does the fake ID? I don't think he'll be easy to find, given his skills, but he doesn't deserve to have De Vere after him.'

'I could care less,' Silver says. 'None of my business.'

'Maybe you should care that De Vere favours a scorched earth policy. Anyone who knows what he's been up to has a tendency to disappear.'

Silver looks at his watch.

'You've only got about two minutes left with your daughter. I wouldn't waste it chatting shit to me if I was you.'

'He's right,' Ruby says. 'And don't beat yourself up about any mistakes. You did an OK job. There are worse parents.'

'But they still found us in the end, didn't they? I was so careful but I must have slipped up somewhere along the line.'

Ruby shakes her head. She's been thinking about this a lot over the last day or so, especially since she started reading Alex's letters. She's pretty sure that it's down to her that they found them.

'I think it was me,' she says. Alex looks puzzled. 'Liv persuaded me to put something on Facebook about my birthday party. With a photo.'

Alex grimaces.

'I'm sorry,' she says.

'It might not have been that.'

She looks back at Silver, hoping he might get her off the hook. As she does she catches a small movement outside the window. Someone is watching them. Have the others followed them here? Silver seems to see her look and starts to turn but she distracts him.

'You seem to know stuff, Silver. You must know how they found us. How about you put me out of my misery? It's not like we can do anything about it now.'

The soldier turns back to her, clearly considering his options. At least he's not looking at the window now. Whoever's out there won't be caught just yet. And anyway she wants to know the truth. Has all this been her fault? She waits, confident he'll spill the beans, knowing how much men like to show off.

'You're probably right,' Silver says eventually. 'As far as I understand, there's been someone running image searches on you on a regular basis using aged-up pictures based on your mother's looks. They've been doing it for years, apparently, but this time they got a hit. Of course, it probably helped that they knew roughly when your birthday was.'

'I knew it,' Ruby says. 'I really messed up.'

'It's not your fault,' Alex says.

'You told me not to use social media.'

'But I didn't tell you why, did I? And I should have given you a much different birth date on the fake ID right from the start. Back then I reckoned that if there were any medical issues in the early days any health visitor or doctor would realise if it was too far away from the reality. I adjusted it by a couple of weeks but couldn't risk anything more. Ironically you were a healthy kid so it was never an issue.'

Ruby glances at the window again but there's no sign of anyone now. Hopefully they're in the building. Maybe it's not too late to get out of there. She needs to keep Silver distracted.

'Was it earlier or later?' Ruby asks Alex.

'Was what earlier or later?'

'My real birthday.'

'Earlier.'

'So I'm actually sixteen already?'

'What's the date? I've been out of it with the morphine so I've lost track of time.'

'I haven't a clue.'

They both turn to Silver.

'It's February the fifth.'

Ruby looks back at Alex who smiles.

'Happy birthday,' he says, and starts singing the usual song. Ruby takes his hand but before he gets to the end they both hear another sound, coming from outside. It's a long way off but clearly getting closer.

'Time to go,' Silver says.

'That's him, isn't it?' Ruby says. 'That's Simon De Vere's helicopter.'

68

Gold bursts in through the doors waving a pistol around.

'Time's up, get the girl out of here. The minister doesn't want an audience for his first meeting with his daughter.'

Ruby backs away from the two soldiers, edging around her dad's bed. Where have the cavalry gone? She's sure it was Danny she saw outside the window.

The answer comes quicker than she would have liked as the man himself is suddenly bundled through the doors and shoved to the floor by Grey, the guard that Silver picked up at the barriers earlier.

'I found him snooping around outside,' Grey says.

'You on your own?' Gold demands, kicking Danny in the ribs. Danny groans in pain but ignores the question.

'Well?' Gold gives him another brutal kick.

'No,' Danny says. 'I've got 3 Para lined up outside to back me up. Did you not see the parachutes?'

His last few words are almost drowned out by the helicopter descending towards the house. Ruby puts her hands over her ears – it must be landing on the lawn right outside.

Gold turns back to Grey.

'Get back out there and protect the minister, just in case there are more of them,' he shouts. The soldier nods and runs back out through the door. 'And no more prisoners. Shoot to kill,' Gold yells after him.

'Keep a close eye on this one,' the leader instructs Silver, giving Danny one final kick, before going to the window and pulling open the curtains.

'It's the beginning of the end, ladies and gentlemen,' he says.

Most eyes switch to the outside where a small helicopter is hovering about twenty feet from the ground. Grey appears from around the front of the house, keeping his distance from the rotor blades. No one speaks. There'd be no point with the noise coming from outside but Ruby manages to catch Danny's attention. She mouths 'Lucas?' and he tilts his head slightly towards the window. He must still be outside somewhere. She hopes to God he isn't going to attempt anything stupid.

As the helicopter gets closer to the ground Ruby feels Alex squeezing her hand. He's nodding towards Silver and the door.

Ruby glances across and sees that the guard has one eye on Danny and the other on what's happening outside and has moved well away from the door. If she's quick there's a chance she can escape. The noise the chopper is generating will cover any movement she makes and everyone else in the room is focused on the landing – particularly Gold, who also seems to be trying to smarten himself up at the same time. He's put his pistol back in its holster and is now smoothing out his hair. He's clearly a bit of an arse-licker.

She gets slowly to her feet. Alex nods in encouragement. Silver's now got the added distraction of the presence of Grey, who has appeared outside the window waiting for the helicopter to land, but the medic is still roughly between her and the door so will almost certainly see her when she gets closer. She needs one further diversion.

It comes from an unexpected source.

'What the hell?' Gold exclaims loudly, pointing at something outside the window.

Silver takes a couple of steps further forwards to see what the fuss is about and Ruby makes her move, edging along with her back to the wall, just out of his field of vision. She's about halfway there when she stops in her tracks in terror.

Through the window she can see the helicopter has now landed on the lawn. The rotor blades are still spinning around but the chopper itself is stationary and the noise is decreasing. That's not why she's scared.

Outside, there's a blur of movement sprinting towards the chopper from the back of the house. It must be what's distracted the others. The closer the blur gets, the more obvious it is that it's Lucas. He's about thirty metres away from the helicopter and shows no signs of slowing down.

Outside the window she sees Grey raise his rifle to his shoulder and take aim.

'No,' she screams and runs towards the window, brushing past Gold and banging frantically on the glass.

'No, stop,' she shouts again, even louder this time, but

it's too late. She's not sure which comes first, the sound of the gunshot or Lucas collapsing to the floor, it all happens so fast.

'No,' she screams again and sinks to her knees.

'Stay where you are,' Silver shouts behind her and she glances back. Danny ignores the command and crawls over to her, taking her hand and trying to turn her away from the view. She holds firm though, willing Lucas to get to his feet. Danny gives up and she can sense him joining her in some kind of silent prayer but Lucas still isn't moving.

Grey is though, running towards the body on the ground. When he gets a few feet away he raises his rifle again and there's another shot and Ruby feels Danny flinch. To her astonishment, Grey collapses to the ground this time. She turns to Danny, hoping he has some idea what is happening out there.

'Baldwin,' he whispers.

'Lucas needs help,' she says to Gold, trying to get to her feet.

'Not my problem,' he says, drawing out his sidearm again. 'Stay where you are.'

She glances at Danny, looking for help, but there's none forthcoming.

'Do what he says,' he mutters. 'No point you getting shot too.'

Ruby drops his hand in frustration and looks back out of the window. Lucas still hasn't moved. She stifles a sob.

The rotor blades have now stopped and a few moments later a door on the side of the helicopter opens and the pilot steps out cautiously, looking around and clearly making sure that he's keeping the chopper in between him and wherever the shot that downed Grey came from.

He glances at the two bodies on the floor but makes no attempt to see if either of them are alive. Instead he's looking at the house as if expecting an armed escort, or at the very least a welcoming committee. Even from this distance she can feel a sense of entitlement pouring off him. It's that, even more than the smart suit he's wearing, which confirms what Ruby had suspected the second he stepped from the helicopter. The pilot is Simon De Vere.

Out of the corner of her eye she sees another movement. Baldwin comes out from behind a sculpture of some kind at the back of the lawn. He's holding a rifle and limping heavily towards the helicopter.

Gold unlocks the double doors and rushes out towards De Vere, screaming at Silver to make sure no one follows him out. The second he's out of the doors he unleashes a volley of shots towards Baldwin.

Ruby has no idea what the range of a pistol is and it seems quite literally a long shot that he'll hit anything that far away but she sees Baldwin hesitate, looking around for cover. He's in the open though and either has to turn back to where he came from or keep going and hope that he gets Gold first. He chooses the latter and continues to edge forward, firing the occasional shot at the soldier. There's obviously something wrong with his leg – he's moving very erratically – and he stumbles every time he shoots.

Gold seems to realise his target is already hurt and stops

running. He adopts a more rigid stance, his feet apart and his arm steady. He takes careful aim at Baldwin this time and hits his target. The mechanic falls to the floor and makes no attempt to get back up. Gold starts to move towards Baldwin but then there's a shout from behind him and he turns back and jogs over to De Vere.

Ruby's 'father' has stayed firmly behind the helicopter waiting for Gold to get to him and he now allows the soldier to escort him back to the house at the double. She notices that he's taking no chances, making sure there's something in between him and Baldwin, just in case the man isn't dead yet. Only this time it's the clearly expendable Gold rather than the helicopter.

'Everyone over by the bed,' Silver shouts as the two men get closer to the doors.

Ruby helps Danny get up, it's pretty obvious from the grimace as he tries to stand that he's broken a couple of ribs from the kicking he took just now but she manages to guide him over to Alex and props him up against the bed. The two men nod at each other as if meeting up in the pub.

'Heard you stabbed someone,' Danny says.

Alex nods again.

'Not much fucking point me teaching you to shoot then, was there?' the old soldier adds.

'How can you be joking when Lucas is lying out there?' she says, angrily, but before Danny can respond Gold and De Vere burst through the doorway. Gold immediately closes the doors behind him and draws the curtains again.

'Is Grey dead?' Silver asks.

'Yes,' Gold says.

'What about the others?' Silver glances at Ruby.

'I think so. I wasn't going to get close enough to be sure just in case they weren't.'

De Vere hasn't said a word yet, seemingly transfixed by the sight of Ruby, who's now standing to the side of the bed holding Alex's hand tight, desperately fighting back tears. She doesn't want to show this man any weakness. The minister pushes his hair back, straightens himself up to his full height and steps towards her.

'Hello, Ruby,' he says. 'I've been looking for you for a long time.'

69

Nigel is showing some signs of life. His eyelids are flickering and his hand twitches occasionally, like he's trying to nudge something away from his leg.

Boris is nestled at the foot of the sofa, happier than he's been in an age now his master is settled back in the house, seemingly not caring that he's unconscious. The dog is snoring away in the same rhythm as Nigel's chest rises and falls.

Margaret sits on the armchair across the room with one eye on Nigel and the other on the street, hoping that Danny and the rest of them will return any moment now with Ruby and Alex in tow. If she was the religious kind she might even offer a prayer up for them. Not for Nigel though, she realises; let whatever god exists out there make that decision on his own. That's how far he's fallen in her eyes. And in her heart.

She glances back at him and sighs, remembering how attentive he was when they were first married even though he knew she didn't love him. What he did know was that she believed in the sanctity of marriage and would never break her vows. Nothing was too much trouble at first but over the years his attention slowly eroded, like a cliff face that had crumbled into the sea, replaced by anger and frustration. It's amazing what can change without you even really noticing until it's too late.

Maybe it would have been different if she'd been able to have kids but despite their best efforts – at least in the first few years – it never happened and the army became his family, leaving her both alone and lonely with very few friends.

She knows that some of that was her fault. She's always had a sharp tongue and was too ready to use it, alienating half the villagers and putting the fear of God into the other half. Baldwin was probably right about his wife being frightened of her. The only reason they let her run the Neighbourhood Watch was that they were all scared what she might do if they didn't. If only she could have somehow told them how vulnerable she was at home things might have turned out very differently. But she could never find the words.

Margaret's too anxious to sit still so goes out into the kitchen to make a cuppa, thankful, now the power's out, that she has a gas cooker and plenty of spare bottles. She takes her time, in no rush to go back into the front room. Her tea-making routine has always been like a comfort blanket, two teabags in the pot, leave it to stew for five minutes. Milk in the cup first, then the tea. Three sugars. None of which was the way Nigel liked it. Especially the sugars.

'You'll get fat,' Nigel used to say when he first realised what a sweet tooth she had. He was right as well. She glances down at her stout form. Maybe that was why he went looking elsewhere even though he was no male model himself. She shakes her head, knowing that she's kidding herself; the main reason he left was because she never had a good word for him and he was the kind of man who needed one, regardless of how badly he treated her. Even someone as dense as the church organist could see that so why couldn't she? Things could have been so different with just a little effort on her part. She hates the bit of her that still thinks it was up to her to fix their ultimately disastrous marriage.

Tea poured, she treks slowly back into the front room, cup in hand, not bothering to bring him one for obvious reasons. He'd never liked the way she made it anyway. He was a coffee man by preference and since he left she hasn't had it in the house just to spite him. She can do vindictive in her sleep. She puts the cup down on a little side table and goes to sit down but quickly realises something has changed. Boris is still snoring away but Nigel's chest is no longer rising and falling.

'Nigel?' she says quietly but there's no response.

She hastens over to the sofa. His eyes are open now but they're staring sightlessly at the ceiling. She feels for his pulse again. This time there's nothing. Leaning over him she puts her cheek against his mouth and nose. Again, nothing. Instinctively she goes to the phone to call for help but as soon as she hears the lack of dialling tone she remembers that it's useless. She thinks about trying to resuscitate him – she's seen them do it on *Casualty* often enough – but knows deep down that she doesn't care enough to try. He's gone. Her unthinking, brutal, wish has been granted.

She feels like she should be crying but there's nothing there. Slowly, she walks back over to him and gently closes his eyes.

'Goodbye, you stupid, stupid man,' she says.

70

'Don't touch me,' Ruby says, as De Vere steps towards her. She backs away so quickly that her head hits the wall with a thud. She's damned if she'll show him it hurts though.

De Vere stops, but he's still smiling, a tiny twitch of his eye the only indication that he's not entirely relaxed. He holds his hands up, palms towards her, to show that he's no intention of closing the gap. He's studying her closely which makes her skin crawl.

'You look just like your mother,' he says.

'Are you going to kill me too?' she fires back.

He sighs and glances at Alex.

'I don't know what you've been told but I can guarantee you it's not true. Emma's death was a tragic accident, a chance in a million. I loved her very much.'

'And what did your wife think of that?'

He pauses, clearly trying to work out a way to get past her defences. Ruby has no intention of letting him do that but he tries anyway.

'You're very direct. I like that. Chip off the old block. I've come to take you home.'

'She already has a home.' Alex, like Ruby, has clearly had enough of this bollocks.

'Ah, the child-snatcher has a voice.'

'I notice you didn't answer the question Ruby asked you. What did your wife think of you screwing other women? Or should I say girls.'

'My wife is dead. God rest her soul.'

'Another non-answer. Has one of your lackeys given you a few trite soundbites to remember?'

De Vere ignores Alex and returns his gaze to Ruby.

'I feel like we've got off on the wrong foot. It's a little crowded in here. Could we go somewhere else for a chat, get a little privacy maybe?' He looks back at Gold who nods but Ruby has other ideas.

'Fuck that. I'm not going anywhere with you. If you wanted to talk to me, why didn't you just come and knock on my door like any normal person would instead of sending in your own private army?'

He hesitates. 'That's a fair question.'

'Then just answer it like a human rather than a politician.'

De Vere waves a hand towards Alex.

'This man had already hidden you away from me for sixteen years. I was afraid that he might see me coming and whisk you away again. I wasn't prepared to take that chance. I wanted to have the opportunity to get to know you properly.'

'I bet you did. But I wouldn't hold your breath.'

Despite his outer calm, Ruby can sense De Vere's growing impatience. He's a man who's used to getting his own way and none of this is quite going to plan. She's sure that he'd expected her to be overwhelmed with joy and gratitude that he'd come to 'rescue' her and wonders what will happen if she presses some more of his buttons. Can't really see what she has to lose.

'You used to be in the army, didn't you?'

'I did,' he said. 'Joined straight from school. The army taught me everything I know.'

'But one of your men was just shot and you walked straight past him. Didn't even check to see if he needed help. Disposable, was he?'

'Not at all,' De Vere says, 'but in any war there will always be casualties.'

'And what about my friend? You left him lying there too.'

'Was he the man who tried to kill me?'

'His name was Lucas. And he wasn't a man. He was a boy – though he was clearly more of a man than you'll ever be.'

'I'm truly sorry about your friend,' De Vere says. 'I told my men very explicitly that no one should be hurt in this operation.' He's such a bullshit artist; Ruby wonders how long it takes to learn to fake sincerity so well.

'What about Janet Moore? Did she try to kill you?'

'I have no idea who that is.'

'She was my mother's midwife. You had her killed for taking me to Alex.'

De Vere shakes his head.

'Do you understand how crazy that sounds? I was a respectable businessman back then, not a gangland boss – why on earth would I do that? On the contrary, after her unfortunate death I set up a charity in her honour to help get knives off the street.'

'And yet you couldn't remember her name? Is that what's going to happen to my dad now?' De Vere grimaces. She knew he would hate her calling Alex that. 'And what about all the other people who've helped me? Danny here, and Margaret. Will they all end up as unfortunate "casualties" too?'

De Vere smiles. She has a sudden flashback to the tiger in *The Jungle Book*.

'Don't worry about them,' he says. 'You have my word they will be taken care of.'

Silver isn't the only one in the room who picks up on the double meaning of that. Ruby seems to miss it but Gold can't keep the smirk from his face and the old man sitting on the floor that Grey dragged in looks like he'd strangle the politician with his bare hands given half a chance.

Silver is starting to get a bad feeling about this. He's been in this kind of situation before and it never ends well. There are too many people in a small space and if anyone starts firing, particularly someone like Gold, who probably hasn't discharged his weapon in years before today, then a lot of people are going to get hurt. They started this mission with a 'leave no trace' brief but he's starting to think that the body count is going to leave a trail you could see from the moon. He has no wish to be part of another bloodbath and vows to keep an eye on his so-called leader.

Alex can sense a growing restlessness amongst the soldiers and maybe De Vere can too as he decides to change tack, trying gentle persuasion rather than a display of authority. He turns towards the bed and addresses him by his name for the first time.

'Alex, you must acknowledge that I can give Ruby opportunities she couldn't begin to dream of under your tutelage,' he says.

Despite himself, Alex nods, it's undoubtedly true.

'I can give her access to the finest schools in the country immediately and then to Oxford or Cambridge or even one of the American giants, Harvard or Berkeley perhaps. I'd just have to say the word and a place would be hers almost anywhere in the world. I can give her a life that you can't imagine.'

'And what if she doesn't want that life?' Alex says. 'Are you just going to take her anyway? Why not give her a choice?' He realises immediately that he's opened up a can of worms. De Vere looks like he's caught a large rat in a trap. The man's treating this like a university debate.

'Like you did?' the minister says. 'You're in no position to lecture me. You took Ruby away from her real father, changed her identity and locked her away for sixteen years, denying her the prospect of a life beyond your wildest dreams. When did you ever consider what she wanted?'

'Never mind what I wanted, what is it you want?' Ruby asks suddenly.

De Vere looks a little startled, almost as if he's forgotten that she's there. It's the moment Ruby realises that this isn't really about her, that it probably never has been. It's about winning. He clearly can't stand the idea that someone got the better of him and has spent a lot of time and money trying to turn that around and he's not going to stop until he's got her back. She doubts that he gives a toss what happens to her after that. She needs to end this.

'Is it me?' she says.

He recovers his composure.

'Of course. You're all I've ever wanted. I've spent a small fortune searching for you from the day this man stole you from me.'

Of course he would mention the money. People like him always knew the cost of everything.

'Not just any young girl then?'

'I don't know what you mean.'

'I heard you've got a thing for them.'

She steps forward. For the first time he seems less sure of himself.

'Do you want to fuck me, Daddy?' she asks.

Danny is watching the confrontation with a growing sense of anxiety. This is not how he saw this playing out. He's not sure what Ruby's game is but she's definitely getting to De Vere. His mouth is opening and closing but nothing's coming out. Despite the cold there's a thin bead of sweat slowly moving down the man's temple and he's clenched his right fist so tightly his fingertips have gone white.

Gold is equally tense. His pistol is still down by his side but he's almost bouncing on the balls of his feet, clearly expecting it all to kick off any second. Only Silver seems in control of his emotions, though he looks like he'd rather be anywhere other than in this room. The medic has glanced at the door a couple of times as if he's contemplating doing a runner. Danny has decided that if Silver does make a break for it he's going straight for Gold. Despite his broken ribs, he reckons he'd have the gun out of the man's hands before he could blink. He starts to gently flex his muscles, preparing to leap up when the moment comes.

'No! That's disgusting. Why would you say something like that?' De Vere says eventually, though Ruby thinks it's taken him far longer than it ought to have to deny it. 'I don't know what poison he's been feeding you but that's insane.'

'Are you sure?' Ruby says. 'You don't want some of this then?'

She thrusts her hand down the front of her jeans.

'No! Absolutely not,' De Vere insists, edging away slightly though he's staring at her hand in a way that makes it seem obvious he's lying.

'Ruby, I don't think . . .' Alex says from behind her, every word saturated with concern. She wishes she could explain but he'll find out soon enough.

'Stop this please,' De Vere says, stepping forward again, his fist unclenching and reaching towards her.

She licks her lips suggestively and he looks away as if worried what his expression will give away.

That's when she pulls the small gun out of her knickers and points it right at his face.

De Vere blinks twice then starts to back away.

'W-what are you doing?' he says.

'Put the gun down,' Gold shouts, raising his pistol and aiming at Ruby. He glances back at Silver. 'How did she get that in here? Didn't you search her?'

Ruby snorts at that. Did he really think the medic would search in her pants? Maybe they're all fucking paedophiles.

Gold turns back to her. 'It's not funny. If you don't put the gun down I will shoot you.'

'If you harm a hair on her head I will end you,' De Vere says. He points at the bed. 'He, on the other hand . . .'

Gold gets the message, turning his sights on Alex.

'That's enough,' Silver says suddenly. 'Lower your weapon.'

Ruby ignores him and keeps her hand steady but then realises he's not talking to her, he's talking to Gold, who's only just seen that Silver is pointing his rifle at him.

'Have you lost your mind?' Gold says. 'You really don't want to be on the wrong side here.'

'The only thing I want is to get away from this shitshow like almost everyone else you recruited has had the sense to.'

Gold stares at him like he's grown a second head.

'You're going to regret this, Silver, we know where you live. We know where your family lives.'

'Won't matter if you're dead, will it?' Silver says.

'Can we please calm down?' De Vere says, desperately trying to reclaim some authority. 'No one's going to end up dead here. Are they, Ruby?'

Ruby can feel her hand starting to shake a little. De Vere can clearly see it too and he half-smiles. He steps forward one more half-pace. Almost within reach of Ruby's gun.

'If you put down the gun we can get out of here. I'll make sure you have the best help you can get to recover from this whole thing. Your kidnapping and imprisonment by your uncle. And this ordeal. It's all clearly had a terrible impact on you.'

'Don't forget the murder of my friend.'

De Vere looks puzzled so she nods towards the window.

'Lucas. You walked past his dead body ten minutes ago. Shouldn't be hard to remember.'

'I already said I was sorry about that.'

She doesn't respond, all her efforts going into controlling her hand.

De Vere edges closer still, his face radiating sincerity.

'And I'm really sorry about your mother.'

'Me too,' Ruby says and pulls the trigger.

71

The only sound that breaks the shocked silence is the gunshot's echo. Gold is staring open-mouthed at the dead body of the Secretary of State for Defence stretched out on the floor in front of him, an almost perfectly round hole in the middle of his forehead and a growing pool of blood underneath him. Silver glances around the room wondering what the hell happens now. Ruby hasn't moved an inch since firing the shot, holding the gun in exactly the same position as if the man who let her mother die is still standing in front of her. Alex is the first to respond physically, reaching out for her, but the handcuff that's restraining his other arm prevents him from touching her. Instead it's Danny who gets to her first, climbing to his feet and gently removing the small pistol from her hand. He guides her back to sit on the bed where her dad wraps his arm tightly around her, whispering in her ear.

Silver watches Danny cautiously, as the man trains the gun on both him and Gold. He recognises it now as the tiny Beretta Pico that young Green used to keep in an ankle strap as a reserve. They really should have noticed that had gone missing.

He realises that he's going to have to play his cards carefully and hopes that his earlier intervention on Ruby's behalf has bought him some credit here. The locals have the upper hand now – there are more of them and Danny is armed. Unless Gold is prepared to kill them all it's hard to see how this ends without some deal being made. It's such a mess that – at this very moment – he just wants to get out of here with his life intact.

Gold comes to life, lifting his head up as if he's had a brilliant idea.

'I can fix this,' he says to no one in particular.

He turns to Silver and seems shocked that he still has his rifle pointed towards him. But then he glances down and suddenly appears to remember he's got his own pistol in his hand. He holds his hand up in apology, puts it back in its holster and turns his attention back to Alex and Ruby.

'I can fix this,' he repeats.

Ruby doesn't seem to realise the man has spoken at all, her head buried in her dad's shoulder, so it's Alex who eventually responds.

'What do you mean?'

'I can make it all go away. Like it never happened.'

'Seriously? There's a dead cabinet member on the floor.'

'Yes. I think so. No, I know so. They won't want this getting out. It's too calamitous politically now. We can bury it.'

Gold turns to Silver.

'You have a problem with that?'

Silver shakes his head. He can't imagine anything he'd like more but he pushes his luck.

'I still want paying.'

Gold sighs as if he has enough to think about but then shrugs.

'I'm sure that money won't be an issue.'

Not everyone is convinced.

'You're expecting us to keep quiet about all of this, are you?' Danny says.

'Up to you,' Gold says. 'But your girl here just killed the Secretary of State for Defence so I'd think it would be good if that didn't become public knowledge.'

Danny nods at the obvious benefit but Silver can tell he knows that's not the only problem here – for any of them, including him.

'How do we know they won't come after us later though?' the older man asks.

'Who's "they"?'

Danny laughs bitterly.

'People like you two, I guess.'

'It definitely won't be me,' Silver says. 'I'm done with this shit.'

'And I'm pretty sure when word gets round about this debacle my phone won't be ringing again,' Gold adds.

'So how's it going to work?' Danny asks.

Gold glances around the room as if there's someone else watching them and then turns back to Silver.

'You might want to make yourself scarce. The less people who know the details, the better.'

Silver doesn't need telling twice. He's about to head out of the door when it swings open. The boy Lucas walks in supporting a heavily limping fat man that Silver assumes is the guy who was hiding behind the sundial earlier. The pair of them stop right in front of him and there's almost a confrontation but after a moment of hesitation Silver steps aside and lets them pass. The fat man immediately slumps to the floor, his back against the wall to keep himself upright. Silver gets out while the going's good, the door slamming shut behind him.

Ruby hears the commotion and turns out of her dad's arms. She stares open-mouthed at Lucas.

'I thought you were dead,' she says.

Lucas rubs the side of his chest.

'Not quite. Might have cracked a rib or two though.'

'I don't understand.'

Lucas nods at Danny. 'My man here made us put on body armour before we set off. He only had two vests so I wouldn't take one at first but he insisted. Told me if I didn't wear his I had to stay and look after Nigel.'

'How is Nigel?'

Lucas points at De Vere's body on the floor.

'I don't know. But better than him, I'd imagine.'

72

Margaret cycles over the cattle grid and grimaces as her backside bounces up and down on the saddle and Nigel's old shotgun bangs against her back. She wishes she'd strapped it on a little tighter, worries that it might somehow go off.

She looks ahead but there's no sign of her friends yet. When she first set off she heard several gunshots coming from the direction of the manor house and then, just as she was approaching the driveway, there was another one. She hopes she's not too late to help.

As she turns the final bend the house comes into view. There's a body on the lawn. She skids to a halt on the gravel drive and steps off the bike, unstrapping the shotgun and walking slowly towards the prone figure. It's one of the soldiers.

She nudges him over with her foot. She doesn't recognise him, though it's hard to be sure, what with half of his face missing. Definitely dead though so she doesn't waste any more time on him. Danny's rescue mission has clearly passed through this way. She turns away from the dead body and heads towards the main entrance of the house.

Silver walks down the corridor, grateful that he's putting the last few days behind him. The less he knows about Gold's plan to cover all this up the better. He wonders about taking the helicopter – De Vere will probably have left the keys in the ignition. He's never flown one before but he's been a passenger many times and knows that it's a lot simpler than flying a plane. He could be home in twenty minutes – though where he'd land it in the middle of Newcastle he doesn't know – the Town Moor maybe? Not exactly flying under the radar. But at least he'd be back in time to buy a birthday present for his wife.

She'll be delighted that he's packing it all in – she's begged him to quit in the past but he's always talked her round. Not this time. He won't even try. He smiles as he walks through the doorway into the fresh air. It's the start of a new life. As he moves down the steps he suddenly becomes aware that he's not alone. The old lady, Mrs Carr, is standing in the middle of the driveway, shotgun in hand. He automatically raises his hands.

'Don't shoot,' he says, jokingly, but she's not smiling.

Margaret stares at the medic, her finger poised on the trigger of the shotgun.

'You killed my husband,' she says.

Silver frowns, like he's having trouble understanding what she's just said.

'I hardly touched him,' he says eventually.

'Heart attack. I think. He wasn't as strong as he thought he was.'

'I'm sorry. I didn't mean to hurt him.'

'Yet you did.'

Silver nods. 'True.' He pauses, a sly smile creeps onto his face. 'Can you even use that?' he says, nodding at the shotgun and taking a small step forward. Above them there's a whirring sound. Margaret pivots on her heel and blasts the drone out of the sky. She looks back at Silver who laughs.

'I'll take that as a yes.'

Margaret wonders how she really feels about this man. Unlike the brute who threatened her in the garden, Silver has always been polite, respectful almost. Did she really want to shoot him? Depends what has happened since he brought Ruby here, she supposes.

'Where are my friends?'

'Inside.' He nods his head backwards for emphasis.

'Alive?'

'Very much so.'

'I heard a lot of shooting.'

He nods at the dead body on the lawn.

'Mostly involving Grey there.'

'Mostly?'

He hesitates, clearly reluctant to say any more. She pumps the shotgun to encourage him.

'You really don't want to know.'

'Assume I do.'

He takes a deep breath.

'On your own head. Simon De Vere is dead.'

For a moment she thinks she's misheard him but by the look on his face she knows she hasn't.

'How?'

'He was shot.'

'By whom?'

'By Ruby,' Danny says, appearing behind Silver in the doorway. He looks exhausted and is holding his ribs like they might fall out if he doesn't. Margaret isn't as shocked by his news as she would have expected – she knows a fighter when she sees one.

'Nigel's dead too,' Margaret adds.

'I'm sorry to hear that.'

'Don't lie. He was a dick.'

Danny nods. 'True. But there are a lot of dicks out there and we can't wish them all dead.'

Margaret smiles. She's surprised how little Nigel's death has affected her. When he finally walked out on her she vowed that he would never be able to hurt her again and she's mostly managed to stick to that vow.

'Also true. The question now is whether Silver here is one of them.'

Silver goes to say something but Margaret puts her hand up to stop him.

'What do you think?' she asks Danny.

'Maybe that's enough shooting for today,' he says. 'It's not a bridge you want to cross anyway. Once you do it's difficult to go back.'

'Is Ruby all right?'

Danny hesitates. 'She will be. It might take a while though.'

Margaret nods. She knows he's speaking from experience.

'You can help her.'

'Maybe.'

'D'you think she'll get into trouble?'

'Unlikely. There'll be some kind of cover-up. The powers-that-be won't want De Vere's involvement in any of it hitting the headlines. Gold is trying to negotiate a deal in there to buy our silence and make this all go away. I was just getting in the way – I'm not much good at compromise.'

'I hope you're right. She's got a bright future, that one. We need more badass girls.'

'Aye, maybe, but you're already badass in my book, Margaret, no need to prove it again. In any case, we should probably let this one go. He stopped Gold from shooting Alex before it all kicked off.'

'You sure about that?'

Danny nods.

Margaret wonders if this will come back to haunt her but knows that Danny's right. There have been enough deaths for one day. She lowers her gun.

Silver doesn't hesitate. He nods his thanks to Danny and legs it down the steps. He glances at the helicopter but decides it's not worth the faff, he just wants to get out of there as quickly as he can. He'll take the ambulance.

He heads over to the abandoned vehicle, dropping his rifle on the driveway before he gets in and drives off. He's not really certain what he needs to start up as a window cleaner besides a bucket and a sponge but he's pretty sure he won't need to be armed.

73

Simon De Vere obituary

Simon De Vere, who has died in a hunting accident aged 60, was the Conservative MP for Harrogate and Knaresborough and a minister in successive governments.

De Vere was appointed Secretary of State for Defence in 2019; a controversial appointment given his links to the arms industry and a growing concern over Saudi Arabia's involvement in attacks on Yemen.

De Vere, however, rode out the early criticism, forming strong links with his US counterparts and earning the steadfast support of the Prime Minister due to his robust approach and unblinking loyalty.

His forthright manner and polished appearance ensured he became a prominent spokesman for the government, being seen as a no-nonsense safe pair of hands. He did not suffer fools gladly and many an under-prepared journalist wilted in the face of his withering criticism.

Born in Richmond, North Yorkshire, Simon was the eldest

child of Sir Peter De Vere, a former army brigadier, and his wife, Irene. He was educated at Ampleforth College, before attending the Royal Military Academy Sandhurst, after which he was commissioned into the Green Howards. He rose to the rank of captain, however he was medically discharged after suffering injuries in Saudi Arabia in 1991 during the Gulf War.

After leaving the army he formed Claustra, a security company, which provided services and personnel to private industry and the military, building it into a FTSE 100 company before switching to politics, winning Harrogate and Knaresborough for the Conservatives at the 2010 election.

With his party in government he rose swiftly through the ranks, first becoming the PPS to the Secretary of State for Northern Ireland in 2013 and then a Minister of State in the Department for International Trade in 2016.

Despite his fierce reputation, De Vere was well-liked by both colleagues and underlings and was particularly well-known for his enthusiastic mentoring of younger members of staff. He was also an avid advocate of hunting and was instrumental in attempts to overturn the ban on fox hunting in 2022.

De Vere married Audrey Stewart (daughter of the American oil industry tycoon Elmore Stewart) in 1993. She died of cancer last year. They had no children.

A full obituary will appear in later editions.

74

Six months later

Ruby watches as Baldwin pulls another pint for the vicar. He's had to keep the man topped up with free beer since the pub reopened. It's a small price to pay for him turning a blind eye to the mysterious appearance of three new graves in his church's cemetery. It was hard to think of a better place to hide a few dead bodies.

Baldwin hobbles across and hands the dodgy minister his drink before taking a seat on a stool behind the bar. His broken ankle hasn't healed perfectly but he was never much for exercise anyway so as long as he can sit down behind the bar he's a happy man.

Ruby's happier too now. It hasn't been easy, there were a few nightmares to begin with – what would you expect if you'd killed two people on your sixteenth birthday? But time really is a great healer and gradually they've eased and she only thinks about it every other day. Danny's been a star. Initially he was reluctant to talk about his demons but he eventually loosened up – it's not like she could chat to a proper counsellor – and his tips for moving on have helped her a lot. As has his insistence that both men deserved it so she should take any regrets she has and put them in the bin. Maybe she's helped him a bit too. He'll never exactly be Mr Chatty, mind.

There's a plaque on the wall behind Baldwin thanking the donors responsible for the £200,000 crowd-funding which has been raised in the last six months, enabling them to buy the pub from the previous owners and run it as a community venture, providing both post office and library facilities to the village as well as beer. Ruby suspects that Baldwin only insisted on the library element so he could continue his 'friends with benefits' relationship with Peggy from the mobile van. Surprisingly, he's managed to keep a lid on his own drinking and her dad reckons they're actually making a profit on the takings at the moment, with most of the holiday lets being used all summer.

As promised by Gold in the deal Alex had hammered out after De Vere's death, the crowd-funding was almost entirely made up of a large, supposedly anonymous, donation from a mysterious benefactor that Danny insists on calling Mr Hush Money, though only when there are no outsiders listening in. Ultimately it was no surprise to any of them that the current government were prepared to do, and pay, pretty much anything to cover up their minister's misdemeanours as long as it was off the books. They had previous for that and Alex had insisted on them paying a high price for the villagers' silence. The coroner had clearly been leant on too – he recorded a verdict of misadventure on De Vere's death which no one had challenged.

Baldwin had mischievously suggested that Ruby try and claim her rightful inheritance from the De Vere estate but that idea was quickly quashed. The late minister was a sleeping dog that was definitely best left to lie.

Ruby is sitting with Lucas and his mum, Laura, who's been back at home for four months now. She has no idea what really happened in her absence, only that Lucas's stock has risen considerably. They've told her that it's because he helped raise the money to get the place open again and in a way that's true, Ruby supposes. Lucas is still a little nervous that having a pub in the place will send his mum back to her bad old ways but so far she's managed to stay dry since coming out of rehab – not least because Danny has explained in very graphic terms what he will do to Baldwin if he ever serves the woman an alcoholic drink.

Danny himself is sitting in the corner with Margaret. Unlike Ruby and Lucas, the older pair aren't officially a couple yet but everyone knows it's just a matter of time. Nigel's death has cleared the way for them to resume their childhood relationship and the only thing holding them back now is Danny's surprising sense of propriety. He insists that there has to be a suitable period of mourning for Nigel before they make it official. Lucas reckons it's just an excuse because he's a little bit scared of the old woman and he's probably right.

Aside from De Vere, Margaret's ex-husband was the only victim of the siege to get a proper funeral and all anyone else knows is that he died of a heart attack. No one was very surprised to hear that – the man was overweight and rarely exercised and there were several witnesses (no surprises which ones) to him collapsing as he tried to clamber over a stile on his way into the village. There was a decent turnout at the funeral, though Ruby noticed the only person to shed a tear was his ex-lover, the church organist (or 'that slapper' as Margaret still called her), who blamed herself for throwing him out of the house during a cold snap. Margaret took a gleeful pleasure in not correcting her mistaken assumption. 'Karma's a bitch,' she'd explained over cucumber sandwiches back at her house afterwards.

The door opens and Ruby's dad walks in with a large package under his left arm. Though his leg has healed up surprisingly well he still has problems with his shoulder. Silver had done a decent job patching it up but Alex thinks that there's probably something floating around in there that's always going to cause him a problem. It's not like he can get it checked out as it's difficult to explain bullet fragments to a normal doctor. Anyway, considering how bad things could have been, he's learnt to count his blessings.

'Is that the sign?' Ruby asks, getting to her feet and taking the package from him. She rips open the brown paper wrapping and leans the contents up against the wall. They've been waiting months for this to be ready but it's been worth every second.

The pub's name – Lady Emma – sits above an image of a woman's face. It's her mother's face, perfectly captured from an image of Emma they had found in De Vere's pocket – it was probably the picture they'd used to help track down Ruby but she didn't care about that. Though she'd never known her mum, apart from possibly a few moments together that she would never be able to remember, it feels like they have brought her home. For Ruby has no doubts now that this is her home. She's no longer an incomer.

Silver has only a few houses to go to finish his round. He's looking forward to picking the girls up from school – one of the many bonuses of being a window cleaner is that you can choose your own hours.

The afternoon sun reminds him of the fortnight they spent in Paphos recently, lazy days on the beaches, evenings drinking on the balcony with his wife, the girls tucked up in bed, pure bliss. He can't wait to head off somewhere warm again in the autumn now he can plan ahead; wishes he'd changed his career a lot earlier – it would have saved him a lot of grief.

He's a different man in many ways now, sleeping much better, despite the early starts, and drinking a lot less. He's never going to give up completely but he can finally call himself a social drinker rather than the binge version. Maybe he's just grown up though he's pretty sure it's more that he's at peace with himself now he's not carrying a weapon most of the time.

The woman at No. 53 opens the door before he gets

halfway up the drive as usual. He's pretty sure she's got a thing for him – sometimes the old clichés about bored housewives are true – but he's not interested so he always plays it straight with her.

'Nice day for it,' she says, leaving him to imagine what 'it' might be.

'Aye,' he says. 'Probably take the kids to the park when I'm done collecting this week's money.'

'You'll be glad when they're grown up like mine, eh? More time to add a bit of spontaneity to your life. Do more adult stuff!' She fixes him with a mega-watt smile and he wonders how much she paid to have her teeth done.

'Nah,' he says. 'I've missed too much time with them when they were younger, just happy to be able to catch up now. Have you got your purse?'

Her grin fades and she goes back inside the house to get some money. When she returns she thrusts a tenner into his hand and shuts the door a bit too firmly. He smiles to himself – maybe that's what they mean by an unsatisfied customer! The old fella he bought the round from told him some stories that made his hair curl. He'd thought he was exaggerating, just teasing the new boy, but maybe not.

A couple more houses later and he's done, heading back down the road towards his van with a pocketful of cash. He checks his watch, just gone two p.m. so plenty of time to head to the library to get some new books for the girls before he has to pick them up. Mari's on a late shift today and is going for a drink with her mates so he'll have to give them their baths and put them to bed, which he loves. He's had to read them *The Gruffalo* every night for the last two weeks which was great at first but everything has its limits.

Silver is crossing the road, zapping the van with his key fob to unlock the doors, when the car hits him. He somersaults over the bonnet, and flies through the air, crashing head first into the kerb. He hears someone screaming and the last thing he ever sees is the car disappearing around the corner.

Gold leaves the stolen car in the huge Sainsbury's car park. There's no CCTV coverage in that area and it'll take ages for anyone to spot that it's been abandoned there. He gets out, makes sure no one is watching him, and walks to the other end of the car park where he climbs into his own vehicle. He takes out a list from the glove compartment and crosses off Silver's name. That's the last of his remaining team to be eliminated. The other two didn't see him coming either. He's always thought of himself as a man of his word and he's not happy that the new minister has reversed his initial decision to let sleeping dogs lie and instead ordered him to tidy up the loose ends from the De Vere debacle.

Nothing on paper, of course. There never is in his world. Deniability is everything. Gold's pretty sure that once he's done there will be someone else sent out to tidy him up. 'Leave no trace' isn't just some glib throwaway line. But such is life. Or death. Whatever. He made his bed a long time ago.

Anyway, that moment hasn't come yet. And maybe they'll give him a pass if he finishes the job properly. Those fucking amateurs can't be that lucky again. He reaches over and resets the satnav to his next destination: Coldburn, Northumberland.

ACKNOWLEDGEMENTS

A few years back I was playing for Crown Old Contemptibles CC – a collection of ageing gentleman cricketers – in Bamburgh, right in front of the town's magnificent castle. To our surprise, the captain of the Bamburgh team told us we probably wouldn't be able to play them the following year as it was almost impossible for him to raise a team as no one lived there any more – it was all second homes. Since then I've heard similar tales about another Northumberland town, Beadnell, and much further afield, the Welsh village of Abersoch where the bank, the post office, the doctor's surgery and even the primary school have had to close due to the lack of permanent residents. It's a nationwide problem which affects many tourist destinations, including towns and villages in Cornwall and I'm not a fan. I'm sure you can draw your own line from that to the homeless problems I've written about in previous books.

But it's not the only nationwide problem that bugs the hell out of me and certainly not the biggest. For me that's the systemic abuse of power with impunity that has infected the higher echelons of our society. Time and again in recent years we've seen senior politicians and advisers (Hi Dominic), all over the world, doing whatever they like without consequences. Not in my book. That's one of the best things about doing this job – you can put the world to rights.

Rant over. Now the nice bits.

Huge thanks, once again to my fabulous editor, Jane Wood, who gave the go-ahead to *You Can Run* after reading just a few sample chapters. (She had seen me tweeting about how much I hated writing a synopsis and graciously allowed me to skip that hideous task – other editors take note.) The rest of the Quercus team, in particular Ella Patel, Lipfon Tang and Florence Hare have always had my back too. Thanks also to my copy editor Liz Hatherell, especially for pointing out that teenagers think in metres, not yards, and to Joe Mills for the superb cover design – as striking as a disgruntled rail worker. (Boom, boom). I should also doff my cap to Nicola Howell Hawley for her stunning map of my fictional Coldburn village (I have a map!) based on an original sketch by my wonderfully talented wife Pam Briggs. Many thanks too, to my audiobook narrator Sarah Durham.

Another shout out to my brilliant agent, Oli Munson, who despite being a Spurs fan is a top man. (I'm still going to enjoy teasing him remorselessly when St Totteringham's Day is placed firmly back on the calendar somewhere towards the end of this season. I REALLY hope this bit ages well.)

Early readers were hugely helpful for me in writing *You Can Run*. The move from an ageing homeless narrator to a teenage girl (primarily) was a bit of a leap and I had a huge amount of help from several writers, including my UEA pals Harriet Tyce and Kate Simants and, in particular, my Debut 20 allies Nikki Smith and Andreina Cordani. And speaking of the D20s, who knew that a group of writers that got together on social media when they realised they were about to have their debut novels published in lockdown would end up such firm friends in real life? Love you all.

There are so many others who have continued to help. My small but select Newcastle writing group, who as always have offered considered, constructive criticism on my work in progress. Many thanks to Simon Van der Velde, Karon Alderman and Ben Appleby-Dean. I must also again mention my ever-supportive fellow Northern Crime Syndicate writers, Robert Scragg, Rob Parker, Jude O'Reilly, Fiona Erskine, Adam Peacock, and Chris McGeorge.

A huge cheer too for all the readers, bloggers, reviewers and friends who have supported the books to date. I owe you all a(nother) pint.

I mustn't forget the experts that contributed so much to *You Can Run*. A big round of applause please for physics genius Sylvi Whittle, who, in answer to my vague question, sent me a comprehensive four-page document on signal jamming detailing the many ways that this was possible, 90% of which went way over my head. The other 10% was golden.

A shout-out too, to Dan Jackson, whose brilliant history of North East England and its people, *The Northumbrians*, entertained me hugely but perhaps more importantly filled in a lot of gaps in my knowledge of the area.

Thanks also to the many people who gave me some top tips about the area at the inaugural Morpeth Book Festival last year – I hope to thank you in person when it happens again.

Last, but obviously best, my everlasting gratitude to my wonderful family, Pam, Becca and the furry boys Dexter and Leo who all combine to keep me sane. Ok, saner.